I0746830

Cutler's Return

a John Cutler mystery

by Colin Conway

Love cannot save you from your own fate

- Jim Morrison

Cutler's Return

2004

Chapter 1

Her voice was soft in my ear. "Hi, John."

I closed my eyes, inhaled deeply, and gripped the phone tighter.

"You know who this is, don't you?" Her voice was throaty now, filled with hints of long-ago lust and forgotten playfulness.

Several seconds passed before I slowly exhaled.

"It's me, baby."

Opening my eyes brought back my current reality. Several empty beer cans and a discarded pizza box cluttered the coffee table. Nearby, a pile of dirty clothes lay beside a tipped-over laundry basket. In the kitchen, dishes and glasses were stacked in the sink, clamoring for attention. The smell of last night's dinner—the take-out pizza—hovered in the air.

"Are you still there?"

"How'd you get this number?"

"Aw... That's no way to talk to an old girlfriend, is it?"

Pushing down on the footrest, I snapped the ratty recliner upright. "Been a while."

"I'm sorry." She didn't sound it. "I should have called sooner."

It only took a couple of steps to the kitchen, where I pulled the last beer from the fridge.

"But you could have called," she said. The mischievousness had faded from her voice to be replaced by something new. Was she pouting? That didn't seem like her.

After snapping open the can, I took a sip.

"I kept waiting to hear from you." She wasn't pouting. It was guilt—just applied more smoothly than I remembered.

A long pull off the beer now. Then a second.

"Hello?"

"Why'd you call, Paige?"

"Because I missed you."

"No, really."

She paused. "I need your help."

"For what?"

"To get something."

I set the beer on the counter and massaged my forehead with the palm of my hand.

"Somebody stole something," she said, "and I want it back."

"What'd they take?"

"Come to Seattle, and I'll tell you."

From the counter, I shook a cigarette from a slightly crumpled pack of Marlboros. Using a blue plastic lighter, I lit it and inhaled. Grabbing the can of beer, I returned to the recliner. "Why me?"

"I need someone I can trust."

I dropped into the chair, and the footrest snapped back into place. "Call the cops."

"I am."

"Funny."

"Are you blaming me for that?"

I shook my head even though she couldn't see the effect. "I did that to myself."

We listened to silence for a bit until she said, "I'll pay for you to come."

How much would it take for me to see her again?

She must have sensed my question. "A thousand."

Another inhale on the cigarette, then an exhale. A

thousand bucks. How long would it take her to make that much money? Three days? Maybe two if they were good. It was probably a couple of weeks of work for me. Could be three if things were slow—a far cry from my former self.

I said, "Tell me what they took."

"Will you do it?"

My gaze flitted about the small unit. A thousand dollars would give me some breathing room in child support, but it meant going back there—home—where everything went wrong.

"C'mon," she goaded, "it'll be fun to see each other again." It sounded forced. We both knew there was no way it would be fun.

"Make it two."

Half of me prayed she wouldn't agree. I wasn't sure what the other half wanted. That's the part I hated.

"Yeah, okay. A thousand to come over and a thousand when you get back what's mine." When I didn't respond, she chuckled lightly. "I knew you'd do it." Confidence filled her voice. "When can you be here?"

A final swallow of beer, and I set the can on the floor. I slipped the remaining cigarette into the opening, causing a hiss. "Still in the same apartment?"

"I've moved up. Got a nicer place."

I grabbed the empty pizza box from the coffee table and wrote down her new address as she recited it. It rolled off her tongue as if she'd been there for some time. "I'll head over in the morning."

"I start work at one."

"Leave your apartment unlocked."

"I'll put a key under the mat. I can't wait to see you." Again, it sounded forced.

I murmured, "Uh-huh," snapped my cell phone shut, then dropped it to the floor.

My fists clenched, and my jaw tightened. The best thing I could do at that moment would be to throw that pizza box away and ignore any further calls from her. I stared at my handwriting until my jaw hurt.

With a flick of the wrist, I tossed the thin box across the small room. The recliner snapped upright, and I stepped over to the window.

Across the way, an Amtrak pulled behind the combination bus/train station. In front of the building, a Greyhound let its passengers out. A couple of guys in faded green Army jackets wandered away from the building, each carrying a duffel bag. They headed toward Slammer's, a nearby country bar.

They looked the type for trouble.

Chapter 2

The first time I met Paige, she danced under the stage name of Nicolette in a Seattle strip club unabashedly named The Red Light District. Every major city in the northwest has a Red Light District club—Tacoma, Portland, Boise, and Spokane.

Police radio had dispatched me and my partner, Michael Davoli, to eject a disorderly patron from the club. We handled most calls that year as a team and hung out together as families once a month. His daughter was roughly the same age as mine. I brought a date once to our family get-together, but that proved awkward, so I only brought Erin after that.

When Mike and I arrived at the club, it smelled of smoke and desperation. I'd never been to a strip club beyond work and could never understand the allure of a woman hustling men for money. It seemed too ugly of a lie for anyone to believe.

The disorderly patron sat alone and loudly whooped as a naked blond woman pranced off the stage. He was a bodybuilder who wore a tight tank top to show off his muscles. Colorful tattoos climbed the length of his arms. Several bouncers triangulated the man but anxiously jumped any time the bodybuilder made an unexpected move. It appeared as if a fight had already occurred, and the bouncers got the worst of it. Mike and I exchanged cautious glances while we approached.

When I stepped near, the man barked, "The fuck *you* want?"

I pointed at my badge.

The bodybuilder's gaze didn't move from the woman leaving the stage. He muttered, "Rent-a-cops."

"Real cop," I said. "Seattle Police. We got a call there was a problem." I tapped my side-handle baton for emphasis but didn't pull it from its O-ring. "Let's step outside."

"Ain't goin' nowhere," he slurred.

I turned to the bouncer nearest me, a medium-sized twenty-something with spiky black hair.

"He's drunk," I said. "You can't sell alcohol in a strip club."

The bouncer shrugged. "We don't serve booze. He came in this way, but he wasn't too bad at first. He's gotten worse the longer he's been here."

Mike frowned. "Was he sneaking drinks? Or still going up from something he had earlier?"

The drunk kicked his head back and hollered at the ceiling, "Somebody shake some ass!"

One of the other bouncers stepped nervously backward.

I moved directly in front of the bodybuilder to block his view of the stage. "*Sir!*"

"*What?*" he hollered.

"Step outside."

His eyelids drooped. "You step outside."

I looked at Mike and raised my eyebrows. This would be done the hard way.

The lights in the club flickered to the stuttering intro of Ice Cube's "You Can Do It."

The drunk's eyes widened, and he leaned slightly to the side. "Holy shit."

It was a lapse in judgment, but I glanced over my shoulder. An alabaster-skinned woman in a black bikini walked confidently onto the raised platform. She had short bangs but long, dark hair that fell past her shoulders. Her hips swayed in hypnotic rhythm with the song. She made eye contact and smiled demurely. She was a stripper in a swimsuit, for Christ's sake, and like a naïve jackass, I stood straighter and grinned back.

That's when the bodybuilder hit me in the side of the head and sent me sprawling across the floor. I rolled over and looked up.

The big man reared back, stretched his arms wide, and roared like a grizzly bear in the woods. He stood at least a head taller than Mike, who was the same height as me.

Several women screamed. Nearby customers clambered out of the way. The bouncers seemed confused between their duties of helping people to safety or stopping a crazed drunk.

Mike didn't hesitate, though, and latched onto the big man with both hands. He was trying to get to the bodybuilder's back to apply a lateral vascular neck restraint. Unfortunately, the drunk wasn't having any of it. He elbowed my partner while twisting and turning in hopes of shaking Mike free. As the big man moved, Mike resembled a bull rider hoping to hit the eight-second mark.

The two men knocked over tables and chairs while Ice Cube's music thumped through the club's speakers. Patrons and bouncers alike stood wide-eyed during the combat pirouette.

When enough of my wits returned, I scrambled to my feet and slid my side-handle baton from its holder.

"Mike!" I yelled, "Let go!"

My partner pushed away from the drunk, which forced the big man to stagger forward. The bodybuilder's eyes were wild with rage. His lips pulled away from his teeth and his fists clenched. He snarled before he charged—an unsteady bull ready to assert his dominance.

With all my strength, I jabbed the tip of the baton into

the stomach of the oncoming drunk. He stopped mid-stride and clutched his belly. His face pinched, and he exhaled hard. Then he collapsed to his knees and hunched over.

Mike and I jumped onto him—a two-man pig pile. When he could, Mike put a knee across the man's upper back, pinning him to the floor. I yanked an arm out from underneath his body and twisted it behind his back. It took considerable pulling and prodding, but we finally got the other hand free. It took two pairs of handcuffs to restrain the man—one on each wrist with the pairs connected.

We stood and, for a moment, shared a smile of satisfaction. Then I looked toward the stage. The woman with alabaster skin had never stopped dancing. She waved at me and then spun around the pole.

"John," my partner said.

"Huh?"

"You're bleeding." He pointed toward my nose.

I wiped a hand across my face. There was a considerable amount of red on my fingertips.

Mike smacked my arm. "Help me pick this shitbag up."

As we dragged the drunk from the club, the announcer bellowed, "That's Nicolette, gents. Make sure you tip her well."

Chapter 3

The flashlight shone in my eyes for a moment before I turned away.

"You drunk?" the police officer asked in the bored, detached manner that cops perfect.

"Not yet."

The crowd in front of the bar ogled us. Slammer's was known for cheap drinks and cheaper thrills. It attracted every type of low life, from out-of-work drunks to wannabe biker thugs. Anyone who wandered in there risked one of two things: a punch in the mouth or a venereal disease. Music pumped out of the club. It got louder every time someone opened the door.

The cop stood ramrod straight and wore an unimpressed smirk. His name tag read *Higgins*.

A Nissan Maxima full of teenaged boys drove slowly by. Their eyes were wide with excitement at seeing an actual live episode of *COPS*. All that was missing were the television cameras. The teenagers whooped and hollered as they drove away. The car's horn blared.

"Why'd you fight those guys?" Higgins pointed his flashlight at the two men wearing faded Army jackets who now sat on the curb. They were bleeding from various cuts and scrapes and talking with other officers.

I couldn't tell him about Paige's phone call nor the history it represented. "I think there's been some mistake."

Higgins watched the two men interact with the other officers. "No mistake," he said.

I rubbed my hands over my arms in hopes of fighting

off the night's chill.

The officer's attention returned to me. "The bar staff said you came in looking for a fight. Said you went right up to those two and provoked them."

"They said that?"

"Yeah. They said that."

I ran my hands over my face and felt my own scrapes and bumps. "Must be true then."

The cop's smirk deepened. "How's that?"

"That's what accounts for truth in these situations, right? Independent witnesses are more reliable than the victim or suspect."

His eyes narrowed. "Been in trouble with the law?"

"No."

Higgins studied me some more before cocking his head. "Lawyer or law enforcement, then?" He shone the flashlight on my face again, but I used my hand to shield my eyes. "Cop," he said as if stating a fact. "Where at? If it was around here, I would remember."

I considered not saying anything but figured what the hell. Maybe playing ball with him would earn me a little rhythm. "Seattle."

"You quit?"

"It quit me."

"Huh." He absently shook his flashlight in his hand, sending wide arcs of light around the pavement. "You wanna tell me what you said to piss those guys off?"

I looked at the two, and one of them glared back. "I asked if they were on their honeymoon."

Higgins shifted his stance, and then a frown spread across his face. "You wanted a fight?"

My gaze drifted away from the cop. I blew into my hands and rubbed them together.

"Right," Higgins muttered. "Wait here."

He walked over to confer with the other officers. The

cop looked several times in my direction. When I reached into my pocket to pull out the pack of Marlboros, he yelled, "Get your hands out of your pockets!"

I held up the red pack and waggled it. Inside were a couple of cigarettes. I shook a mangled one free and lit it.

Three strikingly similar girls in blue jeans and midriff shirts stepped out of the club to see what was happening. The music from inside seemed to get louder as they held the door open. It was some irritating country song about saving a horse by riding a cowboy.

"Hey," I called to the three.

They collectively turned to me. Each of them flashed a look of disgust.

"Close the door."

"Why?" one of them hollered. She seemed irritated that I dared talk to her.

"Your music sucks."

The three of them looked at each other and must have decided there was more excitement inside. The one I had engaged with indignantly flipped me the bird before disappearing inside.

Higgins sauntered back over. "Making friends?"

"Isn't there an ordinance against noise pollution?"

"Don't like music?"

"Not this kind."

He tucked his flashlight into an armpit and crossed his arms over his chest. "You want to press charges against those guys? They won't if you won't."

I inhaled on the cigarette and considered the men I'd fought. Neither glared at me now. They probably just wanted to go on about their lives.

The officer leaned slightly forward. "Hey, dirtbag. You wanna walk, or do you wanna press charges?"

"I'll walk."

"Figures." Higgins clicked his tongue against his

teeth.

His anger seemed out of place. I hadn't fought with the bouncers or the responding officers. I provided my personal information when asked. Even when the cop interviewed me about the fight, I wasn't overly disrespectful. Maybe a little, but he should have been used to it by now. Higgins seemed to be an experienced officer.

"What did I do?" I asked.

"I hate guys like you. Guys who have it all and throw it away."

"You don't know what I threw away."

"You were a cop." His voice dropped an octave, and he glared at me.

That same intense look used to be in my mirror. It got to the point where I believed the self-righteous son-of-bitch staring back. I stood and brushed the dirt off my jeans. "And?"

Higgins pointed at me. "That means something."

"It means less than you think."

Chapter 4

The night after Mike and I dealt with the crazed bodybuilder, I returned to The Red Light District. Even though most people focus on the uniform and ignore a cop's features, I didn't bother to shave and wore a Mariners baseball hat curled tight and pulled low. It didn't change my appearance much, but I tried.

The doorman charged me fifteen bucks to get in. "Covers your drinks, too."

Inside, a row of chairs surrounded the stage. Behind them were additional tables and chairs.

Unlit booths ringed the outside of the room. This was where the women performed privately for paying customers. The stage's rear wall was mirrored so the dancers could look back into the crowd regardless of which direction they faced.

All the women wore bikinis, and the club smelled like a mixture of sweat and disinfectant. It vaguely reminded me of a gym and didn't seem nearly as depressing as the day before.

I sat in the middle of the room. It must have been the slow time of the day as only a few other men were there. A couple of college-aged guys chuckled nervously and responded timidly whenever a woman approached them.

A heavyset older man sat in a far corner of the room with a continuous line of women stopping by. One would chat with him for a while, and he'd eventually hand her a couple of bills. The woman would then take the money to the stage and tip the one up there, keeping a note for herself.

As a petite black dancer hung from the chrome pole, a deeply tanned woman in a white bikini came by and introduced herself. "I'm Misty." I shook her outstretched hand. "What's your name?"

"John." My name is so ubiquitous that it didn't make sense to lie about it.

"Hi, John. Would you like a dance?"

"I'm just watching."

She stroked my back with her free hand. "All right. I'll come by later and check on you again."

In a moment, a fully clothed woman stopped by. She must have been in her forties and had the disapproving gaze of a mother. "Something to drink?" She put a napkin on the little table next to me.

Washington State doesn't allow liquor in strip clubs, so it was soda or nothing. "Coke."

The server nodded once then disappeared. A little while later, she returned and put a small glass on the table. I handed her a dollar, and she vanished once more.

On stage, the woman finished her set then collected her garments.

When the next woman walked onstage, the DJ announced her as Veronica. She was a curvy redhead with tattoos on her calves. Veronica slinked across the stage as Nelly's "Pimp Juice" bounced from the club's speakers. She made two loops along the edge before returning to the center to jump onto the chrome pole. Veronica wrapped her legs around the bar and hung at odd angles as the music pumped. There was a smattering of applause from the small crowd.

Glancing around the club, I didn't see Nicolette. When my gaze returned to the stage, the redhead met my eyes and nodded. She would make eye contact with the college guys throughout her three-song set and nod the same way she did to me. It didn't take a rocket scientist to figure out what she was doing.

When Veronica finished, the DJ said, "Give her a hand, guys. That was Veronica. Catch her when she comes by."

I sipped from my soda and crunched on a piece of ice while the stage was empty. When the announcer's voice broke the silence, I noticed Nicolette had slipped through the curtain and stood waiting for her call. I sat up straighter.

I'm not a fan of heavy metal music, but even I knew the opening for Mötley Crüe's "Girls, Girls, Girls." It started as she strutted away from the curtain. When the drums and guitars reached a crescendo, Nicolette was at the center of the stage. While the music roared, she clung to the chrome pole with her right hand and swayed around it as if in a trance. She wore a strapless black bra with black panties.

When the song arrived at its first chorus, she opened her eyes. Nicolette slithered around the stage to the beat and soon wrapped herself around the pole. She met my gaze and winked. Nicolette hadn't done that to the college guys or the older man in the corner.

At least, I *hoped* she hadn't done it to them.

At the end of the song, she moved to the back of the stage and crossed her bra with her hands.

Another heavy metal song I'd never heard began, and Nicolette spun around to lift off her top. Her breasts jumped. She danced around the stage once more before slipping out of her panties. With her back to the audience, she fell to her hands and knees.

Veronica, the girl who had just been on stage, broke my stare and stuck out her hand. "I'm Veronica," she said in a deliberately little girl's voice. "How about a dance?"

"No."

She faked a pout then glided over to the older man in

the corner.

Nicolette was at the front of the stage dancing, but she never looked my way again. When the song ended, she grabbed her clothes and hurried into the back room.

A couple of minutes of drinking soda and crunching ice passed while another girl took the stage. I didn't pay much attention to her, though. Instead, I sat there alternating between doubting questions and statements of self-loathing.

What was I hoping would happen here? *You're an idiot for coming.*

Maybe I can talk with her? *Every idiot thinks they can chat up a stripper.*

Maybe she'd want to get coffee? *Don't be stupid. She'll never go for you.*

A hand gently rested on my shoulder, rescuing me from my inner turmoil. She again wore the strapless black bra and panties she had on earlier.

"I'm Nicolette." She stuck out her hand. It was warm and mostly dry.

"John."

She cocked her head. "You're the policeman from yesterday." A sly smile spread across her lips. "Did you come back to see me?"

I glanced around, and my cheeks warmed.

"Would you like a private dance?"

"This is going to sound like a line—"

"You've never done this before."

I shrugged.

She squatted next to me and rested her hand on my knee. Sweat beaded on her forehead. "Here's how it works. For twenty bucks, you get a dance that lasts one song. If you want to go again, it's another twenty, but things will get hotter. It gets hotter each time. Understand? I can touch you, but you can't touch me.

That's the rules." Nicolette wiped her brow and said, "I'm sorry I'm so sweaty."

I didn't mind.

"So, John—" She lightly rubbed my knee. "—wanna dance?"

She held out her hand as if she already knew the answer. Nicolette guided me to a booth cloaked in darkness. "Take off your coat."

While we waited for the music to begin, Nicolette stepped onto a little platform in front of me. She danced slowly to an unheard yet mesmerizing rhythm. Nicolette faced outward as if to show the others what they were about to miss. She glanced back over her shoulder and flashed that same smile she'd shown me the day before. This time, I wanted to believe its demure nature.

AC/DC's "Thunderstruck" burst through the speakers. Nicolette spun and climbed onto my lap. She pushed into me while her cheek touched mine. When she moved her head, her mouth was centimeters from mine. I could feel her breath on my lips. Sweat from her forehead touched my skin. Everything about the moment was a lie, but I didn't care.

When the song ended, she leaned back with a confident smile. "Another one?"

Almost ashamed, I whispered, "Please."

As we waited for the next song to start, she relaxed in my lap and rested her wrists on my shoulders. Neither of us spoke. Me because I was embarrassed. Her because she was sizing up the room. Her head swiveled about the entire time. I leaned slightly to smell coconut oil on her arm.

When Nate Dogg's "Regulate" pulsated through the club, Nicolette ground onto me slowly in time with the beat. Her hands pressed on my chest as she moved. She then brushed her breasts slowly across my face. The texture of the bra felt like spandex. Nicolette was in and out of my lap throughout the song.

When it ended, she stepped back and playfully tapped my chest. "It's nice dancing for someone like you. You work out. I can tell."

I stared at her. She was working me. I knew it. But there was something I wanted to believe—a connection. Did she feel it too? It was a stupid thing to think.

"Do all cops work out?"

"Most."

"You like it?"

"Being a cop? Yeah."

"It sounds cool."

For a moment, there was an awkward silence. I needed to get out of there to think about how out of control I felt. "Do I pay you now?" My voice cracked as I spoke, and I wanted to crawl under my chair to hide.

She smiled. "It's forty."

I pulled out two bills from my pocket and handed them to her. She gently touched the side of my face before leading me back to my chair.

"Don't go far, John." She left me then to make the acquaintance of someone who had just come into the club.

I left then as embarrassed as a teenaged boy who had just gotten his unexpected first kiss.

Chapter 5

When the satisfaction of the fight at Slammer's had worn off, I spent the rest of the night reminiscing with a bottle of Canadian Mist. Somewhere around midnight, I passed out.

Eight hours later, a quick shower and a cup of instant coffee did their best to revive me. I headed toward Seattle in my ten-year-old F150. She was the only thing of value I still owned. After my law enforcement career imploded, everything else of significance remained on the west side of the state.

Unfortunately, that included my daughter.

At twelve, Erin looked more and more like her mother in every picture. When I got mixed up with Paige, she was nine, and I fled Seattle a couple of months after her tenth birthday.

Maria sent school pictures and the occasional holiday photographs to let me know how things were going. Her letters were brief and detached, which was fine since we were never emotional anyway. We briefly dated—if sex without communication can be called dating—and soon realized we weren't right for each other. Maria recognized it long before I did. I'd been okay with the situation.

Things turned into a lifetime connection when Maria discovered she was pregnant after our break-up. I never suggested an abortion, and she wouldn't consider such a thing—her religious upbringing forbade it. I'm glad she didn't.

I wanted to make our relationship permanent to give

the unborn child a two-parent family, but Maria said she didn't love me. She also said that sooner or later, I would let her down. She said she just sensed something in my make-up. I took that worse than the reason for breaking up.

Following my termination from the department, Maria never said it, but she certainly acted as though limiting my access to our daughter had been the wisest decision she ever made.

I sent letters and called Erin on her birthday and holidays, but the conversations were always stilted. I never knew what to say. *I'm sorry, kiddo, but your old man's a screw-up.* She'd probably figure that out on her own.

The phone conversations with Maria were short—usually a quick hello before handing the phone to our daughter. However, she still made a point to include me in Erin's life. She's a hard woman to figure out.

For child support, I sent Maria five hundred dollars every month. It was a lot easier when I was on the department. After losing my job, I never asked for a modification. Instead, I hooked up with one of those hired-hand companies—the ones where they call you when another business needs cheap labor. The company took a cut of my wages, but it was reasonably constant work with the variety I needed. I could've looked for something steady and normal, but I didn't feel like I wanted the daily pressure of a boss breathing down my neck—not now, maybe someday.

As cheap labor, I did everything from construction work to cleaning toilets. I did the work because I had to. I owed Erin that much.

I picked up some decent money bouncing on Friday and Saturday nights for Club Royale, a nightclub specializing in Top 40 and Hip-Hop music. It meant dealing with the same assholes I'd put up with as an officer, except now I shoved the drunks into the street and let the cops deal with them.

By late morning, I was nursing my hangover and eating a Zip's burger in Ritzville, a small community located on the Interstate-90 freeway. My gun was safely tucked into the glovebox. I rarely carried it anymore.

I pulled out my phone to see how many minutes were left on the pre-paid card—less than three. Adding minutes could wait. I had some money in my pocket, but I didn't know where I was staying yet. When I collected the thousand from Paige, I could add time to the phone. Until then, I just had to be thrifty with my calls.

Back outside, I closed my eyes and lifted my face to the sky. The sun warmed me, and, for a moment, it helped ease the hangover and my apprehension. When the moment passed, my head returned to banging, and I climbed into the truck. In a little over three hours, I'd be back in Seattle.

The last place I wanted to be.

Chapter 6

I pulled into downtown Seattle around two in the afternoon. Traffic had gotten worse in the time I'd left. I navigated my full-size truck through the narrow streets and dropped by Mickey Finn's, a bar near Pike's Market. Rain drenched the city, reminding everyone October was just days away. Finn's was only a few blocks from where Paige worked, making it an attractive hang-out when we were an item.

The bar smelled of greasy food, spilled beer, and stale cigarette smoke while a soundtrack of '70s funk played in the background. The owner, Miles Tombari, was big, black, and bald. Before he came to Seattle, Miles played professional football in the late seventies. Throughout his short career, he never started but filled in on the offensive line when necessary. While playing with the Detroit Lions, he took a hit from a defensive lineman that destroyed his knee. His right leg had been stiff ever since. Pro ballplayers at the time didn't have the type of payout that today's stars get, so Miles was forced to go to work to provide for his family. He moved to Seattle after he visited the city on vacation. He purchased Mickey Finn's and has been bartending ever since.

The big man stood behind the bar and wiped down the counter. He cocked his head as I approached. The gears inside his brain seemed to spin as I took off my coat and sat on one of the stools. He set both hands on the bar and leaned closer. He looked mostly the same except for maybe a few more wrinkles around the eyes.

"J.C.?" His deep voice brought back memories of long

talks over cold beers and salty pretzels.

I nodded.

"Where the hell you been, son?"

"Spokane."

"The five-oh-nine? Ain't shit been goin' on there since the World's Fair." He pushed away from the bar and crossed his arms. "When was that, seventy-four?"

"No idea."

"Why'd you pick that dump?"

"It's not so bad." I rested my forearms along the edge of the bar.

Miles waggled a finger. "That didn't answer my question."

"I needed a place to lay low and lick my wounds."

His face scrunched. "You been gone, what, two years?"

"About."

He pointed at my face. "Get in a fight?"

"I fell."

"On somebody's fist?"

I shrugged.

"He must have gotten the better of you." Before I could respond, Miles shook his head and said, "Nah. Not you. Not with that hard head."

"I fell," I repeated. "Like I said."

Miles raised a hand in resignation. "Fine. Don't tell me. But answer me this—what have you been up to?"

"Starting over."

"That so? Doing what?"

"Odd jobs, mostly. Nothing steady."

"Like it?"

"It puts food in my belly," I said, thinking about something Paige once said.

"The usual?"

"Yeah. Got any pretzels?"

"I pulled 'em about five months ago as soon as the bums realized I was giving them away."

"Maybe that's all we get to eat."

Miles snickered, then called over a tall, redheaded kid who was washing dishes. "Danny, take this—" He slipped a few bills into the kid's hand. "—and go get a couple bags of pretzels. Don't cheap out."

Without looking back, Danny hurried out the door. Miles slid open the beer cooler and removed a bottle of Miller Lite. He spun the cap and placed the beer on the bar.

Sly & The Family Stone's "Thank You (Falettinme Be Mice Elf Agin)" popped from the speakers hanging behind the bar. Miles sang along with the song, and I chimed in with him on the next lyric.

We laughed as the music continued.

I asked, "You still running everything through the eight-track player?"

"That broke a year ago. I'm digital now. Got a fifty-disc changer."

"Full?"

He beamed like a proud father. "Oh, yeah. There's a regular who makes me all sorts of mixed CDs. I'll never know where he finds some of these songs, but he told me he downloads most of them off the Internet. *For free.* Can you believe that? You're listening to some of his work now."

"He's got good taste."

"Thank God the classics are still available because music hasn't been the same since Marvin was killed."

I raised my beer.

One of the first things that attracted me to Mickey Finn's was the mixture of funk and soul that played through the stereo. Miles's previous stereo system was an old Wollensack 8075 eight-track player attached to an equally ancient RCA amplifier and Infinity speakers. The first time he showed me the system, I laughed in amazement, but it helped give the place an authentic feel of the seventies.

I grew up listening to Motown because of my uncle, Reuben. He lived in New York City during the late sixties and early seventies and the many crazy years that followed. Reuben couldn't go to Vietnam because of a missing kidney, so he went to the next best war zone. New York didn't draft him, but he invaded its turf, destined to become a successful playwright.

After his dreams of fame and fortune were crushed, Rueben returned to Seattle. The time he spent in New York changed the way he appreciated music. His choice of genre and artist was different than everyone else my mother or I knew. My mother and her friends listened to Joni Mitchell and James Taylor while my friends and I were just getting into rock and roll.

Rueben swore by the music he brought home and never swayed when my mom's boyfriends made fun of him. Whenever she and I went over to his apartment, Rueben would put an album on and tell me to listen to "this amazing hook" or "that powerful beat." Before long, he was letting me take home his albums to listen to them in my room. Reuben was my substitute father until he was murdered while I was in high school. I think his untimely death was one of the reasons I wanted to be a police officer.

Miles slapped his hand on the bar. "Rap music is garbage. The singers— Hell, you can't even call 'em that. They steal their beat from someone else. Those young brothers sell an image that being thugs and thieves is glamorous then showcase it in their music. How can you steal the music from George Clinton, change the words, and call yourself an original? Clinton made music. James

Brown made music. Snoop and Ice, they don't make music."

I thought about arguing that millions of consumers, me being one of them, would disagree with his viewpoint, but Miles was on a roll.

His voice reached a crescendo as he preached. I glanced around the bar and noticed an older couple in a back booth enjoying his tirade.

"The people buying those records are just as bad. Most are stupid kids who've been raised on Barney and old Peter, Paul, and Mary songs. Their heads are so full of mush by the time they hear a rap song that they'll believe anything is music."

"You're being harsh."

"*Harsh?*" He frowned. "How the hell else do you explain the success of the 'Macarena?'"

Miles mimed some dance moves before another couple clapped. When the phone rang, he held up a finger, telling me to wait. After picking up the receiver, he announced, "Finn's."

I sipped my beer and checked the walls for new additions. Miles hung an eclectic mix of paraphernalia throughout the bar. There were Irish flags and Guinness signs amidst seventies blaxploitation movie posters and sporting equipment. The Irish stuff was a holdover from the days before he owned the joint. His prized possession was a pair of boxing gloves Muhammad Ali wore while he trained to fight George Foreman in Zaire, the fight famously referred to as "The Rumble in the Jungle." I smiled at all the stuff and realized just how much I missed the place.

When Miles hung up, he turned back. "Sorry about spouting off. I get emotional when I talk about music."

"Understandable."

He poured himself a cup of coffee then rested against

the back bar. "What brings you home?"

"Business."

Miles studied me. "Paige business?"

"She ever stop in?"

"Sometimes."

"How's she look?"

Miles shrugged. "Same as always."

"I was afraid of that."

"You want her to look old and haggard? That woman ain't ever going to look that way."

"It would make things easier."

When Danny returned with the pretzels, Miles ripped open a bag and poured them into a bowl. We talked for a bit about life in general. I had missed Miles' listening abilities. In all the times I confided in him, he never looked down on me or turned me away. He always stayed steady. That's probably why he had so many loyal customers.

"What time does she get done?" Miles asked.

"Around eleven."

"You still got a few hours 'til then. You gonna drink straight through?"

I took the last swig from my beer and set it down. "I can't be messed up around her. I need to be able to walk away if the business sounds bad." Pulling a fifty from my wallet, I laid it on the bar. "You still got the cot in the backroom?"

"Need it?"

"If you don't mind."

"If I did, you'd just end up staying at her place, and then you'd be in a world of hurt."

I pushed in the bar stool. "I was stupid once. It won't happen again."

A half-smile appeared on Miles' face that quickly turned into a rueful shake of the head. "John Cutler, my friend, if there is one thing that I know, it's that you're a slow learner."

***

Around the corner, I found a payphone. I thought about using my cell, but I might need the scant minutes I had left in an emergency.

I dropped some change into the coin slot then dialed a number I'd committed to memory. Scratches in the Plexiglas window showed the world was full of idiots who couldn't spell.

After six rings, an answering machine picked up. "*Hi, you've reached the Durants. We can't come to the phone right now. Leave your message, and we'll get back to you as soon as possible.*"

"Hey, Maria, it's me. I'm in town. I'm hoping to see Erin for a few. I'm calling from a payphone, so I'll just call again later."

Chapter 7

The first time Paige kissed me was outside The Red Light District.

I'd already returned a couple of times to the club and gotten additional dances. Each visit was a repeat of the initial night, but it didn't lessen my fascination with her. The opposite was true. The simple act of being touched by her but not touching her back intensified my desire. It was stupid and immature, but that's where my head was.

I can't explain why those feelings happened. It wasn't like I had problems with women, although I wasn't some type of ladies' man, either. And I didn't have an issue with confidence. Maybe it was the kind of thing that drug addicts experienced—just a little taste the first time, then one more sample, then suddenly they're jonesing for something they never knew they wanted at all.

The desire for her bumped against the logical part of my brain—the part that knew I was being worked for an extra twenty every time she suggested another dance. But the drug always won out, and soon my self-loathing became less and less. I was headed to a dangerous and pathetic place, and I knew it.

At the end of my fourth visit to the club, I'd paid Paige for a couple of dances, thanked her as politely as I could, and stood. I needed to get out of there and never come back. If I didn't do it right then, I would be one of those weird guys who hung out at strip clubs, justifying the act by saying all men had to somehow pay for a woman's affections.

When I slipped on my jacket, Paige asked, "Leaving

so soon?"

"I've got to go," I muttered.

Something passed over her face. *Concern?* It was too fast for me to make out, and I wasn't going to ask what it might have been.

"Hold on," she said. "I'll meet you outside. Let me grab my coat."

Dopamine rushed through my system when I realized she wanted to talk with me outside the club. My previous concerns magically vanished.

A few minutes later, we stood alongside the building, away from prying eyes.

She wore a long wool coat and calf-high boots. When she moved, there were occasional flashes of skin from where the coat parted. Paige only had on a bikini underneath. Back then, it seemed sexy as hell.

"Can I have one of those?" She pointed at my cigarette.

I handed her my pack of Marlboros and lighter.

"How long is your break?" I asked.

"Thirty minutes. Longer if I want to lose my place in the rotation."

"Is it good? The dancing?"

Paige cast me a sideways glance. "Are you asking if I like it?"

"Yeah."

She inhaled on her cigarette then said flatly, "It puts food in my belly."

"What else would you rather do?"

"Nothing, I guess. I do all right with this. Better than most. Someday, I'll find another gig, but I don't see myself sitting behind a receptionist desk. Can you see me doing that?"

I shook my head.

"What about you? Do you like being a cop?"

"You already asked me that."

"Yeah." Her smile was soft. "But is there something else you'd rather be doing?"

I leaned my shoulders against the building. "It's all I know."

"Chasing criminals is all you know?"

"There's more to the job than that, but even so, would that be so bad?"

Paige looked up as she exhaled. "No. I think it's noble."

We finished our cigarettes then snuffed them out on the asphalt.

She moved directly in front of me, slipped her hands in her pockets, and tugged her coat tighter. "Why do you keep coming back?"

I cocked my head.

"You've got a good job. I assume that means a decent life, too. Are you married? Is this your secret get-away from her? You come to watch us dance then go home to your family?"

"I'm not married."

The corner of Paige's lip scrunched as she thought. "Trouble meeting girls then?"

"Not usually, no."

"I wouldn't think so. So, why?"

Even though it was chilly out, my face warmed. "I thought my being here was obvious."

Her lips relaxed before they turned into a playful smile. "See? I knew there was a reason, but I wanted to make sure."

"How many girls have you seen me get a dance from?"

Paige shrugged. "I don't know. Sometimes I'm in the back. Maybe you get—"

"None."

"Does that make us exclusive?"

"Don't make fun. I already know how stupid this is."

"You're not stupid."

"I've got a crush on a stripper. That's stupid."

"Dancer," she corrected. "And it happens."

"Not to me. This whole thing is ridiculous."

Her eyes softened. "It's not ridiculous."

"Really? How many guy-falls-for-dancer love stories do you know?"

"A few."

"You probably would." I looked down, embarrassed to be admitting how I felt.

"For what it's worth, I think you're nice."

That was about the worst thing she could say. I rolled my eyes.

"Don't do that. Nice goes a long way in my world. Never discount it." She leaned in and gently kissed my lips.

I closed my eyes and drank in the moment. It was a closed-lip kiss—the kind kids do their first time—but it felt like my world imploded. My heart raced, and the nearby sounds of traffic diminished. It was as if everything in the world suddenly became her.

As quickly as it happened, her lips pulled away. She remained close to me, though. I opened my eyes to meet her hers.

"Sooner or later," she whispered, "you should ask me out or something."

She headed back into the club before I could say anything.

Chapter 8

After leaving a message for Maria, I considered going back to Mickey Finn's. That would be a bad idea. I didn't need a belly full of booze before seeing Paige.

Instead, I wandered around downtown, killing time. When I couldn't take more ruminating about my former life, I returned to my truck and headed for the first fast-food restaurant I could find. It was around eight in the evening, and I finally had to give in to my stomach. All the cash I had in the world was inside my pocket, so being choosy wasn't an option until I got the money from Paige.

Besides, Whoppers were on special, and the newspaper I read was free.

It seemed not much had changed in the two years I'd been gone. Crime of all sorts still occurred in every nook and cranny of the metropolitan area. A seven-year-old boy was the victim of a drive-by shooting, and an elderly grandmother was raped by her granddaughter's boyfriend. Disgusted by the continued tales of pain, I closed the newspaper and focused on my fries.

Around ten, I arrived in a north Seattle neighborhood at Paige's apartment complex. The buildings were new, gray, and constructed with a cookie-cutter sameness. Briefly, I wondered what was torn down to make way for them. I parked in a "Visitors Only" spot.

From the outside, the apartments appeared much nicer than her previous place. Back then, she lived in a small one-bedroom apartment not far from the club. It had a nice view of the freeway, but not much else.

Now, she lived in a community whose parking lot was filled with brand names like BMW, Lexus, and Lincoln. I'm not sure what her rent was, but I'm sure one month would have covered my place for several—at least.

A private security vehicle passed through the lot. It was one of those little cars with a company logo and set of emergency lights affixed to the roof. Its presence alone was supposed to deter crime and make the residents feel safer. Usually, these guys worked a route and would pass through one community before moving on to the next.

Underneath the doormat, I found the key she'd promised. I slid it into the lock and hesitated. There were pry marks near the lock, and the doorjamb had splintered slightly. Had this happened after Paige moved into the unit?

Once inside, I wandered through the apartment, taking it all in.

A white area rug lay in the middle of the living room over hardwood floors.

Paintings hung on the walls. On the largest was a flat-screen television.

There were three bedrooms. It was a large place for a single woman.

One of the rooms was set up like an office. A laptop computer occupied the corner of a mahogany desk. There was an empty cardboard box on the floor that the laptop had come in. On the corner of the desk was a *Vanderlinden for Council President* button. Paige must have become politically active in the past couple of years.

The second room was a guest bedroom with a queen-sized bed. Pictures of her family hung on the walls. On the nightstand was a small wooden box with no lid. Inside were dozens of photographs. Her mom and sister were in some. There were random men and women in the others. I wondered if the men might be former lovers. I tossed the photographs back into the box.

In her bedroom was a California King with a black comforter. Pulling back the comforter revealed black silk sheets underneath. A couple of mirrors hung on the wall amidst several modern art pieces. No photographs of friends or family were in here.

I sat on the edge of the bed and opened the top drawer of her nightstand. Inside was a picture of me in my police uniform. A smile creased my face, and pride puffed my chest. I remembered that feeling—tough, cocky, and untouchable. Back then, I had the world by the tail. That was before the fall.

Holding the picture, I wondered why it was there. Did Paige still harbor feelings for me? Did she occasionally look at the image with the regret of what might have been?

No, I thought. Paige was too smart for that.

More than likely, she put the photograph in the nightstand's drawer for this reason. Paige knew how I ticked. She probably went through the pictures in the other room, found mine, and stuck it here for me to discover.

I put the photograph back and closed the drawer.

I left her bedroom, grabbed a Michelob Ultra from the refrigerator, then sat on the living room's white leather couch. After a sip, I picked up the large remote for the television and considered its myriad buttons. Soon, I tossed the controller on the end table. Leaning my head back on the edge of the sofa, I shut my eyes.

The room smelled of her.

***

The dream left me disoriented. That feeling lasted for only a moment, though. Then I was angry that I had *the* dream. It had been months since I dreamt about her.

I figured out the remote enough to watch highlights on ESPN. It had been some time since I'd watched the channel.

When the door to the apartment opened, I dropped my cigarette into my bottle.

She stepped around the corner and smiled. She wore faded blue jeans with a fashionably small tear in the knee and an oversized black sweatshirt from Montgomery Construction. Her hair was pulled back with a scrunchie. Miles was right—she looked good.

Paige dropped her oversized purse near the entryway then fanned away the remaining smoke. "I should have told you that I quit."

"Wouldn't have made any difference."

"Sullen sonuvabitch."

She dropped next to me on the couch. I tensed, and her face pinched with disbelief.

"Relax, John. I'm not going to bite."

She waited for a playful response that I refused to give.

Reaching out to touch my face, she asked, "What happened?"

I pulled away slightly. "Got into a fight."

"Did you win?" Her hand lowered onto my knee.

A man can lose even when he wins, but she didn't want to hear that. So, I simply shrugged.

She leaned closer, and I smelled her musky perfume. "Wanna see my new tattoo?"

I closed my eyes. The game had begun. Hell, maybe it had started back on the phone, and I was too thick to realize it. That's the way it was with Paige. I never knew which way was up until I was headed down.

Paige reached out again. This time, I didn't pull back. Her fingers were cool and gentle on my face. Her voice softened, and she purred, "Poor John, fighting for his life."

I opened my eyes, and her hand jumped off my skin as if it were a hot plate.

"I don't like that look," she said.

"You made a business proposal, and I agreed to it. I'm not here to be reminded of my stupidity."

She clicked her teeth together. "You weren't always this serious."

"Being with you has a way of changing things."

Her cheeks reddened. "Maybe this was a bad idea."

"I think you're right." I stood, grabbed my coat, and walked out of the apartment. I didn't bother closing the door.

My truck started, and I dropped the transmission into reverse. As I backed out of the parking stall, she hurried toward me.

I stopped and waited, which was dumb. Instead, I should have kept going until I was back across the state. That would have been the smart thing to do.

She knocked on the passenger's window. Even though it was now drizzling, she patiently waited for me to acknowledge her. I rolled the window down but refused to face her. It was immature, but I didn't know what else to do.

Turn and say I missed her? *Never.*

Admit that the feelings for her never entirely went away. *Like hell.*

She said, "I'm sorry, John."

My hands gripped the steering wheel.

"I shouldn't have teased you. It means a lot that you came over."

From my peripheral vision, I could see her hands on the door. She was getting wet, but she wasn't trying to get inside the truck.

"You're the only one I could ask for help," she said.

Facing her now, she stared at me the way she did in the early days—with earnest sincerity. It was a lie, though. I knew full well that she was manipulating me. But it felt like the embrace of an old lover, and I missed it.

The rain accumulated on the shoulders of her sweatshirt and had started to weigh down her hair.

"Come back inside, John. *Please.*"

I pulled the truck back into its parking spot and turned off the engine.

A spark of victory flashed in her eyes before she hurried toward her apartment.

Chapter 9

"It's an expandable file," Paige said. "You know—the accordion-type of thing."

We were seated in her living room. She sat next to me on the couch, her legs folded underneath. Her shoes were on the floor.

"What did you keep in there?"

She rubbed the palms of her hands on her jeans. "Important things."

"Like what?"

"You know, things like my birth certificate and apartment lease. That kind of stuff."

That didn't sound important enough for someone to steal or for her to pay two thousand to get back. "What else?"

She shrugged. "And some letters and cards, I guess."

"Cards?"

"Birthday cards, Christmas cards. *Cards*."

The way she said it let me know they weren't from family. I thought about the photographs in the other room. "Which boyfriend were they from?"

Paige stared at the floor and bobbed her head a couple of times as if she were deciding what to admit.

"What's in the letters and cards that makes them so important?"

She looked up. "What's inside isn't important. It's who they're from that is."

"Who were they from?"

She frowned then looked away.

"Goddamn it, Paige. Who took the file?"

She mumbled something I couldn't hear.

"What?"

"Levi."

I lifted my hands in apparent frustration.

"Levi Montgomery."

My eyes flicked to the Montgomery Construction logo on her sweatshirt. "The same?"

"Yeah."

"You two were an item, and now you're not?"

Paige picked at the tear in her jeans. "He liked me fine until his father found out about us. He told him to break it off, or Levi was out of the family business. It seems Levi liked the company better than me."

"Why would his father involve himself in your relationship?"

Paige forced a smile, but it didn't hold. "They're an established business with a lot of old money contacts. According to daddy dearest, it doesn't look good for the face of the company to be seen with a girl like me." She air-quoted 'a girl like me.' Then she jerked a thumb toward the kitchen. "Want another beer?"

"No. Why'd this guy want them back?"

"To hurt me."

"But he broke up with you, right? Why would he care?"

She stared at me for a moment with her mouth slightly opened. Her brow slowly furrowed as if thinking.

"Want me to guess?"

"No. I don't want—"

"He's married."

She glared at me. "I don't hook up with married guys."

I kneaded my temples. A headache was pushing in. "And you know for certain he took the file?"

"Definitely."

"You know this how?"

"I called and asked him to give it back."

"And what did he say?"

"He said, fuck off."

"Sounds like a sweet guy."

With her head, she motioned toward the television. "It worked out all right in the end, though. That's how I got the flat screen." Her expression told me she didn't give a damn about the TV.

I glanced around the apartment, noting the expensive furniture and the artwork on the walls. "Did Levi pay for all of this?"

"I paid for this." She indignantly tapped her chest. "Nobody else. The TV was a birthday present."

"What happened to your front door?"

"What do you think?"

"Levi did that?"

"He had a key. He wouldn't have had to kick in the door."

"You changed the locks?"

"The management company did after he took the file."

"When did this break-in happen?"

"A few weeks ago. They stole my laptop, some jewelry, the cash I had laying around."

My eyes flicked to the new laptop. "Could they have stolen the file?"

"No. It was still there afterward. I made sure."

"Someone broke in and stole a bunch of stuff, then Levi comes in when?"

"A week ago, or so."

"Is that when you two split up?"

Paige nodded.

"Was anyone else in the apartment community broken into?"

"Do you mean was I targeted?"

"That's exactly what I mean."

"There have been other break-ins. So many that the managers hired a security company to patrol the lot. I think the burglary was just bad luck. Levi taking the file, that's something else."

I studied her more closely. "That's what you want? For me to get this file back from Levi."

"Yeah."

"And it's worth two thousand?"

"Uh-huh."

"What else is in there?"

She stood, walked over to the kitchen counter, and opened her purse. She fished out a white envelope.

"That's a steep price to pay for a handful of cards and letters from an old lover."

Paige walked back to the couch and held out the envelope. "For coming over and no more questions about the file. You'll get the other thousand when you bring it back."

I stared at the envelope. Deception wrapped her story in a way that made me wonder if I would ever find the truth. But two thousand meant four months of child support payments—all for finding a stupid folder.

The envelope slipped from her fingers when I tugged on it. Paige dropped onto the couch and tucked her legs underneath her.

Pulling a pen from my pocket, I said, "Tell me about Levi."

"What do you want to know?"

"Where he lives, his age, height, eye color, hair color."

Paige looked up at the ceiling as she thought. "He's thirty-four, has brown hair and blue eyes. Uh, he's about six-three, I guess. I don't know. Maybe two hundred twenty-five pounds."

I jotted notes on the front of the envelope, trying to

keep up as she spoke.

She continued. "The company's office is in Kirkland." She didn't know the exact address but described the building and the intersection. "Levi and his brother are working a job now in Puyallup. They're building a fast-food restaurant or something."

"When's the last time you spoke with him?"

"A week ago."

"Is that when you asked for the file back?"

"Yeah."

"Then how did you know about the job in Puyallup?"

"Come on, John. Construction doesn't happen overnight. They've been on that site for a while."

I considered my notes, looking for things I might have missed. When I didn't see an essential piece of information, I wondered if I missed writing it down. I was sure I asked the question. "Did you tell me where he lived?"

Paige bit her lip and looked at the floor. "I don't know."

"You don't know where your former boyfriend lived or where he's living *now*? It's only been a week."

"He's building a home in Mercer Island. I know that much."

I tapped the envelope against my leg. "How do you *not* know where he's living?"

"He's living with his dad while he's building his house. He never invited me over for obvious reasons."

"He's married, Paige."

"He's not!" she snapped. Her face reddened, and tears welled in her eyes. "He's not," she said softer. "I promise."

I sighed. "All right. What's the brother's name? In case I need to talk with him."

"Max." She gave a brief description of him.

"Anything else you can tell me?"

"Do you want his phone number?"

"Sure."

After reciting the ten-digit number, Paige said, "He usually screens his calls, though."

"Because of you?"

She shook her head. "Unless he knows who is calling, he lets them go to voicemail before calling back."

"When I show up and talk with Levi, how's he going to react?"

"That depends on which John Cutler shows up."

I raised an eyebrow.

"If you go in there to butt heads, I'm pretty sure he won't take it well. If you go in there and smooth talk him, maybe he'll be nice."

"Maybe?"

Paige lifted her hands in a what-can-I-say gesture.

It had been two years since I'd done any type of investigative work. I thought it would be like riding a bicycle. That everything would come back naturally. It didn't feel that way, though. I kept thinking I should have more questions or get more information, but I was stuck on how to get at it. No more questions came to mind. Paige was hiding something; that much was clear. But I needed the money enough to push blindly forward. She watched while the wheels spun in my head.

"What's really in the folder?" I asked.

"No more questions," she said. "You agreed."

I grunted and stood. Shoving the envelope into my back pocket solidified my position. I'd like to say the money felt good, but it didn't. All I'd done is shown both of us how much my soul cost.

"You're leaving?" she asked.

"I'll get started in the morning. Until then, I need to get some sleep."

"You can stay here."

"No."

"I *meant* the guest room."

I couldn't tell if that's truly what she meant. And even if she did, I couldn't be trusted. I'd already sold my soul. My self-respect wouldn't cost much more.

"It's better this way," I said.

"Says who?" She got up and headed toward her bedroom.

I let myself out.

Chapter 10

Before I met Paige, a crack dealer filed a complaint stating that I stole fifteen hundred dollars from him. I never took the money. I've done a lot of shitty things that I regret, but I never stole a dime.

However, the administration was on the warpath to clean up the department's reputation with the community—especially the black neighborhoods. The whole hold-hands-with-a-citizen initiative was some modern Kumbaya bullshit, and patrol officers were forced to play along.

The crack dealer's complaint got kicked up the chain of command before it was sent to Internal Affairs. It irritated me that the department took the claim seriously enough to sic Lieutenant Daryl Crites on me.

If anyone was ever handmade for Internal Affairs, it was Crites. The man was a dog with a bone. If he sniffed trouble, he bit into it and held on until he proved something. He had no friends in the department, and he never seemed to crave them either. Many line-level officers believed the brass hated Crites as well, but the man was good at what he did. There was no disputing his effectiveness. He wasn't blinded by loyalty or friendships, so he wasn't afraid to tear apart an officer's life if it meant getting at some kernel of truth. He believed that the police should be held to a higher standard and, by God, he was going to keep every officer accountable to it.

For my initial interview, we were seated in the Internal Affairs conference room. My union rep, Thomas Jasper, sat next to me.

Across the table was Crites with an open folder and notepad. "At this time, Officer Cutler, you haven't been charged with a crime."

"Then why the hell am I here?"

"Easy, John," Jasper said. "Let the man speak."

Crites smiled. It was a practiced act. The kind a car salesman gives right before you sign the contract. "I want your side of the story."

"You shouldn't need my side of the story, Lieutenant. You should be able to tell that this was bullshit from the get-go."

"We do our job by getting the facts, Officer. Maybe that's part of your problem."

"My problem?"

"Acting impulsively."

"Have I done something to you, Lieutenant?"

Crites shrugged. "Not me, but this citizen—"

"*Citizen?* You're fucking kidding me."

"John," Jasper said with quiet ferocity. He motioned to the small tape recorder on the table between the lieutenant and us.

"Don't hold back, Officer Cutler." Crites smiled again. If I was buying a new car, he was upselling me on the extended warranty. "Tell me how you feel."

I folded my arms and stared at the tape recorder and its little wheels slowly turning.

After that, Crites laid out the crack dealer's accusations. It was clear that the lieutenant deemed me guilty until proven innocent. It wouldn't matter how I defended myself. This case was going to go further regardless of what I said that day.

Jasper sat quietly by. I expected more enthusiastic support, but maybe he'd seen enough of the lieutenant's antics before.

When Crites finished laying out what faced me, he politely asked, "Not going to defend yourself, Officer?"

"You said I hadn't been charged. Did something happen while you blathered on? I might have missed it because I tuned out."

Jasper put his hand on my forearm to calm me.

The lieutenant shrugged. "The last refuge of the guilty is to cast aspersions on the innocent."

My face warmed. "Fuck you, you're innocent."

"Shut it!" Jasper hissed.

Crites closed his folder and smiled. It was one of self-satisfaction. He'd closed the sale. "I've heard enough." He reached for the tape recorder.

"You got dick," I said.

The lieutenant's hand hovered above the recorder. "What's that?"

Jasper's fingers dug into my arm, but that didn't stop me.

I continued. "You heard me. It's the same dick you've been sucking to get your promotions."

Crites raised his eyebrows and pulled his hand away from the recorder. "And who's dick would that be?"

"Chief Faber's, you fuck. It's the only way you can get away with treating cops this way and not getting fired. Did you tickle his balls while you—"

Jasper reached across the table and clicked off the recorder. "Shut up, John." He sighed. "For the love of God, just shut up."

I glared at the lieutenant. He merely smiled and slid the tape recorder to his side of the table.

What I said was unprofessional and immature, but it felt like a pressure relief valve had finally been turned loose.

The next day an official transcript of my interaction with Lieutenant Crites made its way into my file. A copy was sent to the chief's office. As a result, I ended up on Faber's shit list. Until that moment, I'm not even sure if the man knew I existed.

Looking back, I deserved it.

However, I believed then and still believed now that Crites had gone beyond his authority with the way he hounded me. During the initial investigation, Crites never found anything to substantiate the drug money claim. That's because it wasn't true.

But he found something that eventually hurt me far worse.

He found out about my relationship with Paige.

That's when things got ugly.

Chapter 11

"You sure you want to stay here?" Miles asked. He held a cup of coffee as he led me to the backroom of Mickey Finn's. Amid stacks of beer cases, toilet paper, and other paper supplies, an old cot stood in the corner of the room.

I tossed my gym bag onto the makeshift bed. The pillow had a clean cover and sat next to a couple of folded Army blankets.

"I don't need much."

"Things must not have gone well with Paige."

"Why do you say that?"

"You're grumpier than before."

I sat on the cot and rested my shoulders against the concrete wall. "It went fine."

"You sure about that?"

"She's still beautiful." The wistfulness in my voice wasn't hard to detect.

"Didn't I tell you?"

"You told me."

Miles pointed through an open door that led into another storage room. "There's a small shower around the corner, in case you want to clean up."

"When did you add that?"

"About a year ago. Sometimes the wife comes downtown for dinner or to go to a game. I got tired of smelling like this place. It didn't cost much to add." Miles leaned on the doorframe. "You gonna do the job?"

I looked down at my hands.

"John Cutler, you slow-learning son of a bitch. She's

like a gas stove that you keep checking by putting your hand over the flame. Trust me—it's lit."

"Miles—"

"And it's always gonna be lit."

"It's not like that."

His eyes registered disappointment. "Whether you accept it or not, that flame will always burn the hell out of you." He glanced over his shoulder. "I gotta get back out there."

"Miles," I said.

"Yeah?"

"Thank you."

He left me alone after that.

Chapter 12

Montgomery Construction's office was in south Kirkland, just off Interstate 405. Its building was a small, concrete affair that sat in front of a large gravel lot. Chain link fencing surrounded the storage yard, which contained various trucks and other pieces of equipment.

Men in blue jeans, work jackets, and boots milled about the area. Most gave me only passing glances. My appearance was much like theirs, so I didn't rate much concern.

Immediately inside the building was a small reception lobby. A chest-high counter stopped anyone from passing by without contacting the woman seated behind it. A plaque on the front of her desk read *Sandra Beckman*.

She appeared to be in her mid-forties with grayish-brown hair pulled tightly against her scalp. Small glasses rode near the tip of her nose, and she wore only moderate make-up.

When I cleared my throat, Sandra glanced up from whatever she was reading. After quickly appraising me, a scowl formed. She pointed her pen toward the end of the counter. "Applications are over there."

I paused for a moment, then went to where she indicated. From a plastic tray, I pulled a single piece of paper from the top. "Excuse me," I said politely.

With her attention on a stack of documents, Sandra's right hand manipulated an adding machine. It chattered loudly as a length of white tape extended from its end.

"Excuse me," I repeated, louder this time.

Sandra's fingers hovered over the adding machine,

allowing it to quiet. She tilted her chin down and watched me from above her glasses.

"Is Levi in?" I asked.

"Levi?"

"Mr. Montgomery. Is he here?"

"What's this about?"

I waved the application. "I'd like to talk with him about a job."

The receptionist shook her head. "Max does the hiring, but nobody talks with him until they fill out an application." She returned her head to its previous position, and the adding machine clattered back to life.

When I was a cop, the authority that the uniform represented got me an audience with anyone. Blue jeans and a leather jacket weren't getting me past this counter. I thought about simply barging into the back, but I didn't know if Levi Montgomery was even there. There are times a hammer works. There are times when a light touch works. I was hoping the latter would be appropriate now.

"I'm not here for a job," I said.

The adding machine quieted, and Sandra raised a skeptical eyebrow. She didn't say anything, however.

"I only need a couple minutes with Levi. How do I—"

"You need?"

Light touch, I reminded myself. "I'd like."

Sandra carefully removed her glasses. When she spoke, her words were slow and deliberate. "And why would you like to speak with Mr. Montgomery?"

"It's a private matter."

Her eyes narrowed, and I felt as if I were back in school, standing in front of the principal. "No, sir, it is most certainly *not* a private matter. If it were, you would already know how to get in contact with Levi. Since you don't, you are here for another reason, one of which you are trying to conceal. And because of that, you are done. Goodbye."

She put her glasses back on, and the adding machine returned to its chattering. I stared at Sandra for a moment before setting the application on the counter.

I *could* have called Levi—Paige had given me his number—but had the man not wanted to talk with me, all he had to do was hang up. Then where would I have been? Right there in the same situation that I was faced with now.

My face grew warm. I should have turned and left, but Sandra's arrogance annoyed me. I was also frustrated by my lack of ability to get by her. It had only been a couple of years since I was a cop, but my communication skills were rusty. I felt stupid, and that pissed me off.

"I'm here for a friend," I blurted.

When Sandra looked up sharply, I instantly regretted my outburst. Behind her glasses, her eyes narrowed. Through clenched teeth, she asked, "What friend?"

Don't say it.

With a single hand, she snatched the glasses from her face. "Quit wasting my time, sir. Some of us have work—"

"Paige McIntyre."

She grimaced.

"She's asked me to—"

"Leave."

"Ma'am?"

"Get out!" She pointed at the door.

"Shit," I muttered.

I shoved open the door, hoping it would bang loudly and make a scene. It didn't, and that just frustrated me further. I climbed into my truck, started it, and left the lot, much too fast and reckless.

My anger bubbled for two blocks before I punched the steering wheel several times.

Chapter 13

"I went to Montgomery Construction," I said.

Paige looked at her hand, turning it over to examine her fingernails. She wore a white knit sweater, and her dark hair cascaded over both shoulders.

"And I had a run-in with the receptionist."

"Oh."

"That's the best you can do? *Oh?*"

She glared at me.

We were at Dine and Dash, a '50s style hamburger restaurant that Paige suggested for lunch. Booker T. & the M.G's "Green Onions" drifted out of a Wurlitzer in the corner. We had already ordered and were waiting for our cheeseburgers.

"Why would she act that way when I said your name?"

"I don't know. Maybe Levi said bad things about me."

I spun a dull knife on the table. "When I said your name, her head almost popped off."

Paige turned to watch passersby through the window.

"Is this your passive-aggressive way of not telling me what happened?"

"We broke up. It didn't go well. Leave it at that."

"You want me to find that file, but you're keeping secrets."

Paige ignored me and pulled a piece of paper from her purse. She slid it across to the table. On it, in her handwriting, was an address. "That's the job site in Puyallup. I drove down there and got it. You're welcome." Her sarcasm was easy to detect.

"You're hiding things, and it's pissing me off."

She leaned over the table and said very deliberately, "Find the file, John. That's what I'm paying you for."

A woman walked into the restaurant then. She was in her early forties and dressed business professional. She was engaged in casual conversation with a younger man who deferred to her. Perhaps he was her assistant.

When Paige saw the woman, she went white.

"Everything okay?" I asked her.

"What?"

"Who's that?"

Her face slackened, and she turned to me. "Huh?"

I pointed at the woman, but she was already leaving the restaurant with the younger man on her heels. "Who was that?"

"I have no idea."

I slapped the table, and Paige jumped in her seat. Several patrons turned our way. "For once, tell me the truth."

Paige squinted and seemed to fight the urge to say something. She relaxed when the waitress walked up with our order. The server quietly put our plates down and hurried away.

"This looks good," Paige said with a forced smile.

And just like that, she ended the conversation.

While we ate in silence, I argued internally about giving her back the thousand dollars. Every time the thought came up, though, I remembered Erin. I was doing this for child support, not some knight-in-shining-armor bullshit.

I would find that file, collect the remaining thousand, then run away from this woman again.

Chapter 14

With my career as a Seattle police officer wobbling, my personal life seemed to have discovered some semblance of hope. Paige and I began dating and found ourselves in an easy rhythm. There was no pressure in our relationship, although I knew I felt something for her that she didn't necessarily feel for me. I figured that's how relationships went, though. Someone was always a little further out on the teetertotter than the other, threatening to throw the whole thing off balance.

Paige knew about my daughter, and Erin understood that I was seeing someone, but it still seemed too early for them to meet. Besides, Paige wasn't into kids. It was best to keep those worlds separated.

I also didn't want Erin's mother harping at me. Maria was a nice woman, but I imagined her response to my new girlfriend wouldn't play well. We weren't married, but Maria might make negative comments about Paige's occupation. Why force that issue?

Paige and I had already been together for a couple of months when I showed up at the club one Friday night. We had a date planned after her shift. The doorman, Jarod, shook my hand as I went in.

"She's in high demand tonight," he said. I'm sure he meant it as a compliment, but it set me on edge.

Some of the other dancers engaged me in small talk. Paige wasn't on stage, and she wasn't wandering around. That meant she was elsewhere in the darkness. I pretended not to know what was going on.

Def Leppard's "Pour Some Sugar on Me" cranked

through the club's stereo system.

After a few minutes, I couldn't help myself. By then, my eyes had adjusted to the lower level of light, so I scanned the back booths until I found her. She wore a gray sports bra and matching bottoms.

Paige was in the middle of a lap dance, wriggling in pace with the music. I despised what she was doing, so I looked away.

She never apologized for her career choice, and if I wanted to be with her, I had to accept it. Hell, the first time I saw her on stage, it affected me enough to come back to a strip club, something I'd never done before. I ignored the embarrassment of paying her to dance privately for me and did it again. Not one ounce of any of those transactions was real, but I still choose to believe it. She opened my nose wide, and I breathed in the fantasy until everything became real.

In quiet moments away from her, I realized I couldn't have been the only guy that felt that way. Most of The Red Light District customers had to feel it, too. Maybe not just for her, but with some of the other women, too. That's why guys kept coming back, putting money on the stage, and asking for private dances. They wanted to make their fantasies come true.

When Paige was on stage, peeling off her clothes, that was tough enough. Every guy watched her with a hunger I knew intimately. But when she was one-on-one in a booth, that almost ripped my heart out. The jealousy made me want to tear someone's head off.

It wasn't a good feeling for a cop to have.

I wanted her to stop dancing, but I kept those thoughts to myself, especially after only two months of dating. Those weren't the type of things I could admit to Paige. She wasn't the kind of woman to be told anything. Doing so would have gotten me a one-way ticket out of the relationship. Even asking her to stop would have been a display of weakness that she would have disrespected.

I kept getting further out on the relationship teetertotter, which would throw us off balance. I hated myself for letting it happen, but I couldn't seem to stop it. I feared her jumping off and sending me crashing to the ground.

Def Leppard's song pulsated throughout the club.

I fought my curiosity for as long as I could, but I eventually glanced back toward Paige. Her customer reached up and set his hands on her hips. She let him get away with it for a second before pulling them off and pinning them to the back of the booth.

Consciously, I knew it was a hyper-sexualized defensive move. She had removed his hands and was now holding him back. But by restraining her customer this way, she put her breasts in his face.

My fingernails dug into my palms, and I forced myself to relax. I looked away again, but my jealousy quickly got the better of me once more.

I watched her again.

She released her patron but continued grinding on him.

I should have walked outside and taken a lap or two around the block. My entire body felt on fire. I wanted to yell. It was like every night of jealousy from the past two months had suddenly found itself into that single moment.

Why did that simple act of putting his hands on her waist seem so intimate?

Maybe because I did the same thing in the privacy of my apartment.

As Paige wriggled, the guy leaned forward from the darkness. Even from across a poorly lit room, I recognized him. Lieutenant Daryl Crites grinned widely.

He dropped back into the darkness as Paige continued to dance privately for him.

I sprinted across the room, knocking over tables and chairs as I went. Denzell and Hoyt, the bouncers, jumped at the commotion.

Grabbing Paige's arm, I yanked her away from Crites.

"The hell!" she said.

"Get off."

She pulled her arm free. "I'm working."

I pointed at Crites. "Not him."

"Come on, John," the lieutenant said. "Don't be that way."

"Is there a problem?" Hoyt asked in his low voice. Denzell stood beside him.

"You bet there's a problem," I said. "This guy's trying to get me fired."

Crites shrugged. "We don't want dirty cops."

"I'm not dirty."

Paige's face contorted with anger, and she hissed, "Go away, John."

Crites looked past me to Denzell. "Are you gonna comp me another dance because of this interruption?"

"We'll take care of it, sir."

"But I want it with Paige here," he said using her real name, not her stage moniker. To me, he smiled. "I see why you like her, John."

I punched him.

Paige screamed and tumbled backward to the floor.

Denzell and Hoyt tackled me. I struggled to get free. I wanted to fight Crites. I wanted to kill him. I yelled like a lunatic.

A couple of nearby patrons cheered while several dancers hollered at me to knock it off.

With blood streaming from his nose, the lieutenant shouted, "You're under arrest!"

"You started this!"

While the two bouncers pinned me down, Crites slipped handcuffs around my wrists.

Hoyt whispered into my ear, "Sorry, John."

"I've got him," the lieutenant said and lifted me to my feet. "Let's go, Cutler."

"Where's Paige?" I scanned the club, but she was gone. "Paige!"

Crites jerked my arm and led me toward the exit. The whole time, I anxiously searched for her.

Once outside, the lieutenant spun me around and shoved me against the wall. He stepped away and made a phone call.

Alone and cuffed, the hatred for Crites drained from my body. It was then that I realized what I did—not punching the lieutenant. That I would do again. But fighting in front of Paige. By losing control, I pushed myself further out on the relationship teetertotter. Would this be the thing that she would jump off for?

When Crites ended his phone call, he returned to where I waited. His smile wasn't the used car salesman he'd affected in the department's conference room. Now, it held cruelty. It was something I'd never seen before.

"A transport car is on the way. You've done it now, buddy boy."

"How's the nose?"

Gently, Crites touched the side of it. "Hurts," he muttered. "You got a good shot in. I owe you for it."

"Sure, you do."

He punched me in the stomach.

With my hands cuffed behind my back, I was defenseless. It was a line I never thought the lieutenant would cross. I collapsed to my knees and sucked for air.

No one was around us. Fear lanced through me. I was afraid he would hit me again.

Instead, Crites placed his hand on my shoulder. "Mess with the bull, Cutler, and you get the horns."

Chapter 15

Montgomery Construction's Puyallup project was a retail strip center on Meridian Street. Meridian runs through the heart of Puyallup, a town best known for hosting the state fair. On the corner of the lot stood a sign showing an architect's rendering of the building with the words COMING SOON!

To the south of the site was a Jack in the Box. A gas station stood to the north. They were older structures and would likely fall in the future with so much new construction surrounding them.

I parked near a row of dented pick-ups. Men in hard hats milled about as they prepared for the morning's efforts. After exiting my truck, I approached a medium-sized guy who wore his white helmet backward and carried a clipboard.

He eyed me suspiciously. "You with the city?"

"I'm looking for Levi."

The guy briefly studied me before pointing toward a white trailer sitting in the back corner of the lot. "Behind there. He's grabbing a smoke."

As I walked away, several of the men stopped what they were doing to watch me. They seemed to take more than a passing interest.

Behind the trailer, there was a lone guy, smoking a cigarette and leaning on the side of the mobile office building. He wore grimy blue jeans and a red flannel jacket over a blue sweatshirt. Dirty fingers pulled the cigarette from his mouth. He raised his eyebrows, waiting for my question. He didn't look like a guy Paige would go for.

"Levi Montgomery?"

He flicked the cigarette away. "Nope."

"That's what I figured."

A noise from behind caused me to glance over my shoulder. The guy with the backward hard hat was there, along with two men from the construction crew. The cronies, one black and the other white, were both big fellas. They weren't subtle as they flexed their shoulders and rotated their necks.

Hard hat motioned at the cigarette smoker. "Take off."

Footsteps hurried away from us and soon vanished around the building.

"What do you want with my brother?" hard hat asked.

Brother. Max Montgomery, I thought. "I'd like to ask him some questions."

"About?"

"A job."

Max shook his head. "I don't think so. Sandra said to be on the lookout for someone like you. Said he was working with Paige."

"You say that like it's a bad thing."

"Levi doesn't ever want to hear from that bitch again." Max eyed his cronies. "You know what's stopping us from kicking your ass?"

I shook my head.

"Nothing." The two laughed at Max's joke. He pointed his clipboard at me. "Stay away from my brother."

I raised my hands in surrender. Three versus one. Those were odds I wasn't going to challenge.

Max stepped aside, and the sidekicks parted. I walked through them and hurried to my truck. There wasn't any need to try and make nice. I knew the score.

I stopped at one of the few payphones left along Meridian. I could have stopped and bought more minutes for my phone, but I still had some change in my pocket. The payphone wasn't as convenient, but it was cheaper.

No one wanted me to talk with Levi Montgomery except Paige. I needed for him to want to give me an audience.

Flipping through the phone book, it took a few moments to find the phone number. I dropped a couple of quarters in the payphone and placed a call. It was answered on the second ring.

"Montgomery Construction, this is Sandra. How may I help you?"

"Hi, Sandra, this is Bob Ryan with the Eastside Investment Group."

"Hello, Mr. Ryan."

"I represent a group of investors who recently purchased some land in the south Seattle area. We'd like to talk with someone about different options on constructing a mid-sized office building." I didn't know if the words I said were too vague, but I couldn't be any more specific without revealing I was a fraud.

"You can talk with Paul Montgomery, the owner."

I hesitated probably too long before saying, "That sounds fine."

"Or you could talk with his son, Levi." The suspicion in her voice was unmistakable. Maybe she had recalled the sound of my voice.

This time I didn't falter when answering. "It doesn't matter who I speak with as long as they're a decision-maker, and they can give me a quick number. Time is of importance here. So, whoever you recommend."

"In that case, I would suggest Levi. He handles most

of the day-to-day operations of the company. Paul is semi-retired."

"That'll be fine. When can we meet?"

"Let me check his schedule." The phone went silent for a moment before Sandra clicked back on the line. "How about tomorrow morning? He's available any time."

"What time does your office open?"

"The office will open at eight, but our work crews will be out as soon as the sun starts up."

"Could Levi meet me there earlier than eight? Say seven? I have an early flight and would like to give him our specifications for the job."

"I think seven o'clock will be fine. I'll let him know. If there's a problem, is there a number I can call?"

This was a gamble. I could either give her the number of the payphone or my cell phone. If she called back immediately on my cell and it lasted longer than three minutes, then my deception would be revealed. How many high-powered developers were operating on pay-as-you-go cell plans? It was likely that Sandra already had Caller ID. Playing the odds, I read the number from the payphone.

Sandra politely said, "Thank you," and hung up.

I hung out near the payphone for a few minutes. When it rang, I answered on the second ring. "Bob Ryan," I announced.

"Mr. Ryan, this is Sandra. From Montgomery Construction."

"Yes, Sandra."

"I wanted to let you know that everything is set with Levi. He'll meet you tomorrow morning at seven."

"Sounds great. Anything else?"

"No, sir."

She was surprisingly polite when she thought I was someone else.

Chapter 16

Almost an hour later, I pulled into Paige's apartment complex and found a spot between a newer Lexus and an older BMW. Both were shiny and covered by a thin layer of rainy mist. Her car was in its designated parking spot. It was still early, so I hadn't expected her to be at the club yet.

After turning off the truck's engine, I sat with my hands on the steering wheel.

The confrontation at the Puyallup construction site still had me on edge. I hated feeling lost and didn't know how much more I would tolerate. Even though I had scheduled a meeting with Levi Montgomery in the morning, the drive over to her apartment had soured me. I was thinking about bagging it now. To hell with Paige and the money. I'd rather struggle to make ends meet on the other side of the state than drown on the west side with some false promise of a big payday.

Her life and its problems weren't my fault. If she were lying to me—the guy she called for help—then she couldn't get out of her own way. Alone in my truck, I made a decision.

We needed to have a come-to-Jesus talk, or she could deal with this situation on her own.

With my shoulders hunched against the light rain, I hurried across the parking lot then climbed the stairs to her floor. I rang the doorbell and waited. Some kids ran playfully down the steps. They screamed and laughed in the way children do until they made the ground floor and ran off to somewhere else.

My finger pressed the doorbell again. After no response, I twisted the doorknob and stepped inside.

Maybe she was asleep. Or perhaps the apartment community had a fitness center, and she was there.

"Paige?" I called.

The new laptop on the kitchen counter was missing, but the power chord dangled there. The computer's empty box lay on the floor. Maybe she took the laptop and went to a coffee shop. If so, why leave the chord? Did people do that?

"Paige?"

She wasn't in the bedrooms, but they appeared to have been rifled through. Drawers were pulled out, and their contents spilled out on the floor. She'd been burglarized again.

Back in the hallway, I paused long enough to notice the bathroom door was closed. The knob wouldn't turn, so I knocked. "Paige? Are you in there?"

No answer. I knocked again.

"Paige?"

Banging my shoulder against the door did not open it.

Stepping back in the narrow hallway, I had barely enough room to thrust a kick at the door. It burst inward and banged against the far wall.

Paige was stuck between the toilet and the shower enclosure. Her head listed to the side, and she stared up at the ceiling. Blood ran down her temple and matted her hair across her forehead. Her face was a mess. Someone had hit her repeatedly.

"No, no, no," I said and moved to her. Pressing two fingers against her neck, I searched for a pulse I already knew wasn't there. Smacking the wall, I yelled a final, "No!"

I didn't grab her and hold her and tell her I was sorry for everything. I wanted to. Christ, I really did. Instead, I muttered, "What did you do?"

Tears welled in my eyes.

What had she gotten herself into?

Why hadn't she been honest with me?

Thoughts of running home faded.

My gaze drifted to the blood running down the side of the toilet. There was spatter on the wall behind her. Red lines streaked down the glass of the shower enclosure.

I cocked my head and studied Paige again.

The neck of her sweatshirt was pulled tight against her throat but stretched out behind her. Someone had dragged her into the room and tossed her into that position. The rest of the garment bunched up around her midsection, exposing her belly. There were drops of blood on her jeans.

I turned around and walked backward. There were tiny droplets along the hallway. Now that I was looking for them, I could see them everywhere. However, they were too small to have made much of a visual impact when I first entered the house.

No droplets were in any of the bedrooms or the living room. The hallway had several on the wall. A small amount of spatter on the wall.

Had someone hit her as soon as she opened the door, or did she invite them in? Was she rendered unconscious after the first blow, or was she aware that she was being dragged into the bathroom?

Why the bathroom? Why not kill her in the hallway?

Someone might hear the act taking place, I decided.

Better to drag her back to a windowless room.

In anger, I balled my fists.

Facing the hallway that led to the bathroom, there was no need to go back and look at her again. That image wasn't leaving my head.

I inhaled deeply, held it, and exhaled slowly. Then I

removed the cell phone from my pocket.

A tinny voice answered my call. "Nine-one-one. What is your emergency?"

Chapter 17

The small interrogation room held a table and two chairs, one on each side. A metal rail ran the length of the wall. There wasn't much space left after adding in two grown men. Across from me, Detective Donovan Ahern wrote in his spiral notebook.

The detective's belly pushed against his white dress shirt, and old pit stains showed under his arms. The solid brown tie he wore was too short and several years out of style. A five o'clock shadow darkened his face, and his hair was weeks beyond needing a haircut. He reminded me of a frazzled high school teacher.

"This interview is being recorded." He pointed to a camera lens in the wall. "Understand?"

I nodded.

"I need a verbal response for the recording."

"Yeah," I said. "Yes."

For the initial questions, Ahern asked for my basic information—name, address, and the like. He jotted almost everything I said into his notebook. Anything he missed, he could go back to the tape and review later. When he finished, he set down his pen and crossed his arms. "It's been a while, John."

"It has."

Upon clearing the field-training program, I worked with Ahern as part of a graveyard team. He had already been on the job for many years. As a rookie, I looked up to him as an example of how a cop should be. His appearance was always squared away, he worked faster and harder than our other teammates, and he usually carried a pleasant demeanor. Now, he had a look that too many officers get after twenty years on a department. Life held few surprises and too many regular disappointments. We used to be friends, and I hoped Ahern would keep that in the back of his mind.

"Where've you been living?"

"Spokane."

"I got family over there—a sister. Nice area. What brought you back?"

"Paige called."

"Is that the same girl?"

I nodded.

"Rumor was she was the reason you left."

"There were other reasons."

"What did she call for?"

I told him the truth. There was no reason not to. He asked follow-up questions that led to a discussion about Levi Montgomery and the stolen expandable file.

When Ahern finished making his last note, he looked up. "Do you think he could have killed her?"

"I've never met the guy, but maybe. I don't know. If I had to guess, it seems unlikely."

"Why do you say that?"

"He got what he wanted from her. He had the file."

"Maybe she took back the file without you knowing, and he killed her for it."

I shook my head. "He had it and wasn't returning it. She needed me to get it."

"She didn't want you to be an enforcer or something?"

"I was supposed to sweet talk the guy."

Ahern cocked his head. "You?"

"There's varying levels of sweetness."

"Right."

"Didn't matter, though, since I never got a chance."

The detective lowered his head and made a note.

I pulled a pack of Marlboros from my pocket and shook a cigarette loose. Ahern's nose crinkled when I lit up, but he didn't complain.

Instead, he asked, "Was she worried that anyone might have wanted to hurt her?"

"The only thing we talked about was that file. She was adamant that I get it."

"Letters and cards from a boyfriend?"

"That's what she said." I shrugged. "It sounded like bullshit. She said there were also some regular documents in the file as well. Maybe that's what this is about, and I've been looking at it all wrong."

Ahern tapped the end of his pen against the table. "What documents?"

"Birth certificate, car title. Who knows what else was in there?"

"I gotta ask this, John. Were you and her together again?"

"She hired me. That's it."

I ran my fingers along the metal rail and replayed the image of Paige lying in her bathroom. Ahern left me to my thoughts as he made some additional notes on his pad.

"Did she have a cell phone? We haven't found one in her apartment yet. Officers are still searching, but so far, *nada*."

"She had a phone," I said.

"Do you have the number? If we get that, we can get a search warrant and maybe ping its location with the cell company."

I pulled the burner from my pocket and recited her number. Ahern jotted it into his notebook.

The door opened, and Daryl Crites stepped in. It took me a moment to realize who he was. He was a couple of pounds heavier and gone was the salesman's smile I remembered. It was replaced by a look of what I could only describe as compassion.

The detective looked up with surprise.

To me, Crites said, "I saw your name on the computer." His voice was soft and respectful.

Ahern stood. "Sir, can we step outside?"

"I'm not here to interfere, Detective." Then Crites faced me again. "I'm sorry this happened, Cutler. I know what she meant."

Dumbfounded, I didn't say anything. Standing in front of me was the guy who used my relationship with Paige to destroy my career, and now he was showing sympathy about her death.

Crites nodded once more then left the room.

Ahern turned to me with a surprised look. "What the hell was that?"

"You got me."

Chapter 18

After punching Lieutenant Crites at The Red Light District, I was transported to jail for booking. The processing deputy wouldn't make eye contact while he prepared my paperwork. I had seen numerous suspects run through the same process, but everything took on a glaring starkness when I was the one in handcuffs.

The lieutenant stood nearby and filled out my booking paperwork. Upon arrival, he proudly announced to the jail staff his intention to charge me with Third Degree Assault—a felony. Even though punching him should have been only a misdemeanor, he claimed that he was performing his official duties. This allowed him to slip my actions under the higher charge whereby a provision for assaulting an officer lay. I wasn't sure how getting a lap dance from my girlfriend could be considered an official duty, but that would be an argument for another day. Tonight, I was being booked for a felony.

As I leaned against the wall, my fingers absently picked at the pitted concrete blocks, searching for anything to distract from reality. The smell of urine crept into my consciousness, but I couldn't find its origin. The fluorescent lights in the room hummed loudly.

Deputy Shawn Yinger's gaze remained firmly on his clipboard. "Any allergies, diseases, or medical conditions?"

Previously, Yinger and I had spent plenty of time together in the booking lobby, making inappropriate jokes or comments about the suspects I brought in. He was short and trim with an easy smile and sharp wit.

Now, though, his pen froze on the clipboard while he waited for my answer.

"Can't you look at me, Shawn?"

Crites muttered, "Leave him alone, Cutler."

Yinger's eyes flicked up but immediately dropped to the clipboard. "Any allergies, diseases, or medical conditions?" he repeated. His pen remained at the ready.

"No."

The deputy ticked his pen across the appropriate boxes.

The sliding doors opened, and Captain Murphy stepped into the booking area. Even in his civilian clothes, he was a commanding presence. Tall, dark-haired with a thick mustache, he was often accused of being a Tom Selleck clone. Tonight, though, he looked pissed. "Lieutenant," he said, "step outside."

Crites glanced at Yinger and me before saying, "I need to finish the booking paperwork."

"*Now.*"

The lieutenant dropped his pen and walked out into the sallyport.

Murphy eyed me with disdain, exhaled loudly, then spun on his heel. The sliding glass doors closed behind him

I fought back a smile. "Looks like Crites is about to get his ass chewed."

"Who should we contact in the event of an emergency?"

"Huh?" I turned back to see Yinger with his eyes fixed on his clipboard.

"Who should we—"

"I heard you," I said solemnly.

I didn't have a lot of options. It was either my mother, Mike Davoli, or Maria Durant.

I wasn't going to have someone call my mom. As my

only adult family member, I'd rather sit in jail. Okay, maybe that wasn't true, but if I could have someone else called first, that was what I would do.

My partner would come if called, but he'd give me an earful because of Paige. Therefore, Maria seemed the safest bet because of our daughter.

"Maria Durant," I said and provided her phone number.

Through the Plexiglas doors, I watched the captain and lieutenant argue. Crites waved his arms while he spoke. Several times he mimed getting punched in the face. Murphy angrily pointed at him and said something that caused Crites to straighten.

When the captain turned to leave, the lieutenant stalked back into the booking lobby. The sliding glass doors opened with a hiss. Crites scowled at me briefly, then faced Yinger, who waited patiently. "Charge this bastard with misdemeanor assault."

The deputy cast me a sideways glance.

To me, Crites said, "Don't think you got lucky." The lieutenant brushed by me, banging my shoulder, and headed back to the counter to complete the charging paperwork.

Deputy Yinger grabbed my arm and led me from the booking lobby and into the processing center, where another jailer photographed and fingerprinted me. Conversation was nonexistent, and the only words spoken were orders.

"Stand there."

"Turn to the right."

"Turn to the left."

"Move over here."

"Press and roll."

"Wipe your fingers with this."

With processing done, I noticed a phone bank with a

group of inmates waiting for their chance to call their girlfriends, wives, or lawyers.

"Can I use your phone?" I whispered to Yinger.

He glanced at the shift sergeant and made a motion toward the phone in the booking center. The sergeant shook his head.

"Sorry, man. You've got to use the same phones as the inmates." Yinger then leaned in. "We've got a solitary unit for you. We'll keep you away from these animals as much as we can."

"Thanks."

He nodded and glumly patted my back.

I took my place in line at the phone bank. Ten minutes later, I placed a collect call to Maria.

After she accepted the charges, the first words out of her mouth were, "Are you in jail?"

"Yeah. Can you—"

"Oh, my God. What happened?"

"Can you come and get me? They'll release me now if you can. Otherwise, I'm in for the weekend. Normally, they wouldn't book for a misdemeanor, but I'll explain everything when you get here."

"It's past midnight, John. Tell me now."

"I'm standing in a line of guys who are waiting to use the phone. I only get a few minutes."

Her voice raised in anger. "Goddamn it, John, I'm in Portland. It's going to take at least three hours to get there."

I leaned into the payphone. "It's fine, Maria. Never mind. I'll ask somebody else."

She sighed. "Just stop. When I get back, where do I go?"

***

Maria waited until we climbed into her Ford Explorer before flooding me with questions. She'd been asleep when I called and was forced to leave Erin at her mother's house. That meant either she or we would need to make a return trip to get her.

"What the hell happened?" She stuck the key in the ignition but didn't start the engine.

"I punched a lieutenant."

Her eyes widened. "Why?"

"He messed with a girl I'm going out with."

"A girl? I drove three hours because you fought over a girl?"

I grimaced. "It's not like that."

"It's not?"

"No."

Her face hardened. "John, you take whatever it is we have for granted."

"What do we have?"

"We have a kid. Nothing more."

"Then I don't take that for granted."

"We're not a couple, and we're not friends. You can't just call me whenever—"

"We're not friends?"

She shook her head. "You don't pay child support to friends."

"Some people do," I muttered, then looked out the passenger window.

"Where the hell were you when this fight took place?"

I pulled my seatbelt on. "Let's get out of the parking lot."

"Not until you tell me where you were." Her voice was strong, and her eyes searched mine.

Maybe I should have lied to her, but instead, I said, "The Red Light District."

"Isn't that a—" Maria's mouth hung open. "You took

your new girlfriend to a strip club? Classy, John. Real classy. Even for you, that's a new low."

I averted my gaze.

"Wait. Don't tell me. You're kidding, right? Not even you would be so stupid."

"To do what?"

"This new girlfriend is a stripper?"

"Can we leave the parking lot, please?"

"Three hours, John!" She smacked her steering wheel. "Three Goddamned hours to bail you out of jail because of a fight over a *stripper*?"

"Again, it's not like that."

"Well, my friend—"

"You said we weren't friends."

She smacked her hand repeatedly against the steering wheel. "Don't you do that. Don't be smart with me, John Cutler."

I raised my hands in surrender.

"You need to tell me what's going on right now. You're about to lose seeing your daughter."

"You can't do that."

"Wanna bet?"

"This has got nothing to do with Erin."

"Everything has to do with her. Don't you see that? You're dating a stripper. Do you know the kind of life those women lead?" Maria pointed at me. "She's to come nowhere near my daughter. Nowhere near her. Do you hear that? Tell me you understand that."

"Yeah, okay."

"That doesn't sound like you get what I'm saying."

"I get it."

"And why were you fighting? You're a cop, for Chrissake."

"He's investigating me, Maria. He got under my skin."

She paused then, seemingly to think about my words.

"Why's he investigating you?"

"It's nothing."

"Don't do that." She held up three fingers. "That's how many hours of my life I will never get back. I should make you pay for my gas."

"No problem."

"And I've got to drive back, too."

"I'll go with."

"And do what?" She adamantly shook her head. "Stay with my family? No way. I'm so pissed at you right now. I don't want to spend another three hours with you."

"Fine. Can we leave the parking lot then?"

"Tell me what he's investigating you for."

"Maria."

"Tell me, John."

"It's bullshit is what it is."

"So, tell me."

I sighed in frustration. "I've been accused of ripping off a drug dealer."

Her brow furrowed. "Did you do it? Don't give me that look. Answer the question."

"Really?"

"Yes, really. Did you do it?"

"How can you ask me that?"

"I'm picking you up from jail after you were arrested for fighting another cop in a strip club. I feel like 'did you do it?' is a reasonable question based upon the situation we find ourselves in. Now, I've asked twice, and both times you avoided giving me an answer. So, what is it?"

"No, Maria. I did not take the *fucking* drug money!"

"Then why not say that when I asked?"

I shook my head and stared out the window.

"Why does he think you took this money?"

"Because some drug dealer has a hard-on for me."

"Why?"

I lifted my hands in frustration. "I arrested the guy."

"And to get even he called IA?"

"Who knows why he did it? It's bullshit, but the community wants everybody to get along. Like crime is going to go away if we learn to be friends."

She rolled her eyes. "Tell me about this lieutenant."

"What about him?"

"Did you hit him because he's investigating you, or did you hit him because of the girl?"

"I hit him—" The image of Paige wriggling in the lieutenant's lap flashed in my mind. "—because of how he's crossing the line in this investigation."

Maria studied me a moment further, then decided something for herself. She started her vehicle, and we drove in silence to my apartment building. I began to say something several times, but she held up her hand to cut me off each time. At the front of my apartment, she stopped, and I opened my door.

"This isn't over," she said. "You know that, right?"

"Yeah, I know. I just made the whole thing worse by hitting him."

"Not him, you jerk. With me. This thing isn't over *with me*. I'm going to think about how this affects things going forward with Erin."

"C'mon," I pleaded. "This doesn't have anything to do with her."

"That's the problem, John. You still haven't realized this yet, but you're a father. Everything you do affects your daughter. When are you going to grow up and accept responsibility for your actions?"

Chapter 19

After finishing the witness interview with Detective Ahern, I caught a taxi from the station back to Paige's apartment building, where my truck was still parked. Ahern offered to have a patrol unit give me a lift, but I declined.

From the end of the walkway, I looked up toward her apartment. Crime scene tape crossed the door to her unit. There wasn't any need to go closer. Even if I could get inside, I knew what was there.

I absently drove around after that. First, I headed toward Seattle, then I turned around and headed home. What point was there in remaining now? As I passed through Issaquah, I left the freeway.

When night descended, I arrived in Maria's neighborhood. I should have called her to ask permission to stop by, but I was so lost in my thoughts I hadn't even considered it.

Wearing flannel pajama bottoms and a faded blue Seahawks t-shirt, she opened the door with a surprised look. "John?"

"Is Erin home?"

Her surprise turned to confusion. "It's ten o'clock. Are you okay?"

I shook my head.

"What's wrong?"

"It's Paige."

Maria's expression flattened.

"She was murdered this morning."

Her eyes softened, and she pushed the door open.

After sitting in the spacious living room, I explained what had occurred. Maria listened quietly, almost dutifully. When I finished, she simply said, "I'll be back," and went into the kitchen.

While she was gone, I scanned the photographs on the mantles and end tables. There were many happy pictures of her and Erin. Several were of my daughter by herself.

When Maria returned, she carried a bottle of wine and two glasses. She carefully poured us both some before climbing back into her chair. After sipping from her drink, she opened her mouth but slowly closed it. Whatever she was going to say, she kept it to herself.

I stared into my glass. Regrets about my life flowed through me then. Scenes played out in my mind like a disjointed movie montage. Discovering Paige's lifeless form. The fight with Lieutenant Crites. My first date with Maria.

Looking up, I said, "I'm sorry for how things turned out."

"What do you mean?"

On the table next to the couch was a picture of my daughter riding a horse. Erin never told me she had done something like that.

"Maybe we should have gotten married—made everything official."

Maria tsked softly. "But I didn't want to marry you. We wouldn't have worked out. Believe it or not, it's better this way."

"We never even tried."

"I knew better, John. You aren't the marrying type."

The comment stung, and I turned away.

"Some women are attracted to that kind of man," she said. "Not me."

I picked up the picture of my daughter on the horse. Her smile was big, and her eyes sparkled brightly. "Is

Erin asleep?"

"She's spending the night at a friend's house."

"Isn't it a school night?" I muttered, then looked up from the photograph. "Did I interrupt some plans or something?"

"It's after ten, John. If I had anything planned, it would be happening now."

"Yeah. Sorry. That was a stupid question."

Setting the picture down, I wished I had heard about Erin's day with the horse.

Maria shifted in her seat. "Can I ask a question?" She didn't wait for me to agree. "What was the power she had over you?"

I shrugged.

"Don't do that, John. Be honest with me. Be honest with yourself." It wasn't blatant, but she didn't go to great lengths to disguise her contempt. I couldn't blame her.

"I guess—" I rubbed my eyebrow as I tried to come up with the words. "Whenever I was with her, I sort of, I don't know, I felt out of control. Like at any moment, the world would spin me free."

Maria slowly drummed her fingers along the side of her glass. "Sounds reckless."

I shrugged again, knowing she would never understand an answer, even if I could give a better one.

Silence hung in the room. The second hand ticked its way around the grandfather clock sitting in the far corner.

"Why did you come here, John?"

"I called yesterday."

"I got your message. I'm talking tonight. This late."

"I was hoping to see Erin."

"Even if she were home, she would have been asleep."

We were two strangers who had made a child together. What was I expecting from this woman? Staring into my glass, I said, "I don't know what I want."

"You can't stay here," she said flatly—a mama bear protecting her cave.

Slightly hurt and more than a little embarrassed, I said, "I know."

She watched me for an uncomfortable moment before saying, "You can see Erin tomorrow after school."

"Thank you."

I put my wine glass on the end table and stood.

She didn't follow me when I walked out of the house.

Chapter 20

The clock on the wall said it was a few minutes after midnight. I glanced around the bar.

An older couple sat side by side in a booth and swayed while The Meters' "Cissy Strut" played.

In another booth, an elderly black man sat alone, tapping his cane absently to the music. Miles placed a beer on the man's table then shared a laugh. The two shook hands before Miles hobbled behind the bar. He grabbed a bottle of Miller Lite and set it in front of me. He then poured himself a fresh cup of coffee.

I pulled out a cigarette, lit it, and inhaled deeply. "Paige is dead."

Miles stared at me.

"Murdered."

"I'm sorry."

He sipped his coffee while I smoked. Left to my thoughts, I inhaled a couple of times before crushing out the cigarette.

"Run it down," Miles said.

I pulled the beer toward me and clutched it to my chest. "When I got to her place, I found her on the bathroom floor. The cops took me down to a precinct station to be interviewed by a detective. Decent guy I used to know."

"Any witnesses?"

"Only some kids who saw a big man in front of her apartment."

"That's not a lot to go on."

I shrugged. "Especially since it might have been me

who they were describing. I saw them running down the stairs. Even if they got a good look at the guy, they're kids."

His brow furrowed. "Did you tell them why you came over?"

"Wasn't any reason not to."

"That's smart. No need to cross the police. Let them do their job."

"Earn their pay," I agreed.

Miles leaned against the back bar, briefly surveyed his other customers, then returned his attention to me.

"I stopped by Maria's house before coming here," I said.

"To see Erin?"

"It was dumb. I stopped by too late, and she wasn't there."

Miles ran his finger around the rim of his coffee cup but remained silent.

"I wasn't thinking straight."

After putting his mug down, Miles picked up a rag and wiped the bar. "Why did you really come back?"

"Tonight?"

"No," he said gently. "For Paige. Why did you come back? You had to know nothing good would come of it."

I picked at the label on my beer. "I wanted her to say it."

Miles stopped wiping. "Say what?"

It took me a few seconds to admit it. "That she loved me. She never said it once."

He tugged on opposite ends of the rag. "If she didn't say it then, why would she say it now? After two years of not seeing you?"

I stared at my bottle, looking for an answer it wouldn't give.

"If a funeral happens, you should go."

I looked up.

"For closure." Something must have changed in my appearance because he asked, "You all right?"

"Until she called, I thought I'd left everything behind. That none of it could ever touch me again." I tapped my chest with the neck of the bottle. "But everything hurts now, and I don't know how to deal with it."

"That's because you don't deal with things, John. You ignore them."

"Not always."

"Those you don't, you punch."

I eyed Miles. "Well, I'm going to deal with them now."

"How are you going to do that?"

I picked at the beer label some more. "I'm going to find her ex-boyfriend. See what he knows."

Miles grabbed his coffee cup and surveyed the bar. When his gaze returned to me, his eyes were filled with sadness. "What will you do if you find who killed her?"

When I didn't answer, Miles walked away.

Chapter 21

Things soured in my police career by the time I finally revealed my relationship with Paige to my friend and partner, Mike Davoli. We were in the back booth at Mickey Finn's. Curtis Mayfield's "Pusherman" muscled its way from the speaker above us, covering our voices.

"What are you going to do about IA?" he asked.

"Not much I can do now that I'm on leave."

The day after I punched Lieutenant Daryl Crites, the department put me on administrative leave until the criminal investigation was complete.

"You can argue that it's a hardship."

"It's hard to argue that when I'm getting paid."

"It's a hardship because your reputation is in the shredder, man."

My leave of absence sent the department's rumor mill into overdrive. I had to turn off my cell phone due to the relentless calls from guys wanting the inside scoop. Avoidance seemed the easiest course of action. I wanted as few people as possible to know what occurred.

Mike was the exception. He shoved some French fries into his mouth while holding his hamburger in his other hand. "What about the union?" he mumbled through a mouthful of food.

"They agree with the administration."

"The fuck?"

I nodded.

"You got to come clean and tell me what this is all about."

I finished my beer and ordered us two more from

across the room. Miles acknowledged my request.

"It's about a girl," I said. Then I leaned forward and told him about Paige.

Halfway through my story, Mike dropped the burger to his plate. He finished chewing and wiped his mouth. "This trouble—everything with Crites—is over a stripper?" His eyes were challenging. "What's wrong with you?"

"Listen—"

"I asked you a question."

I expected him to react poorly, but not this bad.

"Fucking A, John. You're already in trouble with the crack dealer's accusation. Now, this? Where's your head?"

"Mike—"

"You did this to yourself. Nobody but you."

Miles limped over and set two bottles of Miller Lite on the table. He hobbled away without a word because he could see something was wrong. I grabbed my bottle and held it with both hands.

Mike pulled his beer closer. "When did this start?"

"Couple months ago."

"What the hell?"

I knew why he was pissed. We made a promise to look out for each other—to keep the other guy in the loop on anything going on in our lives. That promise happened after Mike's marriage crumbled, and he fell apart. His wife left him for an up-and-coming pitcher with the Tacoma Rainiers, the farm club for the Mariners.

"Why am I just hearing about her now?"

I shrugged. "I was afraid this would be your reaction."

"Dude, she's a stripper. She's a half-step from a prostitute."

"Hey."

"Maybe she is."

"*Hey!*"

He pointed accusingly at me. "You know some of them do that. They'll step outside the club if the money is right."

"She *doesn't.*" I shook my head. "This is why I didn't tell you."

"Why start messing with her?"

"I don't know."

"If you tell me she's the stripper with a heart of gold, I swear to God, I'll punch you in the teeth."

I smiled. "Then you'll end up in IA with me."

"I'm not joking around, John. Make me understand why you would do this. It's not smart. It's not even close."

I leaned back in the booth, ran my hands through my hair, and let out a slow sigh. "There's something with her. I can't explain it."

"If you can't explain it, then why do it?"

I looked around the bar. Groups of people laughed and drank at various tables in the bar. Not facing him, I asked, "Have you ever met someone that you couldn't stop thinking about?"

"No."

"Not even Tina?"

"Watch it." Mentioning his ex-wife was still a sore spot.

Lifting my hands in mock surrender, I said, "What about love at first sight?"

He shook his head.

"I didn't believe in it either, but that was before I saw her."

"You love her?"

I shrugged.

"Who is she?"

"Her name's Paige."

"That's a stage name." Sarcasm dripped from his voice.

"That's her real name. I'm not an idiot."

His gaze dipped. It was the closest thing to an apology I would get. "Where'd you meet?"

I stared at him, hesitant to answer the question.

His burger had grown cold, and he pushed the plate away.

"The Red Light District," I finally said.

"You're kidding me." Disbelief flooded his voice. "You met her at the strip club?" He clucked his tongue against the back of his teeth. "You're screwing up your life over a whore."

"She's not a *whore*!"

The bar went quiet as everyone stared in our direction. Brothers Johnson's "Strawberry Letter 23" filled the void until people started talking again.

My voice softer this time, I repeated, "She's not a whore."

Mike held up a hand with his thumb and forefinger barely apart. "She's a millimeter of clothing away from screwing for money. What does that sound like to you?"

"I'm not looking for understanding."

"Good, because you aren't getting it."

"You're supposed to be my friend. That's why I'm talking with you."

Mike grabbed his beer. A big swallow later, he set the bottle down and crossed his arms. "You're right. I am your friend. That's why I'm going to tell you this. Pull your head out of her ass. A stripper is a stupid reason to get jammed up. You punched a lieutenant, and now you could lose your career because of it. Is any of this getting through to you?"

I massaged the back of my neck. "Shit."

Mike sat still, his eyes alert with concentration.

"How's Erin?"

"She's fine."

"Has she met this woman?"

"No."

"Does Maria know about you getting arrested?"

"She picked me up from jail."

His eyes widened. "What?"

"I called her to—"

"You called her? Why didn't you call me?"

"I was twisted up that night. I was worried that you would do exactly this." I twirled my finger above the table.

He shook his head. "How fucked up are you?"

Mike had never been this mad at me before, and I now regretted talking to him about Paige.

"Break it off with her," he said flatly.

"I can't."

"Because you love her?"

I met his gaze.

"Son of a bitch," he murmured. "If you think she's got that heart of gold, you're going to be sorely disappointed."

"I know she's doesn't."

"Then what is it?"

"I don't know. There's just something."

He spread his arms wide. "There's something about them all."

Irritation lanced through me. "You don't believe that."

"Of course, I do. They're a dime a dozen. Dump her."

My face warmed. "If they were easily replaceable, you wouldn't be crazy because of your divorce."

Mike's eyes hardened.

"You would have moved on. Instead, you pine away while she's doing God knows what with you know who."

"Careful, John."

"I'm only trying to make a point."

"Don't make it by bringing up my ex. Are you going to marry this girl? Settle down and have babies?"

"She's not that type, but I want to be with her. I know that. But it feels like the harder I hold on, the less she's there. It's like trying to grab water." I opened my hand and stared at my palm.

"Maybe she's the type of girl you don't get to keep." He said it without anger. Instead, it sounded filled with regret.

I closed my fist. "But I want to be with her."

"Sometimes what you want and what you get aren't the same thing."

Those were words I didn't want to hear. I leaned my head back on the booth and stared up at the ceiling.

"So, I ask you," Mike said. "What are you going to do about this girl?"

I shrugged. "Try to love her."

Chapter 22

I parked on the street outside the Montgomery Construction office and waited. My alter ego, Bob Ryan, was meeting with Levi Montgomery in a few minutes.

Sipping lukewarm coffee, I considered the meeting might not occur at all. If Detective Ahern interviewed Levi last night, he might skip coming into work today. For that matter, if Ahern proved Levi killed Paige, he would have been arrested.

Various scenarios like that ran through my mind until a yellow Humvee pulled into the parking lot. A Montgomery Construction logo was emblazoned on the side panels. What kind of arrogant jackass drove a vehicle like that?

The driver's door swung open, and a big man stepped out.

Big man, I thought, just like the kids at the apartment complex described.

The man's brown hair was cut short, and he wore faded blue jeans, a button-up shirt, and clean work boots. He chatted casually into his cell phone while he looked around the lot. After performing a full three-sixty, he closed the driver's door and headed toward the building.

Paige was dead, and this guy didn't seem to have a care in the world.

I dropped my truck into gear and pulled into the parking lot, stopping too close to the Hummer's driver-side for him to get back into it. The guy watched me from the front door and frowned at my park job.

He muttered something into his cell phone and

snapped it shut.

After climbing out of my truck, I said, "Levi Montgomery?"

"Are you Mr. Ryan?"

Even the way he asked that simple question irritated me. The guy seemed full of himself. He was several inches taller than me and physically impressive. He was also handsome and probably rich, too. On top of all that, Levi Montgomery had recently been with Paige. Adding those things together meant I had only hatred for the man.

He asked, "Can I help you?"

"I'm John Cutler. I'm here for Paige."

His brow furrowed, and he shoved his cell phone into his pants pocket. "You should leave."

"We need to talk."

He slowly widened his stance. His fists balled, his breathing deepened, and his shoulders dipped. "Last chance."

I didn't wait for him to decide on a course of action. Instead, I feinted a kick at his shin.

When Levi's gaze dropped to my foot, I hook-punched him in the temple. His head whipped to the side, and he crashed into the building. He took two awkward steps back before collapsing to the ground.

He fumbled around before working to his hands and knees. He rocked backward to the balls of his feet and lifted his arms to protect his head. He was like a fighter refusing to stay on the mat. I hit him in the chest, and he yelped. This time, his fall wasn't as far, but he stayed down.

Levi Montgomery might have been a big man, but it was clear he hadn't been in many brawls. He looked up like a frightened fawn awaiting the wolf to deliver a killing blow.

"Why?" was all he managed.

I leaned over and grabbed him by his shirt. "You killed her."

"What?" Blood covered his teeth and lips. His eyes widened then narrowed as realization set in. When his brow furrowed and his lower lip trembled, I knew the truth.

"Open the door," I said and jerked him to his knees. It took some effort to get him stabilized and on his feet. Slowly, he dug into his pocket and removed a set of keys. After a couple of tries, he got the building unlocked.

We walked by the front counter and into a hallway with rooms on both sides. His office was at the far end. Photographs of construction sites lined the walls.

When we were inside his office, he went straight for his chair and fell heavily into it. He stared at me. "She's dead?"

"Yeah."

He leaned forward and put his head in his hands. "How?"

"Someone beat her to death."

"Why?"

"That's what I came here to find out."

Montgomery pushed back from his desk. "I think I'm going to be sick."

"The police haven't contacted you yet?"

He shook his head and retched. To his credit, he held it in.

It occurred to me then that I hadn't told Detective Ahern that Levi was living with his father while building his new home. If the detective pulled Levi's DOL record, maybe an old address popped up. If that were the case, the detective or a patrol uniform would show up to the Montgomery Construction office after it was officially open.

"The cops will want to talk with you."

"About what?"

"The folder you stole from her."

"That doesn't mean I killed her!" Tears welled in his eyes.

"Where is it?"

He reached over to the bottom desk drawer.

"Hey!" I hollered and stepped closer to him. He pulled back as if afraid of being hit again. I motioned toward the drawer. "Got a gun in there?"

"Huh?"

"Open it slowly."

Levi pulled the drawer. He then lifted out an expandable file and plopped it onto the desk.

Inside were a few personal letters and other documents, such as the title to her car and a copy of her apartment lease. I flipped through the letters and found some from her mom and her sister. I tucked the notes back into the file.

"Why would you take this?"

Levi scratched the side of his head. He glanced up before answering. "I wanted my cards and pictures back."

I sat in the leather chair in front of his desk. "Why would you care if she had those?"

He wiped the tears from his eyes then tapped the desk. "My father."

"What about him?"

Levi looked away. "He said either I left her, or I lost my job with the company. When he retires, he wants me to take over. Otherwise, it's Max, and he's not a financial guy. That's what this is about. Making the right choice."

"And you chose the company."

Levi dropped his hands into his lap. When he looked back at me, he asked, "What would you choose?"

I knew the answer but didn't tell him.

He touched his chest where I had punched him and

winced.

"What happened when you told her?"

"She said she wasted too much time not to get something out of it."

I cocked my head. "She wanted money?"

His shrug was noncommittal. "She didn't come out and say so, but yeah."

Was Paige blackmailing him? That didn't seem like her. More likely, she would have told him to get lost. She knew there were plenty of other men that she could wrap around her finger. I was living proof of that.

"My father told me not to trust a woman like her."

"A woman like her?"

"He said women in her line of work don't have morals, but I didn't listen. She twisted me up. Had me questioning who I was." He paused and touched his chest again. "She showed her true colors when I called it off."

"But why did you need the cards and letters? I'm not understanding."

His eyes moved to the corner of the room. "My father. He said that if I gave anything to her, I should get it back."

"Why?"

"So she couldn't use it against me." He wiped the tears from his cheeks.

"You're married."

"What? No."

"Then what could she use against you? Birthday cards?" None of it sounded right. "How could those hurt you? How could they hurt the company?"

He shook his head. "I don't know." His voice was small.

"Did you say anything else in those cards?"

"No." He lifted a hand in a futile gesture. "I just— I don't know. I said I loved her."

"Then why take the file?"

Tears streaked down his cheeks.

"To hurt her?" I suggested.

"Maybe." He looked toward the ceiling. "I wasn't thinking straight. I loved her. I didn't want to break up. Then I did it for the company, and she got mad." He waved his hand around like a conductor. "That's not what I wanted. I made a mess of everything."

"Did she say it back?"

He stopped waving. "Huh?"

It was a stupid question, and I shouldn't have asked it. I should have left well enough alone.

But he lowered his head, and his lips pinched together. When Levi closed his eyes, his entire face trembled.

She didn't say those words to him either.

It was selfish to think, but her not saying it to him made me feel better somehow.

"Do you have a key to her apartment?" I asked.

He wiped his face with both hands. "Not anymore. She changed the locks after I took the file."

"Did you take anything else besides your cards?"

"There wasn't anything else to take."

"Then why keep this stuff? You could have thrown it all away. No one would ever have known."

"I thought maybe someday she would calm down, and I could see her again."

"Without your father knowing?"

Levi turned away, ashamed. "He's not going to live forever," he muttered.

Absently, I tapped the file, wondering if there was anything I was missing. Deciding there wasn't, I grabbed the folder and stood. "I apologize for hitting you."

"I deserved it."

"I used to think I did, too. Now, I'm not so sure." I held the file in the air. "A detective is going to come looking for this.”

“What should I tell him?”

“Tell him you gave it to me, and he can pick it up at Mickey Finn’s.”

As I left the office, he called out, “The bar?”

***

I returned to Finn’s and grabbed a booth in the corner. Miles wasn’t in yet, but Danny brought me a cup of coffee while he cleaned.

The expandable file sat on the table. I sorted its contents into two piles—one for family letters and one for documents like her lease and car title.

I examined everything.

It felt dirty reading the letters from her mom and sister, but it was clear they loved Paige. Some were several years old. A recent one from her mom said she was glad that Paige finally found a man like Levi. Nowhere was love mentioned, though.

There was nothing of interest in the legal documents. Besides the car title and lease, there were copies of her auto insurance declaration, renter’s insurance, and library card. I packed the papers back into the file and closed the flap. Danny put Detective Ahern’s name on the file and slipped it under the counter.

I went into the back room and sat on the cot.

I’d done my duty and could go home now. I recovered the file Paige hired me to find. I could leave Seattle with a clear conscience.

But was that all I wanted—a clear conscience?

Paige was dead. It wasn’t my fault, and I wasn’t narcissistic enough to even believe so. However, the hole inside me wasn’t going to get filled just because I located a stupid file. It didn’t answer the question about why I was really there.

Beyond that, there was a more significant reason to stay—I could solve her murder.

Even though Paige never loved me, I could bring her killer to justice. It was a simple premise, but the idea of it made me feel better. It made me feel special.

And it was something Levi couldn't do.

To solve the mystery, though, I needed to find someone who knew her. And the only way to do that was to go back to where it all started.

And I hated the idea of that.

Chapter 23

"The cover's fifteen bucks," the doorman said.

He was new. Well, new to me. I was hoping Jarod would have been there. He was the guy who handled that particular duty a couple of years ago but collecting the cover charge for The Red Light District wasn't a career most guys stayed at long term.

"How well do you know Paige McIntyre?" I asked.

He eyed me suspiciously.

"She danced under the name Nicolette."

"Fifteen."

I handed him the money, and he jerked open the door. Music thumped from inside.

"About Paige?" I prompted.

"You a cop?"

"Not anymore."

He frowned and jerked a thumb toward the open door. "In or out?"

The hallway led into the club. The music got louder the further I walked into it. I turned the corner and entered a room lit by neon lights. Three women on as many different stages pranced around to the bouncing rhythm of Coolio's "Fantastic Voyage." They had updated the club since my last visit. It still had the same smell and vibe, though.

I scanned the dancers, looking for anyone that might remember me. No one looked familiar.

A top-heavy brunette with a nose ring sidled up. She almost spilled out of her bikini. "Hey, honey. Wanna dance?"

"No, thanks."

She caressed my back. "C'mon, baby. You look like a guy who needs to relax."

"Did you know Paige McIntyre? Went by Nicolette."

Her hand stopped moving. "We don't talk about other girls."

"Someone killed her yesterday."

She covered her mouth with a hand.

I leaned in. "Were you friends?"

"You a cop?"

"A friend. She called me for help, and then she was murdered."

The woman cringed at the word. Maybe she had considered the same plight for herself. She glanced toward the redhead on stage. I followed her gaze.

"I didn't know her too well, but you should talk with Cherry. They were tight."

When I turned back to her, the brunette was hurriedly walking away.

***

After Cherry finished her set, she grabbed her bikini from the stage and skipped happily into the backroom. It didn't take her long to return to the floor, though.

She wore a white terry cloth robe wrapped tightly around her waist. Her eyes checked the room before landing on me. She walked in my direction. One guy smiled at her and lifted a friendly hand, but Cherry blew by him without acknowledgment.

When she stopped in front of me, I noticed that she was barefoot. She crossed her arms and set her jaw. "Who are you?"

"John Cutler."

"And she's dead? That's what you're telling people."

Cherry's eyes filled with anger. "Nicolette's dead?"

"Paige," I clarified. "Yesterday."

"Who would do such a thing?"

"That's what I want to find out."

Her face hardened further. "Yeah? Well, maybe *you* did it."

"I didn't."

She took a half-step back. "And you're here to get another one of us."

"I'm not," I said softly.

Her eyes narrowed. "Who are you again?"

"John Cutler. Paige and I were old friends."

"She never talked about you."

"We were the kind of friends you no longer talk about."

Cherry appraised me. "Lovers?"

"Like I said."

"Right. The kind you no longer talk about. If that's the case, then why are you here?"

"I used to be a cop. She called for help."

Using a thumb, she wiped something imaginary away from her lip. She noticed a motion on her right and nodded at an approaching customer. After making a just-a-minute gesture to the guy, she faced me again. "Are the cops gonna talk with us?"

"Probably."

"Then why should I talk with you?"

"I already told you. Because we were the kinds of friends you no longer talk about."

She hugged herself. "I wonder if I have any friends like you. Guys who would make sure things were done right if I..." Her voice trailed off, and she shuddered slightly.

"I'm sure you do." I had no way to know if it was true, but the idea seemed to bring her some comfort.

"Okay." She repeatedly blinked as if fighting back the tears I couldn't see. "What do you want to know?"

"Did anyone want to hurt her?"

Cherry shrugged. "I don't think so."

"The woman I talked to—" I searched the floor for the brunette but couldn't find her. "—said you and Paige were tight."

"As close as you can be in this job. The other girls called us the three amigos."

"Who was the third?"

"Destiny."

"Is she working today?"

"She hasn't been for a couple weeks now."

I cocked my head in a questioning manner.

"She's gone." Cherry popped open her hands like a magician. "Poof."

"Anyone call the cops?'

She smirked. "It's not that kind of gone. After she broke up with her boyfriend, Destiny stayed with Nicolette—I mean Paige. Sorry, I'm used to talking to customers, and you already know her real name." Cherry gave a pained smile. "Anyway, things seemed to be going good for the two of them. Maybe they were having a little too much fun living together. Frankly, I felt left out. Almost wished I was living with them. Then one day, Paige came home to find her gone. Destiny moved out. No note. No forwarding address. No nothing."

"What's Destiny's real name?"

Cherry's lips twisted.

"I'm not asking for your real name, but I'm not going to get far with a stage moniker."

She seemed to consider her options, then leaned in. "Amy," she whispered. "Amy Mackey." When she straightened, Cherry said, "These guys can't know our real names because— Well, you know why. Don't you?"

It wasn't mean, and it wasn't snarky, but her statement cut to the heart of the matter. These women lived duplicitous lives. They knew the truth, but the men sitting in the dark wanted to believe the fantasy being sold. Occasionally, the dancers bought into their own lies. When that happened, relationships like the one Paige and I had developed.

"Any idea on how to get in contact with Amy?"

"I'm pretty sure her mom lives in Kent. At least, she did."

"Do you know where?"

She shook her head.

"Would anyone in the office have the address?"

"Maybe, but even if they had it, they wouldn't give it to you."

But they would give it to the cops. If I couldn't find Amy Mackey, I would pass the lead to Detective Ahern and let him get it.

"You can't blame the management," Cherry said. "They're just as worried as we are about some creeper killing one of us." Her face slackened. "I wonder if that's what happened to Paige."

"And you never saw any customer giving her a hard time?"

"Nothing more than usual. She knew how to take care of herself. Paige was a professional. And for those times she couldn't handle a guy, she let the bouncers step in."

"What about Amy's ex-boyfriend?" I asked. "What's his name?"

"Marco." Cherry smirked. "Now, that boy's crazy."

"How so?"

"He's got a bad temper. That's why she left him."

"How can I find him?"

"He's a bouncer at the Pit. And yeah, it's as nice as it sounds."

***

Shortly after two in the afternoon, the Pit was locked up.

The nightclub sat mid-block and bullied its way between two smaller bars. Its bright green door and even brighter green sign signaled its existence to everyone.

A cool breeze blew down the street, and I pulled my coat tight. The overcast sky threatened to drop more rain.

Flyers for promotional nights littered the outside of the windows, and a reflective film covered the inside. I stood there and checked out my reflection. I looked like a broken-down version of The Fonz, the character from *Happy Days*. Beaten leather jacket, blue jeans, and black boots painted a strange picture of the man I had become.

I tried to peek through the reflective film to no avail. Someone could have been standing on the opposite side of the window, and I wouldn't have known they were there.

The sign on the door said the club opened again at seven.

I had almost five hours to wait.

Chapter 24

Dishes clattered in the kitchen of Denny's as I ate my French fries and read the newspaper.

The article that caught my attention was about Councilwoman Elizabeth Vanderlinden's latest stand against homelessness in downtown Seattle. What she proposed sounded like tossing sand into the ocean to stop an incoming tide. It wasn't the homeless problem that gave me pause, though. It was the accompanying photograph.

Councilwoman Vanderlinden stood amongst a homeless camp located underneath a freeway overpass. She looked about as uncomfortable being there as one could imagine. This was the same woman that had walked into the Dine and Dash restaurant and immediately turned around after making eye contact with Paige.

Paige had her campaign button in her apartment. I leaned in to study the picture further. Had Paige known a city council member?

"Cutler, is that you?"

I looked up at a couple of uniforms.

"It is you," Officer Brock Gatlin said. To his partner, "And you said it wasn't him." Back to me, "What the hell have you been up to, man?"

Officer Ty Jenke lifted his chin as a greeting.

Both men slid into the booth across from me.

I pushed my plate away. "I thought I'd drop in and see if I could get my old job back."

Gatlin, the older of the two, laughed mirthlessly. He

had a large gut that hung over his ill-fitting uniform pants. His shoulders were rounded, and he hunched slightly forward. Even though he looked like a sloth, the man had held his own in more fights than I would ever see. "Hate to break this to you, but you ain't ever getting back on the department. Crites made Captain."

Detective Ahern hadn't mentioned that when Crites interrupted our interview. I was being cooperative, so he probably didn't want to send my attitude sideways.

"Fucking Crites," Jenke muttered.

"My feelings exactly," I said.

The server approached then to wait on the two officers. She was in her late forties and had bleached-blonde hair with dark roots. "Weren't you boys just over there?" She motioned to elsewhere in the establishment.

Gatlin politely smiled. "Yes, ma'am, we were. Just wanted to say hello to an old friend."

"Want some coffee?"

"No, thank you. We're on our way out."

"Let me know if you change your mind." She headed over to a nearby table to check on its occupants.

Gatlin leaned in. "So, why are you really back in town, Cutler?"

"Yeah," Jenke said. "Word was you vanished like Houdini."

The older officer rolled his eyes. "Houdini didn't vanish. He escaped."

Jenke's brow furrowed. "What's that?"

"Houdini was an escape artist."

"Well, he escaped. So what?" Jenke pointed at me. "It's not like this guy didn't get what I was trying to say." He asked in a conspirator's tone. "I bet you came back for that girl, huh? She was fine. I totally get why you lost your mind over—"

"She was murdered yesterday," I said.

Jenke's face whitened. "Shit."

Concern filled Gatlin's eyes. "What happened?"

I laid it out for them—every detail including the sympathy from Crites.

When I finished, the older officer said, "I'm sorry, man. The whole thing."

Jenke nodded in agreement with his partner's sentiment. "Who's running the investigation?"

"Don Ahern."

"He's good police," the younger officer said. "He'll knock it down, for sure."

Gatlin studied me so closely that I grew uncomfortable. He tugged a business card from his pocket, wrote something on it, then slid it across the table. "In case you find what you're looking for, call me before you do something stupid. That's my cell."

Jenke cocked his head. "Did I miss something?"

I pulled the card from the table and slipped it into my pocket.

Gatlin shifted in his seat. "Time has a way of healing wounds, Cutler. People learn to forgive and forget. But don't pick open the scabs. Do you hear me?"

"I hear you."

Jenke glanced between his partner and me. "What the hell did I miss?"

A call came over Gatlin's radio, and both men listened intently. A female dispatcher announced a burglary in progress at an address not too far from our location. When the air was clear, Gatlin keyed his microphone, announced his callsign, and said, "Show us clear from lunch and en route to the call."

The two officers slid out of the booth. Gatlin put his hand on my shoulder. "Be safe and be smart."

"Yeah." Jenke nodded. "What he said."

They hurried out of the restaurant then, banging the glass door as they went.

Chapter 25

A week after I punched Lieutenant Crites, the department pulled me off administrative leave and told me to report for duty the next night. At that shift's roll call, Thomas Jasper caught me leaving the locker room.

"Let's take a walk," he said.

I followed him into a small counseling room, and he closed the door after us.

"The brass wanted to keep you on admin leave." Jasper's baritone voice tended to be loud, but he did his best to whisper.

"Why?"

"You know why."

I did—the misdemeanor charge. It wasn't a new phenomenon. Cops have hit other cops. I wasn't the first, and I sure as hell wouldn't be the last. Usually, the incident was swept under the rug, and the guys either made up over a beer or refused to talk with each other for the rest of their careers. Regardless, no one was ever charged with a crime.

I said, "I was set up."

Jasper raised a critical eyebrow.

"Crites," I said. "The same guy who's pushing to keep me on leave."

"It's not just him. The chief, too."

I lowered my gaze. "Which means all those brassholes down the line."

"Relax, man. We've got your back. Marty had a heart-to-heart with the chief."

Marty Walker was the union president. Him talking

directly with the chief about my situation was more attention than I wanted. My career had been spent keeping my head low, staying out of trouble, doing my job like a good cop, and going home safe.

My record was mostly clean. A couple of use-of-force complaints that were deemed justified. A sustained demeanor complaint that resulted with a disciplinary letter. If they do their job right, every cop ends up with some paper in their file.

Jasper shook my shoulder. "Seriously, J.C. It'll be okay. Marty threatened a grievance over past practice. Remember when Lamar and Brad had their incidents?"

I did. Lamar was involved in a bar fight and arrested by county deputies. Brad punched out a guy in an argument over a parking spot at a Home Depot. He was also arrested.

Jasper continued. "They both got to work while their cases were adjudicated. That's precedent, man. If they don't like it, the brass can stick it up their collective ass and break it off."

I reached for the door handle. "Tell Marty I said thanks."

Jasper held up a hand to stop me from leaving. "But realize one thing."

"What's that?"

"Crites wasn't just another officer—he's an IA lieutenant investigating you for taking money."

"C'mon on, Tom. I didn't steal that crack dealer's cash."

"Even if you didn't take the money, you assaulted a superior."

"He was out of uniform."

"Investigating *you*. They're gonna want to set an example."

I sighed.

"Don't forget you went nutso in that interview room and made yourself look out of control. Saying that Crites blew the chief for rank is coming back to haunt you." He tapped his temple. "Next time, think before you act. You're looking like a loose cannon."

"Somebody needs to leash Crites, then."

Jasper frowned. "Stop worrying about him." He tapped my chest. "Worry about yourself."

"If that bastard keeps pushing into my private life, I'm gonna kick his ass up around his ears."

"That's the kind of stuff I'm talking about, John. Don't you get it?"

"He started this. Not me." I yanked the door open and headed to roll call.

***

A heavy thunderstorm made that night of patrol dreary. Rain pelted my patrol car's windshield as I turned the corner onto Occidental Avenue. Dispatch sent me to a reported domestic dispute. In that part of the city, it usually meant a pimp and a prostitute.

The wipers flicked the rain away as I replayed my conversation with Jasper. Several hours had passed since our talk, yet I continued to get angrier the more I thought about it. Every minute that went by only ratcheted me up higher.

The previous call—a stolen auto report—went poorly. A father claimed his sixteen-year-old daughter stole his car because she failed to report home on time. She broke curfew. Yet, the girl had returned safely home along with the car *before* he called the police. He wanted to teach her a lesson by filing a felony report. He justified his actions by saying it wouldn't be on her record after she turned eighteen. I called him an idiot and left. On the way out the door, he threatened to report me. I was sure that encounter would end in a demeanor complaint.

My body tingled with rage. Jasper's warning that I was looking like a loose cannon seemed like a distant memory when it should have been a clanging warning.

At the reported domestic dispute destination, a large black man pointed his finger at a young Asian woman. He wore dark jeans and a puffy black jacket. Underneath an opened winter coat, the woman wore a skintight red dress that stopped barely below her rear. As the rain fell, the two stood beneath the awning of a store long since out of business. They excitedly yelled at each other.

This wasn't a domestic dispute, it was a business quarrel, and the last thing I wanted to deal with was an uncooperative victim. I had no doubt the woman was a prostitute by the way she was dressed. Based upon my prior experience, I imagined the two of them would say nothing was wrong and that they were arguing about something inconsequential. Unless I witnessed something, I would waste fifteen minutes of my life telling them both to be better members of their community.

I keyed my in-car microphone, announced my callsign, and said, "Show me on scene."

"Unit to back?" the dispatcher asked.

"Go ahead and start one. No hurry."

The responding unit was clearing another call and was several minutes away.

Neither the man nor the woman acknowledged my approaching vehicle. The noise from the rain bombarding the awning above them must have hidden the sound of the patrol car's engine. They didn't even seem bothered by the headlights. Usually, one of those things would catch a suspect's attention, and they would, at least, pretend to be doing something legal and uninteresting.

These two continued to argue animatedly.

Then the man abruptly punched the woman in the face, which sent her backpedaling into the nearby building.

I stomped on the accelerator and wound the Crown Victoria's engine up.

The pimp stepped forward and grabbed the woman by the throat.

Slamming on the brake and jerking the steering wheel brought the patrol car to a stop along the sidewalk next to where the two fought.

The pimp's gaze snapped to me, and we made eye contact. He shoved the woman away from him, and she fell into the nearby building.

By the time I got out of the car, he was halfway down the block. I sprinted after him, feeling wild and alive. Nothing else mattered in the world except catching him.

"Stop running!" I yelled.

He didn't, and I laughed once. It wasn't a typical sound, though. It was a simple bark that most men will never make. The pimp glanced anxiously over his shoulder.

Thrilled by the chase, I yelled, "I'm going to get you!"

It didn't take long to catch up and tackle him. We rolled around the wet pavement as the pimp struggled to break free. He slipped an arm free from my grasp and elbowed me in the face. He then scrambled to his feet and headed back the way we originally came.

Anger swelled inside me as I stood. He was visibly slower now. That meant he was gassed and running on fear. I caught him quickly this time.

"I give," he rasped. "I give!"

I grabbed him by an arm and his shoulder and swung him into a nearby brick wall. His forehead bounced off and sounded like a melon dropping to the floor. He crumpled to his knees and moaned, bringing both hands up to hold his head. Blood ran from a cut above his eye.

Grabbing an arm to handcuff, I said, "Why'd you run?"

He grunted something I couldn't understand.

"You bastard!" the prostitute screamed. She ran toward us. I wasn't sure if she was yelling at him or me.

"Stay back," I ordered.

She didn't listen, and I pushed her away. She came back again, but this time she was swinging at the pimp.

I let go of the man to deal with her, and he collapsed to the ground. He wasn't going anywhere, so handcuffing could wait. As the prostitute kicked at the prostrate pimp, I halfheartedly said, "Step back."

I took my time pushing her away until she was out of kicking range. Under a brighter light, I assessed her. Swelling grew around her left eye, and some blood trickled from the same side of her mouth. Redness was around her throat as if she'd been grabbed, maybe choked.

Her brow furrowed as she studied the man on the ground. "Is he okay?"

"He's fine."

The woman moved forward and bent as if now concerned.

"Get back," I ordered, and she froze. I wasn't sure what she was up to.

She held my gaze for a moment. "You didn't have to hit him so hard."

"Me? You were kicking him."

"I didn't do nothing."

Typical, I thought. She already had whore's remorse. "Stay there."

I reached down for the pimp's hand but kept my eyes on her. That wasn't my first mistake of the night. The man grabbed my wrist and yanked me to the ground. As I stumbled and clumsily fell, he stood and ran.

The prostitute kicked at me now and screamed, "Rape! Rape!"

I clambered up, then angrily pushed her away before chasing after the pimp.

He turned into an alley, and I caught him about halfway through. I shoved him in the back, forcing him to windmill his arms for several feet before crashing headfirst into a dumpster. He immediately rolled onto his back and lifted his hands in surrender.

"I give!" he yelled. "I—"

I jumped and landed on his chest. The first punch I threw was to the side of his face. The second went to the opposite side, near his eye. The third punch broke his nose—I'm sure of it.

My fist hung in the air as my heart pounded in my ears. I sucked deeply for air. It felt like a steel band was around my chest, tightening and constricting the airflow.

The pimp was a mess. He was unconscious, and his face bled badly. Slowly, I stood and looked around. No one was in the alley. The prostitute hadn't followed us in.

I lurched back toward the street and looked both ways. A white Lexus drove by, but the driver never looked my way.

The streets were quiet—a casualty of the thunderstorm. And the prostitute was gone.

"Shit," I muttered. "*Shit!*"

A thought seared its way through my worry and fear—a backup unit was still on the way.

I keyed my shoulder mike but quickly let go. I inhaled deeply and held it in hopes of steadying myself. Then I rekeyed the mike and announced my callsign. "Code four," I said softly. "Just a verbal argument."

"Copy," the radio dispatcher responded. She canceled

the additional unit and sent them to a disorderly subject call in the vicinity of Pike's Market.

Inhaling deeply again, I let the breath slowly out through my nose.

As the rain continued, I returned to the mouth of the alley. Puddles danced from the falling drops. Near the dumpster, the pimp lay motionless.

Get up, I mentally begged. *Run away.*

Hesitatingly, I moved deeper into the alley. When the pimp moved, I stopped. It was a simple lift of the hand toward his head. I stood there—frozen in fear—waiting for him to do something more. When he rolled over, I ran out of the alley.

Near my patrol car, I knelt and dipped the backs of my hands into a dirty puddle. I wiped off as much blood as I could before climbing into the driver's seat. I pulled smoothly away from the curb.

The nearest convenience store had a restroom with outside access. I washed up thoroughly before walking inside and buying a cup of coffee. My hands shook as I took several uneven sips.

I drove to a darkened parking lot and used my in-car computer to notify radio I was following up on an earlier call. It was a trick patrol officers used if they wanted to disappear for a while.

How many people saw me on that street? I wondered.

Dispatch had me out at that location. There was a permanent record that I was there at that time.

But would the pimp report an assault? No, I decided after a time. He wouldn't say anything. There were rules to this game, so he'd take his beating, lick his wounds, and go on about his life.

I stayed there for thirty minutes until I calmed down.

Jasper was right. I was a loose cannon.

Chapter 26

As I approached, the man standing near the open door eyed me with suspicion. His bald head glistened under the green neon sign flashing *The Pit*. Techno music pulsated from inside the club. He was a couple of inches taller than me, but his arms and chest strained against his t-shirt. The club's logo—a dancing cobra—was over his left breast.

"Are you Marco?" I asked.

His face pinched. "You with liquor control?"

I shook my head.

"Some kind of cop?"

"No."

"Then how do you know my name?"

"I'm looking for Amy."

Marco stepped forward, and I reflexively took a step back.

His face contorted further, and his fists balled. "You're the bastard stalking her."

"You got it all wrong. Her friend—"

When he moved forward again, I stepped back once more.

"You ain't her friend," he said. "I know them all."

I lifted my hands to a protective posture. "I only want to talk with her."

Veins popped out on his forehead as his face reddened. "So you can fuck her?"

"I don't even know her."

His cheeks trembled. "You think you're too good for her?"

"I didn't say that."

"Then you do wanna fuck her!"

He yelled and wildly swung his fist. I stepped in and heel-palmed him under the jaw. His head snapped backward, and he stumbled, flailing his arms to keep his balance. When his eyes refocused, he screamed and rushed back. I side-stepped his tackle and punched him in the kidney.

Marco dropped to his knees and arched his back. He bleated once before falling to the ground and rolling around, grabbing his side. When he got onto his back, he was pissing himself.

Cherry from The Red Light District had said Marco's temper was bad. Based on his size, I'd guess some of it was caused by steroids. Something needed to cool him down quickly. I removed my gun from the back of my pants but covered it with my free hand—in case a passerby noticed our interaction.

His eyes widened, and he held his hands in front of his face. "*Please.*"

"I don't want to fight. Understand?"

Marco nodded once. Already, his face was returning to normal color.

"Can we talk like reasonable people?"

He nodded again. The rage in his eyes faded.

"You're sure?"

"We're good. Swear to God."

I tucked my gun away and stepped back.

When Marco sat up, he pulled at his pants. "Oh, man, look what you made me do." He rose to a knee. "I oughta bust you in the mouth."

My hand went behind my back.

"No need for that," he said.

I jerked my head away from the club.

A light rain drizzled while we stood in the alley.

Marco stared down at his crotch. "These are my favorite pants." He scrunched his nose and bent at the waist. "I smell like piss. Do I smell like piss?"

"We'll be done soon enough."

Marco looked up. "But I still gotta work."

"About Amy," I prompted.

He straightened and pulled his shoulders back. "I'm not supposed to see her."

"Why not?"

"She's got an NCO."

"How many have you had?"

His brow furrowed.

"Most guys call them restraining orders, but you say it like an attorney." NCO was short for no contact order—the state's standard response to any domestic violence situation. "How many?"

"A couple. Nothing major. They're all total bullshit." Marco shifted from foot to foot as he tried to adjust his pants.

"You seem like a smart guy," I said.

He made a serious face then nodded.

"And I think I'm a smart guy."

Marco gave a half-shrug then a partial nod. I tried not to be offended at his less-than-enthusiastic response to the statement of my intelligence.

"I bet a smart guy like you knows how to keep tabs on his woman even when he can't contact her."

As he considered my words, he absently picked at something in his teeth. Washing his hands after pulling at urine-covered pants hadn't occurred to him.

"Are you trying to entrap me?"

"No."

"Okay, but since I asked, you can't arrest me now."

"I'm not a cop, and I'm not trying to entrap you. I only want to talk to Amy, but she's gone missing. No one knows what happened to her after she left Paige's."

"Pretty girl, Paige. You a friend of hers?"

I nodded.

"After Amy left her place, she stayed with me for a few days."

"Even with the no contact order?"

He shrugged. "The state put that in place. We didn't have no choice about it."

"When did she stay with you?"

"Couple weeks ago."

"What happened?

"The usual. We started fighting the second night, and things got out of hand. Cops were called."

"Did you get arrested?"

He lifted his hands in frustration. "That was total bullshit, too. I threw a toothbrush, and it hit her. Some neighbors heard us arguing and called the cops. She had a little mark on her cheek from the toothbrush. That's all. You could barely see it. Amy didn't even want to report it, but the cops arrested me. Can you believe that shit?"

Washington State has mandatory provisions in DV situations. Because the law is compulsory, most cops will make the arrest regardless of the level of assault just to avoid any possible future litigation.

Marco shook his head in disbelief. "While I was in jail, she took off. Didn't even wait around. Took my stash, too."

"Your drugs?"

His face pinched. "I don't put that crap into my body. She took my money. I had a few grand set aside for emergencies, and she took it."

"Have you tried getting in contact with her since?"

"Hell no. I don't want to be around her anymore."

"Why not?"

"Man, it's time I wise up. Every time we're together,

it's the same stupid thing. I lose my head, and I go to jail." He tapped his head. "It's my temper. I got to work on it. Look at what happened with you. You barely said anything, and I wanted to take your head off. I don't want to go inside again. I don't do so well in there."

"What's her cell phone number?"

"I can give it to you, but it won't matter none."

"Why's that?"

His gaze dropped sheepishly away.

"You called her," I said.

"It gives that little boop—boop—boop sound and says the phone is no longer in service."

"She canceled her phone service while you were in jail?"

"Why else?"

I eyed him. "You don't have any idea where she might have gone?"

"Her mom lives down in Kent. Maybe she can point you to Amy, but she didn't like me none."

"Why wouldn't Amy stay with her mom instead of you? Based on your history and all?"

"Her mom didn't approve of Amy's life choices. Me being one of them."

I knew that feeling.

"I think mom was the destination of last resort."

"Do you have mom's address?"

Marco crossed his arms. "What am I getting out of this?"

I thought about showing him my gun once more but instead pulled two twenties from my pocket. "Take your pants to the cleaners."

Marco slipped the bills from my fingers. He was about to shove them in the front pocket but stopped and slipped them into a rear. Folding his arms again, he said, "What else?"

I should have shown him the gun. "How about I tell Amy you're helping me find the murderer of her friend."

"Who was murdered?"

"Paige."

He covered his mouth with his hand—the same one that had been picking at his pants. "Oh fuck, no way."

"That's why I need to talk with Amy. I'm talking with anyone who knew Paige to see if they can help me find a reason someone would want her dead."

Marco dropped his hand. "So, if I tell you where the mom lives, and you find Amy, you'll say something nice about me?"

"Sure."

"I'm going to remember that. You promised." He recited the mother's address. "It's sort of a nice place, but in a terrible neighborhood. If she wasn't such a cranky old broad, I'd say she deserved to live somewhere better. Why are you looking at me like that?"

"You remembered that address off the top of your head?"

"What?" He said, slightly offended. "You said I was a smart guy."

With that, he headed back toward the Pit, shaking a leg as he pulled the pants from his crotch.

Chapter 27

After fighting with the pimp in the alley, I spent the rest of my patrol shift hiding out. I dodged calls, assigned myself to fictional contacts, and took extended breaks.

I could have easily said I didn't feel well and gone home, but I wanted to monitor the Mobile Data Computer. Every time a new incident popped up on the screen, I worried that it was related to my assault.

And that's how I began referring to it in my thoughts—an assault. I had crossed the line and assaulted the guy. I knew it. Maybe I could defend my actions *before* we entered the alley, but everything went too far once we were in there.

I went too far.

Near the end of my shift, Sergeant Terry McNeil sent me an in-car message via the MDC and requested a side-by-side in the parking lot of a closed restaurant.

McNeil was an old-school knuckle dragger, a throwback to when cops used brutality to solve crimes. He'd seen his share of accusations, but most ended up unproven for one reason or another.

Our patrol cars idled with their driver's side doors next to each other. This allowed us to chat but be situationally aware of any threats.

"Anyone give you a heads up?" McNeil asked.

"About what?"

"The call dispatch sent me. They're trying to keep it quiet."

"How would I know about it?" Some guys had friends in police radio—not me.

"There's a black male at Harborview claiming a cop beat him. Said it happened near that DV you went to earlier."

I tried to remain calm, but my pulse raced.

McNeil studied me. "You okay?"

"Why wouldn't I be?"

"I've checked around quietly, but no one else has been in that area tonight."

My hands shook in my lap. "You think I tattooed him?"

"I didn't say that."

"Sounds like you are." Even I could hear the tremor in my voice.

"Relax, John. Besides, the guy probably deserved what he got. He's got a sheet a mile long."

I looked forward at an abandoned building.

"Since you were in the area where this guy was assaulted, you might want to complete a Field Interview as to *what* you might have seen, *who* you might have seen. Get what I'm saying? Anything that could help you down the road."

"I responded to a call," I said. "It was verbal. That's it."

"You contacted them, decided there was no crime, so no report."

"That's right. No report."

McNeil rolled his lips inward then asked, "If you contacted them, how come you didn't run their names?"

I stared at him.

"We always run their names. Right, John? Maybe they come back with a warrant or a missing person."

"Did he have a warrant?"

"No."

"What about the woman?"

"What about her? She wasn't at the hospital."

I clamped my hands together to stop them from shaking so badly.

Sergeant McNeil tapped the side of his door. "But hey, the fuck do I care? This guy doesn't deserve our sympathy. He's a leech preying on women. I'll do my best to dunk his complaint, but if someone digs it up, you better have a reason why you didn't run their names. And for God's sake, at least file an FI."

***

Three nights later, Lieutenant Daryl Crites caught me in the locker room before roll call. I was in the process of changing into my uniform.

A malevolent grin creased his face. It was nothing like his earlier salesman's one. "They should have never let you come back from administrative leave."

I zipped my pants and glared at him.

"I've got you dead to rights," he said.

"The hell are you talking about?"

"You beat a man, and I can prove it." His voice was almost sing-song with glee.

My stomach turned. "Bullshit." It sounded weak.

"His girlfriend just picked your face from the wall."

Pictures of every officer hung on a board in Internal Affairs. They had it there so citizens could point out the officer who assaulted, offended, or generally disappointed them. It made it easier for lawsuits and terminations. Kumbaya, my ass.

I slipped a clean t-shirt over my head. "You got nothing."

"I've got more than that. She told me the full story—how you chased her boyfriend into an alley and beat him unconscious."

I stared at him.

"You see it now, don't you?" Crites grinned. "Checkmate, pal."

If I did anything except continue to insist that I responded to a verbal altercation, then I was admitting that I lied to dispatch. Changing my story would also acknowledge that I failed to do my duty by not arresting the pimp for beating the woman.

Crites had the victim and witness to my assault, and he was letting them frame the story. I wanted to cry bullshit, but I could not defend myself. Simply doing so jammed me up. Everything after that would be a bonus for the lieutenant.

"You're history, Cutler. I'm going to start counting the days until you're off this department."

"That won't happen."

He laughed. "It's already done—gift wrapped by your stupidity."

I turned my back to him and moved some gear aimlessly around my locker. Crites waited a moment before leaving. For several minutes, I stared at the inside of my locker. Then I took my uniform pants off and threw them inside.

I told Sergeant McNeil to put me out on vacation for the night. He tried to protest the late request, but I walked away without letting him finish.

***

Two weeks passed before I returned home from an afternoon with my daughter to find a large manila envelope in my mailbox. Its return address was the department. A registered mail receipt was affixed to the front. The apartment manager had signed for its delivery.

A copy of whatever was inside this envelope would also be waiting for me when I returned to duty after my days off. I imagined that the union president also got a copy hand-delivered. The administration would not want to be accused of not following established policy and procedure. They'd already had too many disciplinary actions overturned for those reasons.

This meant the department was now overly thorough. They would ensure that proper notice of an impending action could never be questioned.

Once inside my apartment, I opened the envelope and pulled out a folder. On the cover were the capitalized words—CONDUCT UNBECOMING AN OFFICER.

I flipped open the file to reveal an Internal Affairs coversheet. It stated that I was scheduled for a Loudermill hearing with the chief of police in ten days.

Instinctively, I dropped the file on the kitchen counter. "Son-of-a-bitch," I muttered. I knew it was coming but having the actual file in my hand felt like I just picked up hot coal.

The letter advised that my charge was based upon three incidents—the assault on Crites, the assault of the pimp, and the accusation of stealing money from the drug dealer. The files related to those incidents were included in the envelope for my review.

I walked to the couch and dropped into it. The file felt heavy in my hands—heavier than it should have.

It took some time to read the reports. Crites had been thorough. Even those who hated the man respected his efficiency. Now that it was me in his crosshairs, I finally got to see what all the talk was about. Even the bogus claim of stealing cash from the drug dealer appeared damning. I was screwed.

I closed the file and tried to cry.

Nothing came.

Chapter 28

"I Don't Wanna Lose Your Love" drifted from the speakers of Mickey Finn's.

Besides me, there were only two other patrons in the establishment. At the far end of the bar sat an older man with grayish skin. He quietly sipped a brownish liquor. Sitting at a table was a dark-skinned woman who studied a textbook while nibbling French fries.

Miles stood behind the bar, eating an oversized hot dog slathered in mustard.

I motioned to the stereo. "Pointer Sisters?"

"The Emotions. Came out in seventy-six if I remember correctly."

"I'm sure you do. Mind if I use the phone?"

He took another bite of his hot dog before handing me the telephone. He mumbled something through his mouthful of food.

"Huh?"

After swallowing, he said, "That'll cost you a dime."

"It's thirty-five cents now."

Miles shrugged. "I liked things better when they were simpler."

"You and me both."

I dialed a number I knew by heart but hadn't called in years. When she answered the phone, her voice sounded older than I remembered. "Hello?"

Talking with Marco about Amy and her mother got me thinking about my relationship with mine. "Hey, Mom."

"Johnny?"

"Yeah."

"Are you okay?"

"I'm fine."

"The caller ID said you're calling from a two-oh-six number. Are you back?"

"For a couple days."

"Are you going to come out and see me?"

"If that's all right."

"Don't sound so enthused. You might give your mother false hope."

"Listen, I'm meeting with someone now. I'll come over in a bit."

"Johnny," she said. "I'm sorry. I'd love for you to come and visit."

"Okay, Mom."

"You promise?"

"I promise," I said and hung up the phone.

Miles frowned. "You called your mother? You sick or something?"

"I guess I was feeling sad about how things are."

"This might be taking it a bit too far." He slid a Seattle Police Department business card across the bar. It was Detective Donovan Ahern's. "That man picked up a folder you left for him. He wanted you to have that."

I turned the card over. Handwritten on the back was *What the fuck, John?*

Miles said, "I didn't mean to read his note, but there seems to be a lot of that sentiment going around."

***

My mother lived in a large, red brick home in Gig Harbor. Its manicured lawn was visible under the bright security lights at the edge of the property. Two newer cars—a black Audi and a white Lexus—were parked in the concrete driveway that arced perfectly through the middle of the lot.

I disliked the neighborhood's affluence that came from the big, expensive homes with their fancy cars. It hadn't bothered me when I lived in the Seattle metropolitan area. Maybe I'd gotten desensitized to the overt display of wealth. After two years of living in a one-bedroom apartment, struggling to make ends meet, a person can learn to resent the rich—even those who are family.

The door to the home opened, and Vance Mallory studied me with a perplexed look. "John?"

"Hey, Van. Mom's expecting me."

"Of course. It's just that you look… *different*."

"A little older."

"Aren't we all?" His expression changed to that of an easy smile. "Come inside."

After entering, Van closed the door behind me. Even at this hour, he wore a red sweater, khaki pants, and loafers. It looked like he was ready to step into a class and teach at a moment's notice.

My mother put a lot of emphasis on appearances, and Van fit right into her expectations. That was only one of the reasons I no longer got along with her, but it was the main reason she seemed perpetually disappointed in me.

Van gently patted my shoulder. "Let me go find Carol." He turned and moved deeper into the house.

In the foyer was a picture of Van and me following my graduation from the police academy. He married my mother in a private ceremony on the San Juan islands during my second week of training. Vance was the dean of a local college and a nice enough guy, but he and I never really hit it off. He came from a family of money and spent his life surrounded by books and those searching for higher education. My life had been about violence and darkness. That made it hard for us to talk about many things. We hadn't spoken since I left Seattle.

I turned from the photograph when my mother walked briskly into the foyer. She stretched her arms wide and announced, "Johnny." It was the overly warm greeting that holiday movies pretend people give each other.

"Hi, Mom."

She wrapped her arms around me and buried her head into my chest. I hugged her and nodded at Van, who stood a few feet away from us. She clung to me for a few moments until Van touched her shoulder.

"Give the boy some room, Carol."

When my mother stepped back, her eyes clouded over, and she forced a smile. It quickly vanished as concern washed over her face. "What happened?" She touched my cheek.

"I got into a fight."

She studied my bruises and scrapes with disapproving curiosity.

Van motioned us to follow. "Let's sit down."

Dark hardwood covered the floor of the living room, and floor-to-ceiling bookshelves lined the walls. Every book was a hardback, and not a single empty spot existed. A rolling ladder rested in the corner to allow access to the upper shelves.

Roomy green chairs and a matching sofa triangulated the room. Free-standing lamps were used as accent pieces. A richly colored Oriental rug sat under a large antique coffee table in the middle of the room.

Van and my mom settled onto the couch, and I sat in the chair nearest the room's entrance. We remained quiet for a few seconds before Van anxiously got up. "A beer, John?"

"Coffee, if you don't mind."

Van waved my concern away. "I'll make some right now. Decaf?"

"Whatever you've got."

After Van left the room, my mother slid over on the couch to be nearer to me. Her eyes searched mine. "What brought you back, Johnny?"

I considered different answers but settled on, "Business."

"What kind of business?"

"Investigative work."

Her face brightened. "Are you back to being a policeman?"

"No."

"That's a shame. You looked very nice in your uniform."

My gaze drifted over some of the book titles. None of them were familiar, so I turned back to my mother.

She leaned in closer. "Have you seen Maria and Erin?"

"I saw Maria."

"That's good." Then she muttered, "It's the least you could do."

And there it was—even before Van finished preparing the coffee.

"Don't start, Mom."

"I'm just saying."

"I know. You've said it before."

"Maria's a good woman. You should have treated her better."

I'd grown up under my mother's perverted vision of marriage and fatherhood.

My father never wed my mother and left her a month after I was born. Mom repeatedly said he left because he was a weak man and couldn't stand up to the responsibility of a family. She said it so often that it became a mantra for her—*Your father was a weak man, Johnny.*

Her lessons also included that men—*real* men—made sacrifices for their families. They gave up false dreams and selfish hopes to build a home for their wives and children. When I told her that Maria and I weren't getting married, she never let up. When she learned about my relationship with Paige, her venom was a hundred times worse than anything she ever spouted about my father.

For eighteen years, it was her and me against the world. I never felt at a loss for love. Now, she looked at me like a failure. I was a grown man with a child being raised by a single woman. Her judgment stung worse than I wanted to admit.

Even though I'd told her many times before, I repeated it. "Maria didn't want to get married."

"Have you asked her lately?"

I lifted my hands in frustration. "Why would I do that?"

"Maybe she changed her mind. Women have a right to do that. Maybe she's ready now."

"She's not."

"How do you know? You haven't asked her."

My face warmed with anger. "Stop putting your life on me."

"I raised you better than this."

Van returned but stopped when he heard my mother's words.

I stood. "I don't know why I thought this would be different."

My mother pushed herself off the couch. "You still don't see it, do you?" Her face twisted with disgust.

"See what?"

"You're throwing your life away."

"How?"

"It started with that whore and—"

"Carol," Van said.

"What?" she said. "Tell me I'm wrong. He lost his job and moved away. All because of—"

I lifted a hand to stop her. "Enough!"

My mother's eyes widened.

"I came by to maybe reconnect, and it took two goddamned minutes before you're back on the soapbox."

"Don't use the Lord's name in vain!" She crossed herself.

I inhaled deeply. "I'm sorry I haven't lived up to your expectations, Mom, but I'm not sure anyone could."

She frowned. "Maybe if you tried."

"And maybe that's why Dad left."

She stepped forward. "Sometimes you can be a bastard, John."

"Because of you, I thought I was always one."

Her hand smacked my cheek. "You're just like your father."

Your father was a weak man, Johnny.

"You need some new material, Mom."

I turned to Van, who glanced uncomfortably between my mother and me. "You're a better man than me."

"Yes, he is," my mother snapped.

I headed toward the door. Her thin, screeching voice followed me.

"Yes, he is!"

Chapter 29

Before my Loudermill hearing, Union President Marty Walker and I stood outside in the quiet hallway. The fluorescent light shimmered above us. Marty leaned in close, his breath smelling of coffee and cigarettes.

"It's going to be okay, John. Trust me. This'll be a walk in the park."

I cocked my head.

"Now that the criminal charge is handled, all you have to do is get over this administrative hurdle."

In exchange for deferred punishment, I pled to a misdemeanor charge related to punching Lieutenant Crites. The assault would be expunged from my record if I didn't get in trouble again for the next twenty-four months. Supposedly, that upset Crites because he wanted the charge to stick permanently.

Things got worse for the lieutenant. The pimp refused to press criminal charges against me. I didn't know why, and I didn't care. This sudden course change didn't make the Internal Affairs problem go away, though. Crites had the initial written statements from the pimp and prostitute, which was enough for disciplinary charges.

Finally, there was never proof that I took anything from the drug dealer. That was entirely built upon hearsay, but Crites kept that file open. Of all of them, I was least worried about that issue.

The administrative hurdle that Walker referred to still sounded like a mountain to me.

Walker continued. "This meeting is an opportunity for you to tell the chief anything that might not have been in the file."

"Can I tell him that Crites has been out to get me?"

"God, no." He shook his head. "Play ball in there. This is a way for you to mitigate the damage that IA's trying to do. If the chief has any questions, be truthful. Because you know the old saying—lie and you die."

I thought about my interaction with Crites in the locker room.

"The chief won't put up with lies. And if you do, there won't be a thing the union can do to protect you."

I stared down the hallway and absently nodded. The previous night, I'd met Mike Davoli for a couple of beers. He thought Paige was to blame for everything wrong in my life. I tried to convince him otherwise, but he wasn't buying what I was selling. The gist of his point of view was, "I told you so." Our night ended badly after that.

"You listening to me?" Walker asked.

"Yeah."

"Crites won't be at the hearing. The chief agreed that was a conflict of interest so Sergeant Robinson will fill in for him."

Compared to Crites, Robinson was a better person, but she was still an Internal Affairs rat. I rolled my eyes.

"I figured you'd be more grateful," Walker said.

"Isn't that your job?"

"You make things tough when you act like an asshole, John."

The hearing was held in the department's conference room. The American and Washington State flags stood prominently at the north end. Black and white pictures of Seattle's history hung on the walls. The room smelled of new carpet.

Chief Daniel Faber sat at the middle of the conference table. On his left, Sergeant Gayle Robinson fiddled quietly with a handheld tape recorder that would capture the entire hearing on cassette. To Faber's right were the department's legal counsel and the administrative captain who simply witnessed the proceedings.

To my left was Walker and to my right was the union's attorney. The lawyer was a fantastic negotiator at contract time, but his representation in Internal Affairs issues was legendary in its ineffectiveness. Why the union leadership continued to work with him was a mystery to the line-level officers.

When the chief signaled her, Robinson pressed the little red button on the handheld recorder.

Chief Faber read from a script that addressed the ground rules of the hearing. It was my opportunity to speak one-on-one with him and address any issues about the three cases they were bringing against me. I could talk to legal counsel or a union representative on any question, but I had to be the one to answer. Blah, blah, blah, the chief prattled on until he finally looked up and slid the script to the side. "Do you understand?"

I stared at his pocked marked face and nodded.

"We're on tape, so you'll need to verbalize whether or not you understand."

"I understand," I said.

"Do you have anything to say on your behalf?"

"How do you want to do this?"

The chief's brow furrowed. "What do you mean?"

"Do you want to address these charges all at once or one at a time?"

Faber thought for a moment and opened his hands. "Your choice, Officer Cutler."

"All at once then."

"I ask again, do you have anything to say on your behalf?"

"Yes, Chief, I do. These cases are bullshit."

Walker reached out and touched my arm, but Faber

waved him off.

"We're adults here, Marty. Let the man say what he's got to say."

I leaned forward so the recorder could catch my voice. "This is a witch hunt. The first case is a total fabrication. I never stole any money from that dealer. I had probable cause to arrest him for drugs and did so. In my mind, he's taking a pot shot at me, and the department is coddling him by letting it get this far. This will set a bad precedent on the street, mark my words."

Chief Faber interlaced his fingers but did not interrupt.

I continued. "The second case, I'll own. I hit Lieutenant Crites. I've never said anything but that. You've seen the testimony from my interview, and you know why I hit him. He was coming at me through my relationship with a woman. By dealing with the resulting criminal charge, I believe I've been punished enough concerning that incident."

The chief pulled a folder to him and opened it. He flipped through the pages. "Please continue, Officer Cutler."

"I'll wait, Chief. Find what you've got to find."

Faber looked up, and his face flattened. "I've got what I needed." He closed the file.

Next to me, Walker shook his head.

"The final case," I said, "is something out of a *Twilight Zone* episode. I contacted a couple on the corner while they were in the middle of a verbal dispute. I told them to leave the area immediately. They walked off, and I left. I did not assault him. They're lying. Plain and simple."

The chief leaned back in his chair and crossed his arms. "Anything else?"

"No, sir."

Faber remained silent for some time. It was a

technique most investigators used—let the silence work on the subject you're going after. However, this was a hearing, and the investigative work was done. The chief's silence only served to irritate me. I did my best to tamp the anger down, though. Getting mad on record again would not be helpful.

Finally, the chief said, "I think—" He took a breath then sighed. "I think you're lying."

"No, sir," I said. "I am not—"

The chief held up a hand to interrupt me.

"You've got a daughter, Officer Cutler?"

My brow creased. "What's she got to do with this?"

"Were you and her mother ever married?"

I glanced at the union president on my left. "The fuck?"

Marty's eyes bulged. "Language, John, language!"

"But he's bringing my daughter into this."

"No, Officer Cutler," the chief said, "I'm only dealing with you. Did you marry the woman who bore you a child?"

"What does that have to do with any of this?"

"You had a responsibility, and you avoided it."

"I haven't avoided anything. She didn't want to marry me."

"That's a convenient excuse."

"It wasn't convenient. Not for me. I asked her, and she said no. I'm still having trouble understanding how this ties into the hearing."

"You're supposed to set an example, and you can't even do that for your own daughter."

I glared at Marty, then at the noticeably quiet union lawyer. "Are either of you going to speak up here?"

The lawyer shrugged. "He has the right to talk with you. Right now, he's only talking."

I turned to Marty and thumbed back at the attorney.

"We pay this guy?"

"The chief hasn't imposed any punishment yet," Marty whispered. "He's only talking. Relax and listen."

"This is what I'm talking about," Faber said. "You need to set an example, but you think you're above it. You're somehow above everyone else."

Sergeant Robinson stared at the tape recorder.

The chief opened one of the folders. "Take this file—the one with the couple."

"Pimp and prostitute," I said.

He raised an eyebrow. "You know this how?"

I remained silent.

The chief flipped a couple of pages. "Unless I'm missing something, you didn't check their names while on the scene. Did you run them?" His eyes settled on me.

"No."

"Then how do you know they're a pimp and prostitute?"

"I don't for certain."

"Did you run their names after you saw the IA file? By the shake of your head, I'm taking that as a no."

"I didn't run their names."

"Because doing so now might be a violation of policy. There would have been no need to run them at a later date."

"I understand."

"So you're assuming that they're a pimp and prostitute."

I held my tongue. Either answer was a trap. If I said yes, he would ask why I didn't check their names at the scene. If I responded no, then he would ask what about my training didn't allow me to see that dynamic.

Faber's eyes narrowed. "Do I need to repeat the question?"

"No, sir. I rolled up on the scene. Based upon that

neighborhood and my experience, I made an educated guess about their relationship."

He harrumphed then consulted his file again. "Regardless of their relationship, they couldn't make up a story this perfectly. The man was busted up so badly I'm sure the city will have to pay on their claim."

"Are you kidding?"

The chief looked up calmly. "No, Officer Cutler, I'm not. Care to further elaborate on the events in this file?"

I set my jaw and said through clenched teeth, "No."

"Based on their written statements and your responses, I'm left to think that you're lying. So does Lieutenant Crites. He believes you assaulted this man. The woman verifies the story."

I shook my head.

"Maybe you thought you were doing the righteous thing by beating a man senseless, but it was not noble— especially not while wearing that badge. It was illegal. Lucky for you, it's not prosecutable since they won't press charges."

I glanced at the union lawyer, who stared straight ahead. He still hadn't written a word on his notepad.

"You also admitted to hitting Lieutenant Crites, but what else could you do? There were witnesses to that assault, along with the physical evidence of the strike. It seems you two have had negative contacts recently for reasons I'm not entirely clear about. Want to explain those?"

"No," I said flatly.

"John," Marty whispered. "This is your chance—"

"No," I repeated.

The chief looked at the union president before continuing. "You punched a fellow officer— Strike that. You punched a *superior* officer. I believe you were engaging in an inappropriate relationship with a woman of questionable morals—"

"Inappropriate?"

"—who has a criminal record."

My brow furrowed. "What criminal record?"

"Driving under the influence."

I laughed. "Are you kidding me? I can name five guys on this department with a DUI. One of them's a captain."

The chief tapped something in the file. "There was also a conviction for Possession of Drug Paraphernalia."

"A weed pipe? She told me about that. How many officers on this department have kids smoking that shit?"

Faber held up his hand. "Stop deflecting, Officer Cutler. It's not a good look."

My face warmed further.

"I can't do anything about your outside relationships, but—"

"You're damn right you can't do anything about my outside relationships. She doesn't have anything to do with these charges." Marty laid his hand on my arm, but I angrily yanked it free. "I haven't done anything wrong."

"Which brings us back to the first case," the chief said. He slid the last folder to him. "The one with the drug dealer. This was the case that bothered me the most. When I first read it, I thought the allegation was complete garbage."

"It is," I said.

Faber tapped the file. "I figured this was just some drug-dealing maggot looking to tarnish a good officer's reputation. His story seemed ludicrous. An officer from my department beat him in an alley then stole his money? Ridiculous, I thought."

From my peripheral vision, I noticed that both Marty and the union's attorney were looking down.

The chief said, "Then I read the report about the pimp and, guess what, it bears a striking resemblance. Almost a pattern, you could say. I didn't believe it before, but I can believe it now."

"Fuck me," I muttered.

"Language," Marty whispered harshly.

Chief Faber shook his head. "You're out of control, Officer Cutler. I don't like what I'm reading in these reports, and I don't like what I'm seeing at this table. Your behavior seems eerily similar to your outburst during the interview with Lieutenant Crites."

My jaw clenched. The union's attorney stared at the tape recorder in the middle of the table. I glared at him, but he didn't notice.

The chief continued. "One of the things that I hope my officers have is an ability to learn from their mistakes. Maybe I'm expecting too much from you."

Walker must have sensed something emanating from me because he leaned over and hissed, "Relax."

Faber closed the folder. "Your attitude is poor, Officer Cutler, your decision-making is suspect, and your work product is questionable." The chief's gaze drifted around the room. "I'll let you know when I make my decision. Until then, you're back on administrative leave."

"What?" I glanced at Walker then the union's attorney. "Are you two ever going to speak up?"

Walker said, "Now is not the time."

Before ending the hearing, the chief announced the time and concluded the interview. Sergeant Robinson pressed the stop button on the recorder.

Even though everyone else stood to leave, the chief and I remained seated.

"Anything else?" he asked.

"No," I said, fighting the urge to yell.

"Then you're dismissed."

I pushed back from the table and stalked out of the room.

Chapter 30

In the morning, the repercussions of the visit to my mother remained—anger, self-loathing, and an annoying hang-over. I'd had more than a few drinks when I returned to Mickey Finn's.

After breakfast and some aspirin, I drove to the city of Kent. With the address that Marco provided, it wasn't hard to find Amy Mackey's mother's house. It was a modest, yellow home with a small lawn. Cropped shrubs stood guard at the front of the walkway.

Before exiting my truck, I considered bringing my gun. I might not have thought twice about it in another scenario, but I was about to ask a woman I'd never met about her daughter's whereabouts. A strange man asking those questions was a tough obstacle to get beyond. A strange man with a weapon was an entirely different matter. I tucked my gun under the seat and climbed out.

The small, concrete porch appeared to have been recently painted. The curtains in the front windows were drawn. The hanging mailbox next to the front door had *Mackey* written on it. While the doorbell chimed, I surveyed the neighborhood.

The Mackey household stood in stark contrast to the rough area in which it resided. Homes on both sides were in considerable disrepair—missing roof shingles, peeling paint, dead grass. Older, dented cars parked along the curb—one of them was up on blocks and missing a door. Across the street, three stray dogs roamed together in a pack.

When no one responded to the bell, I opened the

screen door—it squeaked—and knocked. A couple of moments passed, and I knocked a second time. Letting go of the door, it slammed shut with a loud bang.

The morning air was crisp as I wandered around to the backyard. Flowers were planted along the edge of the house. The multiple colors formed a floral moat, protecting the residence from the ugliness that had overtaken the neighborhood. The backyard of the Mackey home had the same cleanliness and order as the front.

Behind the house, parked just off the alley, was a black mid-eighties Chevy Impala. I crossed the lawn to get a closer look. There was garbage on the floorboards and seats. The filth inside the car didn't match that of the house's exterior. I removed a pen from my coat, then searched my pockets for a scrap of paper. The envelope I had my earlier notes on was tucked inside the glovebox of my truck.

Finding no other alternative, I wrote the license plate number on the palm of my hand.

At the backdoor, I knocked once more. It sounded as if there were footsteps inside. I leaned closer to the door to confirm. But once again, it was silent. I knocked again, harder this time.

A screen door opened with a squeak then slammed shut.

The front!

I hurried to the corner of the house just in time to see a white male running down the sidewalk. He wore a black stocking cap, a black leather jacket, and blue jeans.

"Hey!"

It was a stupid thing to yell. The man was sprinting away from the Mackey house, and my shouting wasn't going to stop him.

I ran toward the sidewalk. The chase reaction felt natural, but it was all wrong. I should have known better than blindly follow him. I didn't understand why I was trying to catch the guy. Besides, what would I do if I caught him? And what if he had a gun? Mine was safely tucked away inside my truck, where it would provide me no help.

Those thoughts didn't occur to me at that moment because adrenaline surged through my veins, focusing my attention until it was a laser. All I knew—all I wanted—was to catch this guy running away.

After a block and a half, it seemed as if I was gaining on him when he cut through a yard between two decaying homes. When I made that turn, my feet slipped out from underneath me on wet grass, and I crashed into the porch of the farthest home.

Pain cascaded through the left side of my body, and I moaned loudly. With grunts of protest, I scrambled upright. The chase reaction morphed into anger, and now I wanted to catch the man for an entirely new reason—to share the pain I experienced. My lungs burned as they struggled for oxygen, but I didn't let up. Realizing that the guy was heading back toward Amy's mother's house made me push harder.

The man unexpectedly disappeared behind a garage. I slowed to a shuffle as I fought to get my breathing back under control. It came in ragged bursts, and the sensation of vomiting tickled the back of my throat.

Wearily, I moved forward. If the man jumped out, I needed to be ready to strike back.

The Mackey home was up ahead. Noticing the Chevy Impala parked at the edge of the alley, I came to a stop. Exhaust floated out of the tailpipe.

The Chevy lurched in reverse, its tires squealing on the alley's asphalt. With its engine gunning loudly, the car rocketed backward. There was nowhere for me to go—I was between two garages that abutted the narrow alley.

I did the only thing I could. I jumped onto the trunk of the rapidly approaching car. The back of my head slammed into the rear window. The Chevy stopped abruptly and tossed me off. I landed in an awkward heap. Even as pain erupted in my hip and my shoulder, fear lanced through me.

Move!

I rolled to the nearest garage. If the car reversed now, I might be crushed, but it would have to scrape along the structure to get me.

The Impala darted forward.

As I lay on the ground, I watched the car race toward the mouth of the alley. Its brake lights briefly illuminated before it bounced into the street. The motor backfired once as it zoomed out of the neighborhood.

I rolled onto my back and stared into the morning sky.

***

The young cop frowned and shifted from foot to foot. "You're sure you're okay?"

"I'm fine."

I sat with my shoulders against a cedar fence that protected a neighboring yard. Trash cans lining the alley gave the area an aroma of cut grass and rotting garbage.

The officer was in his early twenties, and his name tag read *Johannsen*. "You don't look fine. We should have an EMT look at you."

My fingers gingerly walked their way over my head. A large bump grew underneath my hair. "I'm good." My voice sounded shakier than I felt.

Was it an aftereffect of the adrenaline or the fact that I just hit my head against the rear window of the Chevy?

Johannsen glanced anxiously around. I'd seen that

look before. Once it had been in the mirror, but mostly it was the look of other fresh-faced rookies. He was probably concerned that his Field Training Officer was somewhere, surreptitiously observing him.

The officer tapped the small spiral notebook he held. "Name?"

"John Cutler."

"Is that short for Jonathan?"

"It's not short for anything."

We went back and forth for another minute as he got my home address, employer—I gave him the name of the club I bounced at—and phone number.

I pulled my cell phone from my pocket. It didn't illuminate after flipping it open. There had been enough power previously. I pressed the power button, hoping to get it to turn on. Nothing. Its last minutes were now officially wasted. Luckily, I hadn't spent the money to put more time on it.

"Can you tell me what happened?" Johannsen asked.

"I came here looking for a woman. This is supposed to be her mother's home."

A light drizzle started, and Johannsen did his best to shield his notebook from it.

"What's her name?"

"Which one?"

Johannsen looked up from his notebook. "The mother."

"Mary Mackey."

"And the daughter?"

"Amy."

"Same last name?"

I nodded.

The officer lifted his head, took a quick look around, then returned his focus to me. "What happened when you got here?"

I told him about the quick chase and how the guy got away in the Impala.

"Did you get a license plate number?"

"I wrote it down." I lifted my hand to show him. Most of the number was smeared from the fall in the grass. Besides a single K, all that was left was a blue smear across my palm.

"You don't remember the rest of it?"

I didn't. A couple of years ago, as a patrol cop, I probably could have recited a quick flash of a plate. But not now. And especially not after a foot pursuit and nearly being run over.

He jotted another, longer note. As he did so, he occasionally looked at me then his surroundings. Rookies are hypervigilant against would-be attackers. "Why were you looking for…" Johannsen paused while he checked his notebook. "Amy?"

I wiped my forehead with the back of my hand. "I thought she might have some answers in the death of her co-worker."

"Where does she work?"

"The Red Light District."

He jotted again in his notebook before flipping the cover closed to keep the light rain away. "How'd you get this address?"

I touched the bump on my head again and winced. "An ex-boyfriend. How'd you find me?"

"A neighbor called in. Said she heard some screaming coming from the house. When we showed up, you were back here."

"There was screaming from the house?" I looked toward the little yellow home but couldn't see it from where I sat. "It was quiet when I got here."

The officer tucked his notebook away. "Why'd you beat the old lady?"

His accusation irritated me. "I already told you I never made it into the house."

"That's not what she said."

"Bull." I rolled onto my hands and knees to push myself up.

"Stay on the ground."

I wobbled upright and used the fence to steady myself.

"Sit *down*." Johannsen stepped back into a defensive stance. His eyes were alert as he focused on my movements.

I dismissively waved him off.

"Johannsen, take it easy," a woman called out. When she was close enough, I could read *Sanders* on her name tag and see the sergeant stripes on her shirt. She pointed at me while speaking to the officer. "The vic said he didn't attack her. She's never seen this guy before."

"Maybe he was the suspect's partner."

"Do you have evidence of that?"

The officer shook his head. "No, ma'am."

Sanders considered me for a moment. "According to the neighbor, this guy was almost run over." The sergeant turned back to the officer. "Criminal partners have violent disagreements all the time."

"That's what I'm saying," Johannsen said.

"If they were partners, does it make any sense to try and kill the man then leave him alive to talk with us? Well?"

"Not really."

Sanders eyed the rookie but waved at me. "You've got his info?"

Johannsen dejectedly nodded. "Yeah."

"Then kick him loose."

I pointed to the house. "Can I ask her some questions?"

The sergeant jerked her thumb toward the end of the

alley. "Hit the bricks."

"Yes, ma'am," I said.

She headed back to the house with the younger officer close on her heels.

Chapter 31

Stevie Wonder's "Higher Ground" bounced through the speakers of Mickey Finn's. I was bent over a newspaper, trying to follow a story on Councilwoman Elizabeth Vanderlinden's latest homelessness plan, but my head bobbed along with the funky rhythm. Because of the song's distracting qualities, it took three tries before I understood the sentence I was reading.

The front door opened, and Captain Daryl Crites stepped in. He stopped to survey the bar. After locating me, he headed over. I closed the paper.

Crites slid into the booth. "Only in town a few days and already making a mess."

Gone was the air of sensitivity that he'd exhibited in the interview room after I discovered Paige's body. This was more like the lieutenant I remembered.

Folding my arms over my chest, I said, "What are you accusing me of now?"

"Who said I'm accusing you of anything?"

"Already making a mess—that's what you said. There's an accusation in there."

"If the shoe fits…"

I didn't respond. Instead, I tried to determine what he was after.

He wasn't wrong; I *was* making a mess of things. Two assaults sprang to mind—Levi Montgomery and Marco, Amy's ex-boyfriend. Would either of those men call the police?

Levi might have called, but he had expected Detective Ahern to show up for the file. And the latter happened;

Ahern had stopped by the bar to retrieve the expandable file. So, I was willing to assume that Levi hadn't called the police.

Would Detective Ahern have passed this information along? His note on the back of his business card indicated irritation with me for sticking my nose into the investigation, so maybe he talked with the captain, but it was unlikely. Nobody liked Crites. I doubted Ahern would willingly tattle on me for reading the contents of a file.

Perhaps, Crites was monitoring Ahern's investigation from afar and discovered the info on his own. But how? Could he read Ahern's reports while they were on the detective's computer? That would be some underhanded behavior, and it seemed a stretch. Not only would it require technological know-how, but why would he do such a thing? Would he do it because he still had a hard-on for me two years after getting me terminated from the department? Maybe, but unlikely.

That left Marco the boyfriend. Would the bouncer have reported the assault to the cops? I doubted it since he didn't even know my name. If Marco *had* filed a report, Crites wouldn't have had any way to connect it to me.

Crites leaned forward. "So, you're denying this?"

"I'm not sure what *this* is."

"This is what police work looks like. Maybe you already forgot."

And that's when I knew he was fishing. The Daryl Crites that I remembered wouldn't have tried to weasel me into admitting anything. He would have rammed it down my throat then arrested me. Or arrested me, then rammed it down my throat.

I relaxed my arms. "Why are you here, Lieutenant?"

"Captain."

"Why are you here?"

His lips twisted. "Rumors are floating."

"How's that concern me?"

"You're the flavor of the day."

For spreading gossip, each precinct was worse than a high school cheerleading squad. If the rumor was really juicy, it would spread throughout the entire department like it was on the front page of a newspaper. Half the guys on the department couldn't identify a city council member, but they knew which officers were hooking up with whom.

Crites leaned forward, and maliciousness flashed in his eyes. "You're not getting your job back."

That's what this visit was about. "I don't want it."

"Just so you know."

"It's been made clear."

The captain nodded, satisfied that he'd put me on some sort of notice. "There's also talk that you're poking your nose into—" he paused as he searched for the appropriate words "—the death of your girlfriend."

I cocked my head. The last part he had said carefully, almost respectfully. This was on the heels of his dick-ish behavior. I couldn't figure out the man. "What about it?"

"Don't stick your nose where it shouldn't be."

"Is that a threat?"

He lifted a hand in a calming motion. "What I'm saying is this—" Again, he paused to pick his words carefully. This action was disconcerting and put me on alert. "I know what she meant to you, and you want to help find who murdered her."

"You're right. I do."

"But this is still a police investigation. Don't do anything that will jeopardize that."

"Or what?"

His face flattened. "Or a killer may get away."

Crites slid out of the booth.

"Wait."

He paused and raised an eyebrow.

"I don't get you."

"What's to get?"

"You come down here to bust my balls, but you showed me kindness after she was murdered. And you're still nice about that. I don't get it."

Crites looked away briefly before saying, "No one deserves what happened to that woman. You loved her. It was obvious. No one should have to see a loved one that way. How hard is that to figure out?"

"But why come down and rub my nose in my termination?"

"You dishonored the badge."

"The hell I did."

The captain's eyes flared. "You did," he insisted. "And that's why I will always think of you as a special project, Cutler."

With that, he strode away.

Miles walked over after the captain exited. "Who was that unfriendly piece?"

"That was the guy who ruined my career."

"Huh." His brow furrowed. "I thought you ruined your career."

I looked up at Miles. "Really?"

"Still too soon?"

Chapter 32

Three nights after my Loudermill hearing with Chief Faber, I spent the evening with Paige.

As we lay in bed, I gently caressed her hair. The digital clock on the nightstand showed it was a few minutes after midnight.

A meeting with the chief was scheduled for the following day. He would hand out my discipline then. He'd provided no hints as to what the punishment might be. I read that as a signal for the worst.

"They're going to fire me," I said.

"You're a good cop. They're not going to fire you."

"Even the union president thinks so."

Her breath was warm on my skin. "What happens then?"

"We'll grieve it."

"What's that mean?"

My hand traveled aimlessly up and down her back. "The union files paperwork claiming I was terminated against our contract or established labor laws. The chief will deny it, of course, because it was his decision to fire me. Then the city has to make its decision. If they agree with the chief, then the grievance goes to arbitration where an arbiter will have to decide if I stay fired or if the city has to give me my job back."

"How long can that take?"

"Six months. Maybe even two years."

Her hand rested on my stomach. "Wow. What happens in the meantime?"

"I get a job until there's a ruling."

Paige lifted onto an elbow. "What can you do besides police work?"

"Not much."

I put both hands behind my head and stared at the ceiling. For a while, I listened to her breathing and felt her warmth along the length of my body. Eventually, I rolled on my side to face her. She rubbed a thumb along my lower lip.

"Paige."

"Hmm?"

"I want you to know that you're all I think about."

Her hand moved away from my mouth.

"Even when we're not together, you're always on my mind."

Her eyes narrowed.

"I can't imagine my life without you in it."

She gnawed on her lip as her brow furrowed.

"I guess what I'm trying to say is that I love you."

Paige opened her mouth to say something, but nothing came out. Emotions cascaded over her face. Her eyes darted away. When she finally closed her mouth, her face tightened.

I should never have said the words. If I had only read the signals, I could have stopped myself, but I missed something along the way. "You don't have to say it back."

She sat up.

"What's wrong?"

"I can't do this."

"Do what?"

"Be your safety net."

"I'm not asking for that. I only said I love you. It's okay if you don't feel the same way." I was making it worse, but I couldn't stop myself.

She slid out of bed and snatched her panties from the floor. With a wriggle of her hips, she slipped them on. "You should go."

"What did I do? Are you afraid of how I feel? Of how you feel?"

"I'm serious," she said while clasping her bra together. "You need to leave."

I scooted to the edge of the bed and covered myself with a pillow. "I'm not going anywhere."

"Don't do this."

"What am I doing?"

She glared at me. "Stop forcing things."

"Will you tell me what's wrong?"

"I already told you." She grabbed her jeans and a black t-shirt then left the room.

I followed her, grabbing my underwear as I went. "You said you couldn't do this."

In the living room, she hurriedly slipped into her pants.

I put my underwear on. "What does that mean?"

"It means," she snapped, "exactly what it sounds like. Stop being dense."

"It sounds like you're breaking it off."

She looked up at the ceiling. The muscles in her jaw strained. She then shook her head and put on her t-shirt.

"Tell me," I pleaded.

She motioned toward the door. "Call me in the morning."

"I've got that meeting with the chief. I want to talk now."

"I don't."

"Are you breaking up with me?"

She walked back toward the bedroom.

"I can't believe this," I said. "My career— my *life* is falling apart, and you want to break up? That's perfect."

Paige spun. "You did those things." She angrily pointed at me. "*You* did those things, John. Not me!"

"You're a bitch."

Her eyes widened. "Don't you *ever*."

"Then talk to me!"

She pointed at the door. "Get out."

My ears felt warm, and my fingers tingled. "Is this how you get off?" My voice boomed through the apartment. "By smashing my life and then throwing me away like some piece of trash? Maybe I should stuff a couple bills into your panties, so you'll consider staying."

It took two strides for her to get to me. Her hand cracked across my cheek. "Get out!"

"No."

"I'll call the cops."

"Big deal. I've already gone to jail for you. What's one more time?"

She grabbed the cordless phone from the armrest of the couch. I yanked it away from her and threw it against the wall. Small pieces flew around the room.

"Get out!" she screamed. Her face reddened, and she breathed heavily. Tears streamed down her cheeks.

I wanted to reach out and grab her, to hold her in my arms and tell her that I was an idiot. I wanted to beg her forgiveness and say again that I loved her. But instead, I said, "I need my clothes."

While dressing in the bedroom, I heard the bathroom door shut. After tying my shoes, I stopped at the door.

"Paige?" I softly said.

No answer. Her sobs were loud enough to be heard, though.

"Let me in."

Still no response.

"Please."

I tried the doorknob. It was locked. My hand rested on

the door while I tried to come up with the words to say I was sorry. The moment had spun so quickly out of control.

But why? Because I said I loved her?

Why did that upset her?

She refused to say it back. I should have been the one to get upset.

My hand balled into a fist. I wanted to punch the door. The feeling of helplessness angered me.

So, what could I say to that closed door?

Nothing.

My hand relaxed. I left her apartment.

***

The following morning, Marty Walker and I were seated in front of the chief.

Various pictures of Seattle's police officers in action graced the walls of his office. Police knickknacks littered the bookshelves behind him. A frequency scanner sat on one shelf, so he could listen to the patrol teams. He flicked it off before facing us.

The chief opened the manila folder in front of him.

"Whether you believe this or not, John, this has been a hard decision for me." He had dropped the formality he displayed during the hearing. "I've given it a lot of time and thought. The early portion of your career was exemplary, but the last year has been a complete disaster. Your moral character came to the forefront, and I can't ignore it."

He handed both Marty and me a copy of his decision. At the top of the letter were the words TERMINATION OF EMPLOYMENT.

I looked up from the paper, but Marty continued to study his.

"You're not going to read it?" the chief asked.

"Why should I?"

"The evidence was too strong."

"Evidence?" I tossed the document onto his desk. "Are we done?"

Marty reached out and touched my shoulder. "Hold on, John. We haven't even talked about this."

"Now, you want to talk?" I shrugged his hand off. "There's nothing I want to talk about."

The chief laid the document on his desk and handed me a pen. "You need to sign here."

"Sign it yourself."

I stood and left his office without being dismissed. What was he going to do? Fire me again?

In the hallway, Walker ran up from behind. "Hey, this won't help if you want us to file a grievance."

I turned quickly, and he backpedaled.

"John—"

"You and that overpriced attorney didn't help me at all during the hearing. Now, you're saying you want to? You're as full of shit as the administration."

Marty stayed calm. "Listen, John. This isn't my first rodeo. I know how to handle these things."

"You know what?" I waved my hand contemptuously. "I don't care. I don't want this job anymore. I don't even want to be in this fucking town. The next time you see Crites, tell him I owe him one."

"Wait."

"Stay away from me."

I headed directly to the parking lot and climbed into my truck. The engine turned over, and the tires chirped as I sped away from the department. At that moment, I'd made up my mind. I was done with law enforcement. I was done with Seattle.

I returned to my apartment and loaded my truck. I

dropped my keys off at the manager's apartment and told them I was breaking my lease. The manager complained that I still had several months left. I told her to bill me.

After saying a tearful goodbye to my daughter, I pointed my truck east, not knowing where I would end up.

Chapter 33

In the morning, I returned to the city of Kent. Mary Mackey cracked the door after the second knock. A brass chain stopped it from opening it all the way.

The older woman's face was heavily bruised and swollen. A Band-Aid was applied over her left eyebrow. "Yes?"

"Hello, ma'am. My name is John Cutler."

"I saw you yesterday. You were the man out back."

"Yes, ma'am."

"The police said the other man hit you with his car."

"That's correct. He got me good, too."

Mary's gaze traveled my length. "They said you were looking for—" I assumed she paused briefly to consider whether to say her daughter's name. "—someone."

I said it for her. "Amy, ma'am. I'm looking for your daughter."

She swallowed with some difficulty. "Why do you want to speak with her?"

"She might be in trouble."

"A little late to be telling me that."

My smile was polite. "Yes, ma'am."

"How do you know my daughter?"

"I don't. Her former roommate, Paige McIntyre, was my… friend."

"Was?"

"She was murdered a couple days ago."

Additional concern flashed through Mary's eyes. "Murdered?"

"And Amy disappeared a couple weeks prior. I'd like

to know if they're linked."

"Are you a private investigator?"

I shook my head. "But I was a policeman. That's why Paige called me. I think she was in trouble, but I got here too late to understand what was going on."

"What are you hoping to do now?"

I glanced around the neighborhood before facing her again. "I want to find some answers."

She studied me for a moment further then closed the door. The chain noisily slid off. When the door reopened, she invited me in. She clutched a large knife in her right hand.

Mary noticed my focus and said, "Oh," and hid the knife behind her back. It made me feel only slightly better. Once again, I'd left my gun in the truck.

She pointed at the recliner with her empty hand. "Please, sit down."

In the small living room was a sofa with an orange and brown afghan thrown over its back. Country-style knick-knacks cluttered the shelves while pictures of farm settings were hung about. Rays of sunlight slipped through the curtains and gave the room a hazy appearance. In a corner was a stack of newspapers several weeks old.

Mary sat on the end of the sofa and put her hands on her knees. The knife remained clutched in her fist. She realized the weapon was there and tucked it between two cushions, the handle sticking out for easy retrieval. "The man who did this to me," she motioned to her face, "wanted to know where Amy was, too."

"Did he say what for?"

She looked away.

"It's okay, Mary. If you don't want to talk, I understand. I can come back another time."

That was a lie. I didn't want to come back. It was

important to get the information about Amy now. Staying in Seattle on some quixotic quest to find Paige's killer would get costly. The initial thousand dollars would only go so far, which was supposed to be for child support. And forcing this woman to talk about her traumatic incident would only build resentment. To get anywhere, I needed Mary to want to speak with me. Or at least feel safe doing so.

"He never said why." She paused and inhaled a short, stuttering breath. "He hit me when I said I didn't know where she was."

"I'm sorry."

She bowed her head. "He liked doing it. At least, it seemed that way. What kind of person…" Her voice trailed off.

"Had you seen him before?"

The shake of her head was barely perceptible.

"Do you think he knew Amy?"

"I think so." She pointed to the mantle above the fireplace. "He commented on her pictures."

"What did he say?"

"He'd didn't like them. He said she was prettier in person."

I moved over to the fireplace. Along the mantle were photographs of the same woman at various stages in her life. She had long blonde hair, sharp features, and piercing blue eyes. Her smile was practiced—a model in training.

"Ms. Mackey, do you have any idea where Amy may have gone?"

"I don't."

Carefully, I said. "It's important that I talk with her."

"I'm sorry, Mr. Cutler. I don't know where she's at."

I thought about asking more questions, but she didn't look like she was in the mood to answer anymore. She looked like a beaten dog that's too afraid to take food from a stranger. The real damage from the assault wasn't on the surface of her skin.

"If you ever need me," I said, "please call Mickey Finn's bar in Seattle. The owner is a friend."

"Mickey Finn's," she muttered.

"That's right."

She opened the front door. After I stepped outside, the door locked, and the chain slid back into place.

***

I wanted a cup of coffee and a place to think, but Starbucks was the only place that fit the bill. Reluctantly, I went in.

The disappointing thing about Starbucks is they're simply the McDonald's of coffee. It's the same store no matter which city it's in. The coffee, goodies, and other sundries are alike. Even the non-offensive background music is indistinguishable. Big business co-opted the coffeehouse mentality of artistic expression and questioning authority before squishing it into systematic uniformity. And the American people gleefully swallowed it down. If that wasn't a metaphor for our society, I don't know what was.

I ordered a small cup of black coffee.

The barista, a twenty-something with a nose ring and short blond hair, asked, "Would you like Pike or—"

"I don't care as long as it's black."

She smiled cheerfully and filled my order.

With coffee in hand, I found an empty table to lay out the puzzle pieces surrounding Paige's death. I was never a detective. I had been a patrol cop. My job was only a temporary fix until long-term solutions could be applied—whether they be the judicial system, the mental-health system, or the arrival of the coroner.

Detectives were an intermediary step in the same process, but they used their brains more than their brawn. This developed a new skill set that allowed them to see different patterns and connect more things.

Patrol cops stare at what's in front of them and try to figure out an immediate solution. Detectives take in the whole scene and try to figure out what really happened.

If I couldn't get a solid lead in Paige's death soon, then I should pack it in. I couldn't stay in the area forever and chase my tail in hopes of discovering something that would lead me to her killer. Besides, Detective Ahern was actively working on the case. He was the pro. I was doing this out of some hope of vindicating myself in the eyes of a dead woman. Even thinking about it felt foolish.

I sipped my coffee and bit back the bitter taste. From the inner pocket of my jacket, I removed the envelope I'd made my original notes on and laid it on the table. Staring at my handwriting, I wondered how I should assemble this puzzle.

One piece at a time, I thought. Start at the beginning.

Paige called because she wanted the expandable file back from Levi Montgomery.

The file—that's what this was supposed to be about.

But someone broke into her apartment. Not Levi since he had a key. Paige said so, and so did he. Paige said the burglary had nothing to do with the expandable file, though. Other units in the apartment community were broken into. She thought it was a coincidental event. But what if it wasn't? I set that question aside.

When I confronted Levi, he seemed truly upset by the revelation of Paige's death. I didn't believe he killed her. Maybe Ahern would prove me wrong, but it didn't feel like the former boyfriend was lying.

I spun the coffee cup around and watched the green

and white logo repeatedly disappear.

Paige never got to see the expandable folder again. Someone murdered her before I brought it back. Would seeing the file have given her some peace? Would that have been the end of it? Would she have paid me the rest of my fee and sent me on my way?

Had it been that simple, I thought remorsefully.

An espresso machine hissed, and a couple of women laughed.

I thought about the other puzzle pieces that didn't fit together yet.

Amy Mackey, Paige's former roommate, had both moved out and quit dancing unexpectedly. She went missing shortly before the file was taken. And I know she didn't take the file because Levi had it.

I paused.

That wasn't an accurate statement. Levi *had* the file, but I didn't know if *he* took it. He said he did, but perhaps Amy had taken it then gave it to Levi. That was a possibility—one I hadn't thought of until now. But Paige didn't seem worried about Amy because she never mentioned her. I only learned about Amy through the other women at the club. And Levi didn't correct me when I stated he took the file. That was tacit admission to him taking it. But maybe I was wrong, and he was hiding Amy's involvement.

Something *was* going on with Amy, though. A man brutally assaulted her mother trying to find her. Whatever was going on with her was so heavy that a man hit me with his car for it.

It wasn't Marco, the big bouncer with a history of domestic violence. I knew him by sight. But could it have been an associate? That seemed unlikely since Marco pointed me to the mother's house. If he wanted someone to hurt Amy, why send me down there? He insisted he wanted nothing further to do with her.

Besides, Marco knew I wasn't pursuing Amy for any romantic reasons. I had to assure him of such to calm him down. The man was crazy about it when I first arrived. I straightened and replayed back our conversation. After I told him that I was looking for Amy, what had he said?

Elsewhere in the restaurant, the espresso machine continued to hiss, and those two women were laughing loudly again.

Goddamn it, I thought. *What had Marco said?*

Closing my eyes, I concentrated harder and tried to remember that night.

Marco and I were standing in front of the club. His face scrunched in anger, and he stepped menacingly forward. His fists were balled. He was about to hit me because he was jealous.

Not jealous. Mad.

That's not right. It wasn't simple anger.

My eyes snapped open when I remembered his words.

He had said, "Are you the bastard stalking her?"

Marco wasn't jealous; he was protective.

I'd read it all wrong.

My eyes flicked to my watch. It was too early to go to the Pit.

Chapter 34

Standing on the sidewalk in front of the school, it wasn't the joyous reunion I had hoped for. My daughter eyed me with suspicion. Stranger danger, I thought, or whatever they taught kids these days.

Erin wore a black sweatshirt, blue jeans, and gray Converse. An Oakland Raiders baseball hat was cocked to the side and at an upward angle. A backpack slung over her right shoulder, but she gripped the single strap with both hands. "Mom said you called."

"I did—to ask permission for us to hang out."

After getting Maria's approval, she contacted the administrative office to allow me to pick Erin up for the afternoon. A teacher had just escorted my daughter out. Erin still seemed surprised by the change in her schedule.

She shook her head. "Not today. Before. Mom said you left a message or something. I didn't get to hear it because she deleted it."

"I stopped by, too."

Erin smirked. "When I wasn't there."

"That's why I'm here now—to spend time with you."

She glanced uncomfortably around as other kids hurried by. Some boarded waiting buses. Others walked away from the school. Yet more headed toward idling cars.

"Can I have a hug?" I asked.

Erin clung tighter to her backpack. "I guess."

I wrapped my arms around her, but she didn't hug me back. She let me envelop her for a moment. When I let go, her eyes had misted. She blinked several times and looked away.

"We're going to hang out for a bit. Is that cool?"

"Whatever."

"Whatever?"

She faced me now but didn't say anything.

"Anything special you want to do?"

Her eyes brightened. "For real?"

"Of course. Name it."

"Mom never lets me have McDonald's."

***

Erin dragged a French fry through a large glob of ketchup then artistically swirled it across the hamburger wrapper. She'd already written her name in the sauce and was now creating some image. It looked like a dog. Or a ship. I wasn't sure.

We were in a corner booth, and I couldn't think of a better way to spend several hours. Later tonight, I would hopefully find Marco at the Pit. Until then, nothing else mattered.

Erin continued to drag her French fry around the hamburger wrapper. It was a flower, I decided.

"Do you like my picture?" she asked.

"It's great."

She scratched the fry through it and obliterated the flowering dog ship. "It's stupid."

Dropping the fry, she wiped her hands and looked up. Her gaze passed over the various tables throughout the restaurant, checking out the others eating there. My guess was she was looking for kids her own age.

"How was school?" I asked.

"We don't have to do that." She pulled her soda toward her.

"Do what?"

"The whole 'how's school' thing." She rolled her eyes. "Mom does that to me every night."

"Then let's not do it."

Her attention locked onto a Hispanic boy sitting with his parents at a nearby table.

"How long have you liked the Raiders?"

"Forever."

"Huh."

Her eyes remained fixed on the kid. He was a handsome boy with short hair and dark eyes. When he noticed Erin watching him, he smiled nervously then quickly looked back to his parents. That seemed to frustrate her.

She turned to me and forcefully asked, "What are you doing here?"

"Excuse me?"

Embarrassed by her sudden outburst, her face relaxed. "I mean, are you moving back?"

"I came to help someone out."

Erin's eyes flicked to the nearby boy. "Who?" When I didn't answer, her focus returned to me. "Who are you helping?"

"A friend."

"Mom says that's avoidance."

"Your mom is smart."

"And you're still avoiding the question. I know because that's what I do, and she calls me on it." Her eyes drifted toward the ceiling as she thought. "How's that going? Helping your friend, I mean."

"It's tougher than expected."

"Why? Because you're out of practice for being a cop?"

She was on the cusp of being a teenager and smarter than I remembered being at that age. "Something like that."

"Want to talk about it?"

I balled up the wrapper from the hamburger that I'd eaten. "Not really."

"Because you think I'm still a kid? I'm not, you know."

"It deals with murder, Erin. That's something I'd like to keep you from as long as possible."

We remained silent for several moments, and she studied my face intently. The Hispanic boy glanced Erin's way, but she didn't notice. She was too busy concentrating on me.

Eventually, she said, "The person who was murdered was your friend."

"Let's talk about something else."

"Fine," she said and picked up a new fry to stir the remaining ketchup glob. "Why didn't you and mom ever get married?"

Maybe discussing Paige would have been easier.

"Well?"

"Did you ever ask your mother that question?"

"Don't let her hear you say that."

"What?"

"*Mother*. She hates to be called that."

"She does?"

Erin giggled. "I say it to get under her skin. Works every time."

"That's funny."

"How about father? Does it bother you?"

"Not really."

She scrunched her face then pointed the red-dipped fry at me. "Mom said you were too immature to get married, but you don't seem that way to me."

An employee approached a neighboring table to clear some left-behind trash.

"Your mom called it right. I was."

"But you loved her, right? That kind of thing doesn't just go away."

I smiled softly. How does a man tell his daughter that love didn't exist in the short-term relationship he had with her mother? I had only told Maria that I would marry her out of duty but love never entered the equation.

"Maybe you've grown up enough for her to marry you now?"

"Eat your French fries."

She dropped the fry and wiped her hands. "You're avoiding again."

"No, I'm not."

"I do it all the time, and mom busts me for it. Don't you want to be with us?"

I reached out and held her hands. "I would love to spend my life with you, but your mom and me, that wasn't supposed to happen."

"I don't get it."

"You will someday."

"I'm not a kid."

"I know. You have friends with divorced parents, right? Consider your mom and me divorced."

Her brow furrowed. "But you were never married."

"That's because your mom is smart. She didn't need to marry me to find out I wasn't the right guy. Better to stay apart from the beginning and avoid the later divorce. Understand?"

"Being an adult sounds stupid."

I couldn't argue with her.

She caught the Hispanic kid watching her. He smiled and looked away again. She didn't seem as frustrated by it this time.

"Got a boyfriend?" I asked louder than necessary.

"Dad!" she whispered harshly. Her face reddened, and her eyes bulged.

"What?"

Erin tilted her head down and whispered, "He could hear you."

"I see the way you guys are looking at each other."

She turned entirely away from the kid now. "Stop it."

"I can introduce you." I pointed at the boy. "He seems nice."

"Oh my God!"

"Maybe his parents and I could sit together while you two—"

"You are the rudest person ever."

I chuckled. "I'm only trying to help."

"You're being a dork, so stop it."

She grabbed her soda and sipped from the straw. She glanced at the boy, who smiled back.

Her eyes were bright and happy.

***

After McDonald's, we aimlessly drove around so we could continue talking.

When I left Seattle, I did it in a fit of selfish anger. I didn't give much thought to how it would impact Erin. Would things have been different if I were married to Maria? Who knows? Maybe she would have been a rock for me to cling to after the firing. More than likely, we would have been divorced, and it would have been one more thing pushing me out of Seattle.

But the reality was that Paige did not cause me to lose my temper, assault the pimp, and later lie to the administration. I did that all on my own. I was also the one who hit Lieutenant Crites when he came after me. There was a common denominator in all my troubles, and it wasn't Paige.

"What's wrong?" Erin asked

"Huh?"

"You look sad."

I forced a smile. "I was thinking."

"About what?"

"Life."

"And that makes you sad?"

"Sometimes."

When we pulled into the driveway of her house, Maria was already on the porch. She walked down the sidewalk toward us. "How was the afternoon?"

"We went to McDonald's," Erin announced.

Maria's eyebrows raised. "You did?" She tried to hide her displeasure, but it still slipped through.

"I insisted," I said.

"Uh-huh. I'm sure."

"It was so we could have some girl talk."

Erin snorted. "You're such a dork."

"He's something," Maria agreed.

My daughter hugged me. "Thank you for the fun time. I love you."

"I love you, too."

When we stepped back from each other, she slung her backpack over her shoulder.

Maria asked Erin, "Got any homework?"

"Some."

"Better get started."

"Yes, mother."

Maria's face darkened, and she lowered her chin.

Erin glanced at me, smiled mischievously, then trotted toward the house.

"That kid," Maria muttered. When the door closed, she faced me. "Want to stay for dinner?"

"I would like that, but I've got something to do tonight."

Maria twisted her lips.

"Thank you, though."

She nodded politely, patted my shoulder, then headed toward the house.

For a brief moment, nostalgia flashed through my mind. Even though I already knew the answer, I wanted to ask why she didn't want to marry me. The conversation with Erin and my mother had stirred up that old ghost. Maybe my daughter was right. Perhaps I had matured enough that Maria would give me another chance.

"Hey."

Maria stopped and turned back. "Yeah?"

But hadn't I recently thought that we were two strangers that had made a kid? If Maria didn't want to marry me then when she knew me better, why would she want to be with me now when she no longer had any idea of who I was?

"You've done a great job with Erin. She's a wonderful kid."

Maria studied me for a moment. "Be safe, John, with whatever you're doing tonight."

With a bit of a wave, she went inside.

After the front door closed, I stayed there for a few moments pretending what might have been.

Chapter 35

The sun had fallen a couple of hours before, and now bass-heavy techno music pounded from inside the club. In the doorway stood Marco, along with a handsome black man and an attractive white woman.

The bouncer waved a small blue light over the two driver's licenses he held. He frowned, asked the young couple a question, then reconsidered the identification cards. This was the job I did back in Spokane, and I would have keyed on the same thing Marco had. It was too early in the night for experienced club goers. At this time of evening, it was usual for after-work get-togethers or married couples to go out. Either this attractive couple was underaged or new to the club scene.

Marco noticed me approaching, and the flashing sign above the doorway reflected off his bald head. "No." Using the licenses, he pointed at me. "Keep the hell away."

"I only want to talk."

"I pissed my pants the last time we talked."

The young woman snickered.

Marco's face flattened, and he thrust the ID cards back to them. With a jerk of his head away from the building, he said, "Fuck off."

Shocked by the sudden dismissal, the young couple exclaimed in unison, "What?"

"You two aren't getting in."

The young man pointed at the open door. "But you've got to let us in."

"Yeah," the woman agreed. "That's profiling."

"Fine. He can go in." The bouncer bent over the woman. "You can still fuck off."

Her eyes bulged. "You can't speak to me that way."

Marco stared at the young man until the guy snatched the licenses back. Then he pulled the woman away from the front door. She yelled a string of vulgarities while the two walked away.

The bouncer shouted, "Keep it up, and you won't ever get in!"

"Marco," I said.

His gaze shifted to me. "Go away."

"You asked if I was the one stalking Amy."

He pointed down the street. "I said—"

"Someone beat up her mother. They did a number on her, too."

Marco's brow furrowed. "She all right?"

"She's going to be okay. Whoever did it is trying to find Amy. She's in real danger."

The bouncer petulantly looked away.

"You can help her, and you don't have to violate the no contact order."

He cast me a sideways glance. "You think I'm scared of an NCO?"

"You don't want to go back to jail."

"Whatever."

"I'll tell her you helped me. I already promised that."

His expression softened.

"I'll even say that you were worried about her."

"I am."

"I know. That's why I'll say it."

Marco wiped his thumb over his lower lip then turned toward the club.

"Yo!" he hollered to a skinny guy in a STAFF t-shirt. "Watch the door."

"Where you going?" the thin man asked.

Marco lifted his hands in frustration. "Just watch the door." Then he motioned for me to follow.

Several young women ran across the street toward the club. They weren't wearing any jackets, and their short skirts barely covered them.

When we were in a quieter place, Marco asked, "What do you think's going on?"

"That's what I'm working out. Who's the guy stalking her?"

The big man leaned his shoulders against the building. "Some creeper she met at the District."

"What was so creepy about him?"

"During lap dances, he would ask about Paige."

"Paige?"

"Yeah. Weird, right? Amy is fine as hell, and this guy wants to ask about Paige."

"He asked about Paige and not Nicolette?"

Marco frowned.

"Her stage name."

"I get what you're after, but maybe he asked about Nicolette, and Amy said Paige."

"But if he did ask for Paige..." I let my words trail off.

Marco knew that world as well as I did. "Then it definitely wasn't right."

"Did Amy know his name?"

"She did." His forehead wrinkled in concentration. "What was it?" he muttered to himself.

A black Impala drove by with a white male behind the wheel. He had sunglasses on even though it was night. It looked a lot like the car that had run me over behind Mary Mackey's house. I couldn't be sure, especially at night, but it was close. And there couldn't be a lot of '80s Impalas running around.

I faced Marco. "The guy's name?"

"Sounded something like macaroni."

"Your name sounds like macaroni."

He smirked. "My name doesn't sound anything like that. The guy's name was something Italian. All those pricks sound the same."

"Like macaroni."

"Now, you're getting it."

As he thought, he closed his eyes. After a couple of seconds, he opened them. "Oh man, I almost had it."

"Try again."

Marco turned around and put his head against the building. "What was it?" he murmured. He rhythmically patted his hand on the building as he said in a sing-song manner, "Macaroni. Baloney."

I thought Mike Davoli sounded a lot like macaroni and had a fleeting thought that my former partner might be mixed up in this somehow. It vanished when Marco said, "Albertoni,"

He patted the wall several times and repeated the same name. "Albertoni. Albertoni. Albertoni." He spun around and clapped his hands. "I got it."

"Albertoni."

"What? No. Alfieri." Marco's face widened in a smile. "The dude's name was Steven Alfieri."

"That doesn't sound anything like macaroni."

Marco opened his palms. "It worked for me."

Chapter 36

Using the phone behind the bar at Mickey Finn's, I called Officer Brock Gatlin. Tapping the business card that he'd given me, I waited for him to answer. He picked up on the fourth ring.

"Gatlin," he said.

"It's Cutler. I'm calling for that favor."

"That didn't take long. Only back a few days and already— Wait. What's that noise? Where the hell are you calling from?"

The Commodore's instrumental "Machine Gun" played through the bar, and several people nearby were cheering as an older Asian woman swung her shoulders and hips in time with the song.

"Mickey Finn's," I said.

"You dog. I'm working, and you're playing."

"You're still on duty then?"

"Almost done. Finishing some paperwork, then I'll clock out. What do you need?"

"Name check a Steven Alfieri. Not sure of the spelling."

There was a long pause before Gatlin asked, "Does this have something to do with your girl's death?"

"Maybe."

"Don't play games. Running names for personal reasons is a violation of department policy."

"It's not a game. I don't know if this guy has anything to do with anything. His name came up in connection with a woman I'm trying to locate. And, yeah, it might have something to do with her murder."

Another long pause. "How long are you going to be at the bar?"

"You might say this is my home away from home."

***

An hour later, Gatlin walked into Finn's. He wore civilian clothes and a blank expression. In his left hand, he carried a folder. When he saw me, he pointed at an empty booth.

I slipped off my stool and headed in the direction he indicated.

The O'Jays' "Backstabbers" grooved through the bar. As I passed the older Asian woman, she grabbed me and insisted I twirl her. Her Caucasian boyfriend didn't seem put out by her demand. He simply said, "Whatever she wants," and lifted his drink.

I raised my hand and let her spin underneath. She laughed happily, kissed me on the cheek, then fell happily into her boyfriend's arms. He nodded his approval.

Slipping into the booth, Gatlin said, "New friend?"

"People having a good time. Want a beer?"

"I didn't do this for my health."

Miles noticed my wave then nodded in understanding.

Gatlin laid the folder on the table. "You picked a winner, John."

Inside was Steven Alfieri's Triple-I report. The Interstate Identification Index report is generated through the National Crime Information Center. A quick scan of the document showed Alfieri had been convicted and served time for robbery, assault, drug possession, and intimidation with a weapon. He was forty-two years old, and his criminal record went back to when he was eighteen. All his crimes occurred in the Seattle-Tacoma metropolitan area.

Miles walked over and sat a beer on the table.

"Thank you," said Gatlin.

"Are you a friend of John's?"

"Yeah."

"That's good." Miles clapped a hand on my shoulder. "Because the boy can use some help staying out of trouble."

Gatlin laughed. "I don't know what good I'll be with that."

I glanced between the two of them. "You guys know I'm here, right?"

"We do what we can do," Miles said, then eyed me. "The rest is up to the Lord." He playfully shook my shoulder before walking away.

"Seems like a nice guy," Gatlin said.

"The best."

I turned my attention back to the folder. Underneath the Triple-I report were several more pages. Gatlin reached out and tapped them.

"Those are copies of field interviews that officers in the region have had with Alfieri."

The first FI was a simple contact made by a Seattle patrol officer. The address where the contact occurred was just around the corner from The Red Light District. Alfieri had been lingering in a parking lot, and a business called in to complain. Alfieri moved on after the contact.

"Notice the date?" Gatlin asked.

I did. It was the night before Paige's murder.

The second field interview occurred several months prior outside a convenience store in Tacoma. Alfieri had a scuffle with a drug dealer. There was no crime committed, so the officer had no reason to detain either man. Therefore, only the short informational report was filed.

The third FI detailed a contact an officer had with Alfieri outside a Seattle bar. Wasn't much to the report beyond the location and time of day. He'd written the report primarily due to Alfieri's history.

Staring at the folder, I realized this wasn't enough. I wanted Paige's killer, but this wasn't the missing piece of information I had hoped it would be. Maybe Alfieri was messed up in Paige's murder. Maybe he wasn't. However, I wasn't Clint Eastwood, and this wasn't a movie. I couldn't hunt the guy down and just extract some type of Old Testament vengeance.

Gatlin pointed with his beer. "You're thinking something."

"This guy," I said and tapped the file, "might have been stalking the former roommate of my…"

"Your girl."

I nodded.

"How did you find out about it?"

I told him about Amy Mackey and her mother, as well as my contacts with Marco.

Gatlin leaned forward. "So, this guy shows up at the club to ask questions about your girl before her murder?"

"Yeah."

"Why didn't he ask her directly?"

"Huh?"

"They were roommates, right? Which means your girl was still alive at the time. If Alfieri wanted to get to your girl, he could have gone straight to her with his questions. Why pussyfoot around with this other woman?"

I folded my arms. He was right. That's why it was good to bounce ideas off another person. Sometimes they helped shine the light in a new direction and expose things that were missed.

"So," Gatlin continued, "why was this piece of squeeze going to Amy instead of going to your girl?"

"I don't know." Closing the folder, I slid it back to Gatlin.

He rested his hand on it. "I should give this info to Detective Ahern. He's running the investigation into—"

"I know." I kicked my beer back and took a healthy swallow. "There's something else."

Gatlin mimicked my action and took a large drink of beer. "Hit me."

"Crites."

"What about him?"

"He's snooping around."

"The sonofabitch investigated you, Cutler. He probably knows you better than anyone. Are you sure this isn't some sour grapes or—"

"It's not that." I told him about the visit Crites made to the bar. He remembered my earlier story about the sympathy the captain displayed during the interview with Detective Ahern.

"Got to admit that sounds strange," he said. "But I'll tell you this—Crites likes to think himself a chess player. If he's doing something, he's got ulterior motives."

Gatlin lifted his beer and drank two big swallows. He picked up the file and slid out of the booth.

I pointed at the folder. "Can I have that?"

"What are you going to do with it?" When I didn't answer, Gatlin glanced around the bar then tossed the folder on the table. "I shouldn't have to tell you this—"

"But you're going to say it anyway."

His smile was humorless. "Don't do something stupid you can't take back."

"I did that a couple years ago," I said. "I'm making up for what I did then."

Chapter 37

Even though it was late, I returned to Kent and Mary Mackey's home. She let me in, and I followed her into the kitchen. Pictures of ducks adorned the walls, and figurines of the waterfowl lined every flat surface. A towel imprinted with two kissing mallards hung from the stove's handle.

A pot of decaf percolated nearby.

We sat at a small table with the folder I brought between us. The bruising around Mary's left eye had darkened.

I opened the folder and pointed at the picture of Steven Alfieri. Since I wasn't a cop, I didn't have to go through the song and dance of a six-pack lineup to prove impartiality. What I was doing didn't need to stand up to the scrutiny of a court review. "Is this the man who hurt you?"

Mary looked away.

"I believe this is the man who assaulted you. If that's true, this man stalked Amy. He wanted information about my friend, Paige, the woman who was murdered."

Her eyes returned to the picture. "Do you think he could have…?""

"Murdered Paige? Maybe. And I'm concerned he may have hurt Amy, too."

Mary stood and moved to the counter. She hugged herself as she spoke. "Amy's father died two months before her second birthday."

It wasn't lost on me that Mary hadn't responded to my statement that Alfieri might have hurt Amy.

She continued. "His death was sudden. An aneurysm. Thirty-two years old." She closed her eyes. "Still seems like yesterday. A quiet, sunny morning. Sunday." Mary inhaled deeply. "He got up and took our beagle for a walk." She opened her eyes. "He was usually gone for thirty minutes. After an hour, I started to get worried. When a policeman showed up at the front door with the dog, that's when I knew. Amy hid behind me when the officer broke the news."

She didn't cry while she spoke, but her gaze grew distant, and her hands squeezed tighter together. "I did my best, you have to understand, but it was hard being a single mom. No one was there to back me up with the little things. I didn't have family around, so there wasn't anyone to help keep me together when the bad stuff happened."

Images of Maria and Erin popped into my head.

"Would you like anything in your coffee, Mr. Cutler?"

"Just black."

She removed two cups from the cupboard. "When Amy was eight, I got involved with a man who said he loved me. He was an assistant manager at a seafood restaurant. That part's not important, is it? But he seemed like a nice man. I thought being nice went a long way at the time."

Paige had said something similar once.

Mary filled the two cups with coffee then handed me one. She cradled hers with both hands.

"I let him move in with us. He said all the right words and did all the right things. He spoiled us with presents and attention. Everything seemed perfect. When I went back to school to get my nursing degree, he spent extra time with Amy. I thought God had finally given me a break."

Her head lowered at that revelation.

"He lived with us for a year before Amy finally told me her secret. The school taught her that the touching was inappropriate." She looked up. "I never talked to her about stuff like that." Mary's eyes misted, and she lightly tapped her chest. "It should have been my job, but the school had to do it. Do you know what that's like? Having your child show you how you failed as a parent?"

She turned her eyes from me. I sipped my coffee and gave her time to work out whatever she needed. When she faced me again, her eyes filled with tears.

"The police investigated him, Mr. Cutler, but they said they didn't have enough evidence to do anything. Can you believe that? He claimed he never did the things Amy accused him of. He said she was a little girl with a wild imagination. What child imagines that kind of stuff?" Mary lifted her chin toward the Alfieri file. "I promised I would never let another man hurt her, but I failed. I failed my little girl."

I covered Alfieri's face with my hand. "Did this man hurt Amy?"

She bowed her head and sobbed.

"Mary?"

I heard the soft footsteps in the next room and turned to see a blond woman standing there. Bruises covered the left side of her face, and the bright eyes from the pictures on the mantle were now scared. Her arms wrapped tightly around her waist.

"Amy?" I asked, already knowing the answer.

She nodded once.

***

Amy poured herself a cup of coffee then sat at the table. Mary had already left the room.

Pointing to the bruises on Amy's face, I asked,

"Marco?"

She lightly touched her cheek. "No."

I opened the folder.

Her eyes drifted down to Alfieri's photograph. She reached out and closed the file.

A piece of the puzzle had firmly clicked into place.

"Alfieri knew you were Paige's roommate."

Amy nodded.

"That's why he came to you and asked questions."

Another nod.

"Did you tell Paige about him? About his questions?"

She swallowed, and her lip quivered. It was apparent she was drowning in guilt. Her motion toward the living room was barely perceptible. She lowered her voice. "Mom was behind on her house payments." She touched the file. "He said he would pay me three thousand if I brought him something Paige had stolen."

"Stolen?"

"That's what he said."

Paige was a lot of things, but a thief didn't sound right. "Start from the beginning. Tell me how it went down."

She stared into her cup. "He showed up at the District one night and ignored the other girls just to pay attention to me. Every guy has their favorite, but new guys usually spend time with all the girls before focusing on one."

A fleeting memory of Paige invaded that moment. I'd focused only on her after that first night. What was it about Paige? What was it about me? Was it love at first sight? Stupid.

"But not Steve," Amy said, interrupting my thoughts. "He zeroed in on me. I should have known there was a problem right away. But I didn't. He was patient. I think that's what threw me. The first night he bought several dances, didn't ask anything out of the ordinary, then left."

I wondered if Paige had any initial concerns about me. Lost in her thoughts, Amy sipped her coffee.

"And the next time?" I prompted.

She swallowed. "He made some comments about Paige and me. Little ones, you know? Nothing out of the ordinary."

"Like what?"

"He knew we were roommates."

"Did that worry you?"

"Not really. Some guys find out things about us almost like we're celebrities. It's sort of flattering. But then they ask crazy questions or make weird comments. He wasn't there yet, so I figured he was just curious. I think it was his fourth time in—he always came by when Paige wasn't working. I overlooked that at first. When he asked if I wanted to make a few thousand for a quick job, I figured he was talking about sex. That didn't make sense, though. Plenty of guys have propositioned me but never for that much." She wasn't embarrassed at the admission. "Steve made it clear his proposal had nothing to do with that."

"And you didn't tell this to Paige?"

"She wasn't working when he asked. That night he caught me outside on the way to my car. If he hadn't, maybe I would have told her about it when I got home. Who knows?"

"What did he say?"

"He wanted me to find a CD in her apartment."

"That's what he claims Paige stole?"

Amy nodded.

"Did she steal it from him?"

"He didn't say, but I got the feeling it belonged to someone else. Steve said if I brought him the disc, he'd give me three grand." She shook her head. "I would have normally said no to something like this, but I was thinking about quitting the club, so I sort of listened to what he was saying.”

“Why were you going to quit?”

Regret passed over her face. “You can’t imagine what it’s like.”

“Tell me.” I wanted to know. Not only to understand Amy better but to get a better understanding of Paige.

“Dancing ate my soul.” She slowly turned her coffee cup. “Everyone that comes in thinks of us as meat for their fantasies.”

Did Paige ever think that of me? How long did it last until she changed her opinion? What caused her to look at me differently?

“It’s an ugly view of life,” Amy said. “And a hole develops inside. A big, dark one. Some of the girls can ignore it, but it’s always there. Others fill it with drugs. I filled it with Marco. That’s why I kept going back. He wasn’t right for me. I knew it. But in a twisted way, I thought I deserved him. Even when he hit me, I figured I earned it somehow.” She grimaced at the memory. “When Steve offered the money upfront, I figured I could walk away from the District and still help Mom.”

“Three thousand, though. That doesn’t seem enough to take something from a friend. I thought most of the dancers made decent money at the club.”

Amy seemed embarrassed. “But I wasn’t saving any of it. The hole needed to be filled. When Marco wasn’t around, I filled it with clothes and shoes and parties.” She patted her chest. “Even now, I feel like I deserve the bad things that are happening to me.”

“Did you find the CD?”

She flicked the rim of her coffee cup with a finger. “It was in Paige’s bedroom, in her closet.” Amy looked up. “She had this file folder, the expandable type? Do you know the kind?”

And there was the truth behind Paige's initial phone call to me.

She didn't care about the folder or the letters from Levi Montgomery. It was the CD that Amy had taken that she wanted me to recover. However, Paige didn't realize the disc was already missing when Levi stole the expandable file. Otherwise, she would have pointed me in a different direction. Or contacted Amy herself. Regardless, Paige operated under a false assumption which meant I spun my wheels because of bad information.

Another puzzle piece snapped into place.

"Anyway," Amy said, "that folder was where she kept important papers and stuff. It wasn't the first place I looked, but when I found it, I knew the disc had to be in there."

"Did you see what was on it?"

"I took it to a friend's house and checked it out. I didn't see what the big deal was."

I put my cup down. "What was on there?"

"Some pictures of Paige and a woman and a few voicemails."

"Paige and a woman?"

Amy nodded.

"What were the pictures of?"

"The two of them hanging out. Sort of everyday pictures. They seemed friendly, but that was it. Nothing dirty."

"And the voicemails?"

She shrugged. "It sounded like they were taking a trip. Then there was one that sounded like a butt dial, and the other woman called back to apologize."

"Did you give the disc to Alfieri?"

"I was going to, but I couldn't." She started to sip her coffee but paused. "*Wouldn't* is the better word. I started thinking about Paige. She was good to me, you know? She let me stay with her after Marco and I broke up. I couldn't treat her that way. So I decided to move out and quit dancing."

"That's when you moved back in with Marco?"

She shrugged. "It wasn't the smartest decision."

"Why not come stay with your mom?"

Amy glanced toward the other room. "I didn't want to add more stress to her. Besides, we don't always see eye to eye. She didn't want me to go into dancing. Maybe I should have listened to her."

"What were you going to do with the CD?"

"I dunno. I was scared to give it back to Paige. I just hoped she wouldn't notice it was gone. I wasn't going to give it to anyone. I promise."

"And you couldn't give the money back to Steve because your mom used it to get right with the mortgage company?" I snapped my fingers. "But you tried, didn't you? When you left Marco's, you took his money. You were robbing Peter to pay Paul."

More pieces of the puzzle clicked into place.

"Robbing Marco to pay Steve," she muttered. "But Steve wouldn't take the money. He told me to bring the disc or else."

I pointed to her face. "Those look too fresh for that threat."

She touched her cheek again. "This was from yesterday."

"He found you?"

Amy shook her head in frustration. "I don't know how he did it. I never gave him this address. After I split from Paige's, I stayed with Marco, then some other friends. Steve must have known where she lived beforehand and been patient. I only came back after what happened to her."

I glanced to the living room, working it out. "He didn't come here looking for you so much as to use your mom as bait. Assaulting her got you to come out from wherever you were hiding."

She sighed. "Yesterday, he caught me at the grocery store. I had just gotten out of my car when he dragged me into his. He told me if I screamed, he'd kill me. We drove behind an abandoned building." Her voice cracked. "Before I could tell him I didn't have the disc, he hit me. Just to let me know what he was willing to do. I told him I still had the money, but he didn't want it and hit me again. He kept hitting me until I told him I'd bring the disc."

"Did you give it to him?"

"I'm meeting him tonight."

"He didn't insist you get it right away?"

"I told him it was with a friend. If I don't give it to him, he threatened to finish the job with Mom."

"Where's the CD now?"

"Why?"

I pushed my coffee aside and leaned forward. "If you don't want to give it to me, that's fine. But the stuff on that CD may put me one step closer to finding the person who killed Paige."

She stared at me for a moment then stood. "Wait here."

Amy and her mother exchanged hushed words in the living room. In a moment, Amy came back holding a shiny, unassuming disc. There were no markings on it. Was this really why Paige was murdered?

"That has to go to him," she said. "I can't let you leave with it."

"I'll take it to him. Just tell me where and when."

"You can't. He's expecting me, so we've got to go together."

I set the disc on the table. "All right, but we to do things my way. Can you agree to that?"

"Do you think you'll be able to hurt him?" She pointed at her face. "Even a little would go a long way."

I examined her bruises and thought about Paige's lifeless body. "I don't think that will be a problem."

Chapter 38

Shortly after midnight, Amy and I were parked behind a regional grocery store in east Tacoma. The front of the building was lit up like an arena, but sporadic lighting in the rear led to large, shadowed areas.

I lay in the tiny backseat of Amy's car, a Chevy Cavalier.

Her head anxiously swiveled from side to side. "He's late."

"He'll be here. You have what he wants."

Trying to calm my nerves, I slowly counted down from one thousand. *Nine hundred ninety-nine. Nine hundred ninety-eight. Nine hundred—*

"I came home once, and Paige was on the couch with a picture of you."

I didn't know what to say. Thoughts raced through my mind. Did that mean Paige missed me? Did she regret how we ended? Maybe she longed for what we had?

"She liked to do that. Look at old photos and reminisce, I mean. Sometimes it was a boyfriend. Maybe a family member who had died."

The thoughts of Paige quieted in my head. I had never witnessed her do anything like that.

"I don't know why she did it. Maybe to take stock of her life, I guess. She never read a book or listened to music. She just looked at her pictures and sipped her wine. She wouldn't say much when I asked. She wasn't good with sharing her feelings."

"What did she do with my picture after she looked at it?"

"She put it away."

Just like her feelings, I thought.

Amy leaned forward to look out the windshield. "When I asked about you, she only told me your name. Nothing else."

I closed my eyes and saw visions of Paige. Some happy. Some sad. When I saw the image of her lying dead, I opened my eyes to the darkness. "I would have done anything to be with her." The wistfulness in my voice wasn't hard to detect.

"I don't want this to sound bad—" Amy twisted in her seat to peer down at me. "—but you weren't the only one who felt that way."

I wanted to turn away, but where the hell was there to look? Her seat? The backseat? I simply stared up at Amy—a wounded animal about to take its medicine.

"I don't think she understood how love was supposed to be. It was the damnedest thing. Guys would do anything for her, but she wouldn't do anything for them. And that's how she seemed to want it, but what do I know?" Amy turned around and looked out the windshield.

I lay there in the darkness and considered her words. Paige didn't want me the same way I longed for her. Relationships are often unfair as one person loves or needs the other person more. We hope for a level playing field, but it's never like that.

"Here comes a car," Amy whispered.

A loud engine approached.

"It's his," she softly said.

The car stopped nearby but left its engine running. A door opened and closed.

"He's walking over," she whispered, her voice frantic.

"Tell me when he's close."

"He's right here."

I popped the door open and scrambled out of the car. I hit the ground and looked up.

Alfieri was already running back toward his Impala. I sprinted after him. I caught him as he opened his car door. He grabbed the steering wheel and tried to pull himself into the driver's seat. I yanked him back by his shirt and hair.

When Alfieri let go of his car, he swung wildly. His punch bounced off the top of my head. I held him as we tumbled to the ground. We wrestled on the asphalt, each struggling for control of the other.

Amy's Cavalier squealed its tires as she fled the parking lot. She did exactly as we planned.

I rolled over onto Alfieri and punched him hard in the side of the face. His head whipped and bounced off the ground. In a split second, he looked peaceful and stopped moving.

After climbing into his car, I backed it into the shadows. Then I grabbed Alfieri by his shirt and dragged him behind the Impala. Now, no one could see us.

From his back pocket, I removed his wallet. Inside were several credit cards. When I found what I wanted, I removed it and threw the billfold onto the hood. I slapped him until he awoke.

"Remember me?" I asked. When he didn't answer, I slapped him harder. "Take a long look."

He closed his eyes, waiting for the next blow.

"You hit me with your car."

Blood flowed from his nose and a cut over his eye. Dark locks of hair were matted against his forehead.

I removed the gun from the back of my pants. "Hey."

He opened his eyes and flinched as if preparing to be shot.

"You killed my girlfriend."

"I didn't kill anyone," he sputtered.

"Don't lie."

He lifted his hands toward his head. "I didn't kill—"

"Don't lie!" I shouted. "You killed Paige."

"No!"

I thrust the gun toward him.

Alfieri turned his head away and closed his eyes. "I didn't kill her," he whispered. "I swear to Christ, I never touched her."

I stepped back. "Sit up."

He scooted until he was upright and leaning against the Impala. "I swear, man. I didn't hurt her."

"Convince me."

He clasped his hands together and shook them back and forth in anxious prayer. "What do you want me to do? Tell me, and I'll do it."

I lowered the gun. "What's on the CD? Why do you want it?"

"I don't know what's on it. I was only hired to get it."

"Who hired you?"

"A guy named Levi."

My mouth went dry. "Levi Montgomery?"

"I don't know. Maybe. I only know his first name."

Had Levi fooled me that well? I believed him. But if he did know about the CD, maybe that's why he took the expandable folder. Except the CD was already gone because Amy had taken it for Alfieri, who claimed Levi hired him. The story looped back on itself and collapsed. It didn't make sense.

These pieces of the puzzle didn't fit together.

"What do you know about this guy?" I asked. "What did he look like?"

"I don't know," he said.

"White, black, Mexican? Dark hair, light hair?"

"He was white. And he wore a hat."

"That's all you got?"

"I met him once in a bar. It was dark, and he was big. Real big." His words flew fast and sounded honest. Alfieri was too scared to lie.

Levi Montgomery was big. Not real big, but maybe he seemed that way to Alfieri.

"How did you two meet?"

"At the bar, like I said. He approached me."

"Didn't you find that weird?"

Alfieri looked down. "He didn't look like a cop. And the way he talked didn't feel like he was trying to set me up."

"How do you stay in contact?"

"He finds me."

"How does he do that?"

Alfieri shrugged. "He just does."

"Where's your phone?"

"I don't have one. The government can track you with that. GPS and such."

"Why did Levi want the CD?"

"He didn't say."

I held up Alfieri's driver's license so he could see it before slipping it into my back pocket. "If I find out you killed Paige—"

"I didn't. I swear to God!"

After switching the gun to my left hand, I clenched my right into a fist.

He cocked his head. "Aw, man. You don't have to do that."

"This is for those women you hurt."

"Shit." Alfieri shut his eyes and covered his head.

I kicked him between the legs. His hands dropped to his crotch, his eyes widened, and he expelled a giant whoosh of air. Then I punched him across the chin.

He slumped to the ground.

I walked out of the shadows and into a dimly lit area

of the parking lot. A moment passed before Amy's car returned. After shutting the car door, I faced her.

Tears covered her cheeks, and worry filled her eyes. "Did you get your answers?"

"Some."

She leaned over her steering wheel to look deeper into the shadows. "Is he dead?"

"No."

"Is he hurt?"

"Yeah."

A smile grew at the corner of her lips. "Good."

She dropped the car into gear.

Chapter 39

I arrived back at Mickey Finn's just as Miles was leaving. He let me in, said goodnight, then locked up.

There was a small office that wasn't more than a closet. It had a desk, a computer, and a phone. On the wall were state-mandated posters about worker rights and employer responsibilities. The wooden chair squeaked as I leaned forward and stuck the CD into the tray.

In a moment, a little window appeared on the computer screen. Using the mouse, I opened a folder to reveal multiple pictures and several sound files. I cycled through the photographs first.

There were three pictures of Paige and a woman in her mid-forties. They were hanging out in a few different locations. One of them was at a restaurant, drinking wine. Another they were arm-in-arm, smiling, standing on a pier somewhere. The third picture seemed overly friendly. Paige's head rested on the woman's shoulder. I couldn't tell where it was taken.

I'd seen the woman before. Even in the relaxed settings, I knew who she was. On the corner of the desk was yesterday's newspaper. Just to make sure, I flipped through it to find the article I'd read about the homeless plan. There was her picture—Councilwoman Elizabeth Vanderlinden.

I moved the mouse back to the folder from the CD and found three mp3 files labeled *message1*, *message2*, and *message3*.

I double-clicked the first one, and the sound file started playing.

"*Paige, it's me. I've got my ticket booked. San Francisco is going to be wonderful this weekend. I can't wait. Call me back when you can.*"

The second message was harder to hear, as if the phone was far from the woman's mouth. It started in the middle of a conversation.

"*... don't care what they want. I'm not voting to rezone... that bastard... the council will vote the way I vote... know that.*"

"*But Elizabeth—*" said a male voice. He was hard to hear but clearer. Probably due to his volume and tone. "*—they're contributing to your campaign. They want your support. They've got a lot of money riding on this deal.*"

"*Tell Montgomery to shove that request up his ass.*" Elizabeth's voice was more robust now as if she were nearer her phone. "*Paul should have thought about that before he backed the competition.*"

"*He's contributing to us both,*" the man said. "*Besides, Mitchell says—*"

"*I don't care what my— Damn it.*"

"*What's wrong?*"

"*My phone—*"

And the call ended.

I double-clicked the third message.

"*Paige, it's me.*" She was whispering now. "*Hey, I'm sorry about the previous call and message. It was an accident. Do me a favor and delete it. And call me back about this weekend. I can't wait to see you.*" It didn't sound as sincere as the first message.

I reopened the photographs on the computer—my gaze traveled from them to the newspaper and back.

Had Paige gotten romantically involved with a Seattle councilwoman? Was that even possible? She had never told me that she was bi-sexual or admitted to feelings of such. We were only together for a short time, though.

Maybe that's something she never felt the need to share. Or perhaps it was something that she only recently discovered. I thought about the box of photos I found in her apartment. There were pictures of her with various men and women. Why had I assumed only the men could have been former lovers?

I replayed the scene from the restaurant. The two women made eye contact, and Paige looked immediately away. She turned white then pretended she didn't know the councilwoman. As for Elizabeth Vanderlinden, the woman spun around and left the restaurant.

What could have made those two women so wary of each other to get that reaction in a public place?

I called up a search engine and entered 'Elizabeth Vanderlinden Seattle.'

The first result was her campaign website. It extolled her virtues, featured her platitudes, and plastered her smiling image wherever there was white space. Conventional party mantra was splashed over everything like heavily scented perfume. I took as much of the political rhetoric as I could stand before leaving to visit other sites.

Next, the Washington Chapter of the Gay and Lesbian Alliance Against Defamation named Vanderlinden the number three political opponent of tolerance and acceptance. I paused on this and called up one of the pictures of Paige and Elizabeth. Their reaction in the restaurant was starting to make sense.

A local newspaper wrote an article questioning if Elizabeth Vanderlinden was indeed a Republican or a Democrat in sheep's clothing. If things had been different, I might have laughed. It seemed this woman couldn't catch a break. The article's author argued that outside of her stand against domestic partner rights, her voting record pointed to an eclectic mix of political ideas.

Maybe, the author argued, she should be reclassified as an independent.

Another website had a different take on the councilwoman. At forty-two years of age, Elizabeth Vanderlinden was taking her game to the next level. She ran a campaign against a weak incumbent. She had a strong approval rating and a conservative message.

It seemed everyone had a different view of the woman and the only consensus on her was her age and marital status. She was married to Mitchell Vanderlinden.

Paige had been adamant that she would never date a married man. Would that same apply to a married woman? Was I misreading the pictures, the voicemails, and the eye contact at the diner?

I entered 'Mitchell Vanderlinden Seattle' into the search engine and got way more results than I would have expected.

An article in *Seattle Living* magazine provided a wealth of information. Elizabeth and Mitchell were married after she graduated from college. They never had children and lived affluent lives due primarily to Mitchell. His grandfather made his millions in the timber industry and left it to his only son. Mitchell's father was now in his early seventies and in failing health. Mitchell stood to inherit the entire estate.

Mitchell was repeatedly listed as an independent businessman with various interests. One article discussed his recent successes in real estate speculation.

I replayed the voice mails again with the new information about Elizabeth and Mitchell in mind.

This time I concentrated on Elizabeth Vanderlinden's reference to Paul Montgomery, the owner of Montgomery Construction and Levi's father. Per the second voicemail, it was clear that Montgomery Construction wanted a rezone that the councilwoman wasn't willing to support.

Could those pictures and audio clips be damaging to her political career? If that were the case, would they be critical to the Montgomery rezoning efforts? The more I thought about it, the more I realized this was about one thing—money.

Levi Montgomery must have known about the CD. He then hired Steven Alfieri to get it for him, which led to the assaults of Amy and Mary Mackey. But the CD was already missing when Levi stole the actual folder.

There was the rub. Something wasn't adding up.

Yet, one thing was for sure. Levi Montgomery must have known about the voicemails. Why else would he have broken into Paige's apartment to steal the expandable file? Not for some stupid letters and cards.

The pieces of the puzzles were on the table, but they didn't seem to fit.

Chapter 40

I slept restlessly for a few hours until Danny returned to open the bar.

Until then, I'd been dreaming about Paige, except she wasn't her—she was Elizabeth Vanderlinden. When we made love, it was the councilwoman who looked into my eyes and made me believe I was the only man in the world. When we broke up, Elizabeth crushed me in a way I didn't think was possible. After I found the body in the bathroom, it was Mrs. Vanderlinden who would never allow me to rescue her.

That's when Danny burst into the back room like a SWAT team drug raid. I bolted upright on the cot and threw the first thing I could find.

"Huzzah!" he screamed and ducked as my pillow floated over his head.

We were both lucky I couldn't find my gun. It was on the floor under the cot.

Danny quickly backpedaled out of the storeroom, and I flopped backward. For several moments, I breathed heavily and tried to remind myself that what I had experienced wasn't real.

Elizabeth Vanderlinden was not Paige McIntyre. I didn't even know the councilwoman. But damn if it didn't feel real. I sat up and groaned. A headache banged inside my skull.

After a shower in the storeroom, I stepped into the same clothes I wore the day before. I hadn't planned on being in Seattle more than a couple of days, and I hadn't made it to the laundromat. I'd need to either go home soon or, at least, do some laundry. My shirt was getting ripe.

Danny eyed me with a mixture of concern and caution as I walked behind the bar to fill a Styrofoam cup with coffee.

"Got some aspirin?" I asked.

"Under the counter." He motioned in the direction he meant.

Finding the bottle, I shook out four. "Sorry about earlier."

"It's cool." His expression told me it was far from that.

"I didn't mean to scare you."

He frowned. "You didn't scare me."

"Well, you scared the hell out of me."

That brought a slight smile. "For real?"

"So much it gave me a headache." I popped the aspirin into my mouth and washed them down with a swig of coffee.

***

My first stop was the office in Kirkland. Not seeing Levi Montgomery's Humvee, I headed to the job site in Puyallup. His rig wasn't there either. Playing the odds, I returned to Kirkland. It seemed the most likely place for him to be sometime during the day. When I arrived, his yellow Hummer was parked in front of the building. The lot was full, which meant there were too many witnesses to confront him.

I parked across the street in the lot of a dentist's office. It was almost noon, so I figured Levi would take a lunch break soon. He didn't. Around two o'clock, Levi walked out of the building. He wore blue jeans and a red jacket. The Humvee backed out of its parking stall before slipping onto the street.

He drove to a newer housing development on Mercer Island. Several houses were under various stages of construction, and they all had Montgomery Construction signs in front of them. Workers moved in and about each of the homes. No one bothered to look in my direction.

Levi's truck slowed as he neared a house that had a For Sale sign in the yard. It had a double car driveway but no landscaping. The garage door slowly opened.

I stopped my truck on the street and hopped out. As the garage door closed behind Levi's vehicle, I sprinted toward the home. I didn't glance around to see if any of the workers might notice me running.

Near the house, I ducked below the descending garage door. There was a momentary fear that Levi would be there, waiting for me. As I straightened, I prepared for a fight. There was no need, though. I was alone.

Inside the house, the kitchen and living room were empty. There was no furniture, no accessories, and no Levi Montgomery.

Behind me, the garage door opened again as another car pulled in.

As quietly as possible, I moved into the nearest bedroom. I stood in the furthest corner and out of view from the door's opening.

"Buddy?" a male voice called. The name echoed throughout the house.

A toilet flushed. Seconds passed before more footsteps were heard, and Levi said, "Hey, Pop."

Paul Montgomery, I thought.

"We've got a problem," Paul said. "Investors are backing out."

"What for? The zoning?"

"They're worried it isn't going to happen."

They sounded as if they were standing right outside

the room that I was in.

"It'll happen," Levi said.

"We need that CD, Bud."

"We don't need it to get the change approved."

"It would make things a hell of a lot easier. The committee swings with her."

I moved closer to the open door.

Paul continued. "What could have happened to it?"

"How would I know? It doesn't help anyone else."

"I'm not sure about that. It'll help anyone that hates that bitch."

Levi must have been uncomfortable with what his father said because he remained silent.

Paul once more. "Should you search her apartment again?"

"She's dead, Pop. I'm not breaking in."

"What would she care?"

"I care. And what if the cops find me?"

"I'm grasping," Paul mumbled. "I don't want to lose this project."

"Can't you just tell her that we know about the relationship?"

"Without proof? Maybe that crazy broad of yours made the whole thing up."

"Maybe she did."

"Don't get mouthy with me, Bud. I wasn't the one—" There was movement. "Who the hell did this trim work? It looks like shit."

"I'll get it fixed." Levi sounded exasperated.

"Then fire their ass. We don't want them on the next job. Quality is our reputation."

More movement. It sounded like they were walking away.

Paul said, "We'd better figure something out soon, or we're going to lose the next project."

It seemed as if now was the time to move, so I left the room. "Excuse me."

The elder Montgomery spun around. "The hell?"

"You," was the only thing Levi managed to say.

Paul's brow furrowed.

Levi pointed at me. "He's Paige's friend. The one who came by." To me, he said, "I already gave you the file. What more do you want?"

"You lied. You never mentioned anything about a CD."

Paul touched his son's arm, but Levi pulled away. "So?"

"How about the truth?"

Levi half-shrugged.

Paul stepped forward. "Don't say anything, Buddy. Call the cops. This man is breaking and entering."

"Yeah, Levi. Call the cops. Let's talk with them about the CD."

The younger Montgomery asked, "What do you want to know?"

"*Levi!*"

"Relax, Dad. I got this." Levi moved closer. "Ask your questions."

"How'd you find out about it?"

"She told me. How else would I know?"

A puzzle piece clicked into place.

The elder Montgomery shook his head and turned slowly in a circle.

"How did you meet?" I asked.

"She approached me at Olive Garden."

"And she just told you about some voicemails?"

"Not right away but something like that. Yeah."

"She set him up," Paul snapped.

Levi lifted a hand to calm his father. "She was using me." The way he said it seemed like he regretted its ending more than that it happened.

"Did she play it for you?" I asked.

Levi shook his head. "She dangled it like bait."

Now, I was confused. "Why would she do that?"

"She wanted to be able to tell Elizabeth Vanderlinden that we knew about it."

And there was another slice of the truth. "What would she get from your interest?"

Levi laughed. "She'd get even with Elizabeth."

My brow furrowed.

"They were in a relationship," he said, "but Elizabeth broke it off. The voicemails were proof of them being together. She said our zoning request was mentioned in one of the calls."

Paul Montgomery watched me with open hostility.

I asked Levi, "So your relationship was also a way for her to get even?"

He averted his gaze.

"Of course, it was," Paul said. "You know how women are."

The younger man sighed. "Give it a rest, Pop. Even if it was, so what?"

"So what?" the father snapped.

I didn't want this to devolve into a family fight, so I asked, "How'd she meet Elizabeth?"

"Let's go, Buddy." Paul anxiously shifted from one foot to the other. "We don't owe this yahoo anything."

"It's okay," Levi said. "He's trying to find her killer, not jam us up." He turned back to me. "As far as I know, Paige worked her campaign."

"When did Paige get into politics?"

"I don't know." He inhaled deeply and averted his gaze. "There were a lot of things about her I didn't know."

"Did you see the CD in the file before you took it?"

He nodded. "One day, while she was showering, I snooped around and found it. I figured I would have plenty of time to come back later and make a copy."

"What happened?"

"Later that night, she said she was done. That she didn't want to be with me anymore." He looked down at his hands. "Out of the blue. Like a switch flipped. I don't know what happened. Just like that, we were over. Maybe she figured out that I snooped around. I don't know."

I glanced at Paul. He seemed uncomfortable by his son's sadness.

"I told her I would do anything for her," Levi continued, "but she didn't care. When I finally realized she wouldn't take me back, I let myself in and stole the file."

"And when you got home, you realized the CD was no longer there."

He looked sheepish. "I went back, but a maintenance man was already changing the locks. He wouldn't let me in. Later, she called and demanded the file back. I told her no. Just to be spiteful. I wanted her to hurt like she'd hurt me."

"But the disc wasn't there."

"No."

"Did you tell her it was missing?"

"No."

"Why not?"

"Because I thought she moved it, and I was the chump for stealing the stupid folder. I couldn't understand why she made such a big deal for some legal documents and love letters."

That meant Amy had taken the CD right before Levi stole the folder. Paige had to assume it was still in there, and Levi didn't call out that it wasn't. That was the confirmation I needed.

"That's when you hired Alfieri?"

"Who?"

"Steven Alfieri. The guy you hired to get the CD."

Levi looked to his father. "Did you hire someone?"

"News to me," the older man grunted.

I motioned to Levi. "He's claiming you hired him."

The younger Montgomery pointed at himself, and his face scrunched with confusion.

"By name, in fact. Although, to be fair, his description of you wasn't that great."

"I didn't do it."

The three of us stood in the silent house, staring at each other.

"Did this Alfieri fellow get the CD?" Paul asked.

"No."

"Would you consider selling it?"

"Not a chance. I might turn it over to police, though."

The elder Montgomery spread his arms and flashed his best salesman's smile. "Can I make a different suggestion? Why not turn it over to the media instead? The newspaper would be happy to investigate it."

"No," I said flatly. "Who else knew about the disc?"

"No one," Levi said.

"No one," Paul agreed.

"You two knew about the CD. Her roommate knew about it. Alfieri knew, which meant the person or people who hired him knew. That's a lot of people talking about a CD with destructive potential."

"We didn't tell anyone," Paul said. "I promise."

"Even your son, Max?"

"We didn't tell Max. We love the boy, but he wouldn't keep the secret."

Reluctantly, Levi nodded in support of his father's statement.

I took a step toward the door. "Unfortunately for you,

it looks like you're going to have to get that zoning change the same way as everyone else."

Paul and Levi remained silent as I walked out of the house.

Chapter 41

I followed her after she left the *Vanderlinden for Council President* headquarters. She got into a white BMW and left downtown. Tailing someone through Seattle proper is troublesome enough. It was made worse by the size of my pick-up.

Once we made it out of the city, she pulled into a Starbucks, eschewing the drive-through to walk inside. I considered my options for making contact. None of them were great. Finally, I decided on an honest and bold approach. I climbed out of my truck and stood next to her car, waiting for her to return. The sky was cloudy, and a light mist now fell.

In a couple of minutes, she approached with a coffee cup in her hand.

"Excuse me," she said. "That's my car."

"Councilwoman Vanderlinden?"

She slowed. "Can I help you?"

"I'm a friend of Paige McIntyre's."

Elizabeth watched me like a cougar evaluates an approaching hiker—deciding whether to attack or flee. "What's this about?"

"It's my understanding that you two were in a relationship."

She glanced around then stepped to the driver's door of the BMW. "Get in. Unless you're finished with your accusations." She climbed in without waiting for my agreement. It seemed odd for her to invite a stranger into her car, but I hurried to the other side.

Elizabeth pulled a *Vanderlinden for Council President*

button out of the cup holder and tossed it onto the nearby tray. Then she carefully settled her coffee cup down before guiding the car out of the parking lot.

"Where are we headed?" I asked.

"Away from prying eyes."

I remained quiet until we entered the freeway and got stuck in bumper-to-bumper traffic.

"Paige is dead," I said.

Her face hardened. "And?"

"You don't seem upset by the news."

She glared at me. "How dare you? You don't even know me."

"I know what grief looks like."

Her lips pressed tightly together. "Is this what you wanted to talk about, Mr. Cutler? How I express my grief?"

Hearing my name surprised me. So, I wasn't a stranger. But how would she know about me? How would she know about Paige's murder? She had to know a cop, I decided. She was a councilwoman, so that made the most sense. Back when I was on the department, even I knew a couple of council members. But they were cursory relationships at best. No, the real connections into the department were made with the brass—those at the level of lieutenant or higher.

Elizabeth checked the mirrors before changing lanes.

Lately, there was one cop that kept popping up in my life that carried administrative juice. "Daryl Crites."

"What about him?"

"He's the one who told you about Paige. Told you about me."

"Is there a question in there?"

"How's he know you?"

"He works for the city."

"How did he know you and Paige were connected?"

She cast a sideways glance. "He's a cop. He knows things. I certainly wouldn't tell him about us."

It was too simple of an answer. "How long have you known him?"

"Several years, I guess. We met when I was involved with getting a new domestic violence shelter off the ground. Daryl was assigned to the project. He seemed nice and helpful and interested in the political game."

Nice and helpful would not be how I would ever describe Crites. However, if he were interested in politics, perhaps he would behave a different way. "And you've been friends since?"

She smirked. "If you want to call it that."

"What would you call it?"

"Expedient."

The car moved forward on the freeway as the truck ahead changed lanes.

"What does your husband think about this expedient relationship?"

"He doesn't."

"He doesn't think? Or he doesn't know?"

Her face soured. "Don't be flippant. I don't know you well enough to put up with that kind of shit."

"You should tell him about Paige."

Elizabeth scowled. "Don't tell me how to handle my husband."

I pointed ahead. Another hole opened, and a Toyota Corolla attempted to move in. She zoomed forward and cut it off.

"There are others who know about you and Paige," I said.

"I'm not worried about them."

"Were you worried about the recording of your voicemails?" She didn't respond. "Paige must have told you about them. I understand her better now, but I want to know why she would threaten you."

Elizabeth nodded as if coming to an agreement with something—a slow bounce of her head that grew faster. "I wanted it to stop. She didn't."

"So, you were in a relationship?"

She glanced over her shoulder and aggressively moved the car into a new lane. The car behind us honked. "It was supposed to be casual." Her hand lifted from the steering wheel then fell back into place.

"And you took it too seriously?"

Disdain flashed over her face. "Don't be dense, Mr. Cutler."

I stared at her. "Paige?"

"Well, it wasn't me. I knew the rules."

My eyes narrowed. "Explain it to me. Please."

"Why should I explain anything to you? You could be working for the press for all I know."

"You know Daryl Crites, and you know my name. That means you already know everything about me."

Elizabeth's fingers drummed on the steering wheel.

"Did you meet at your campaign office?"

A wistful smile formed. "That's what we told people. We met in yoga class. Had a coffee afterward."

I frowned. "I didn't know Paige to be bi-sexual."

"She said I was her first."

It might have been a lie. Not what Paige said, but that it had been Paige's first time with a woman. After what I'd learned the past few days, everything about Paige seemed to be a falsehood wrapped in a layer of deceit. I wondered if she ever told the truth.

Traffic began to flow. Elizabeth's shoulders relaxed as she drove. "I'll tell you this. She was far more experienced at it than me. I'd only done it once in high school, and I was too scared to do it again. The ramifications of family expectations and all."

"Why the sneaking around?"

"You're being dense again, Mr. Cutler."

"Your husband."

She rolled her eyes.

My gaze drifted to the *Vanderlinden for Council President* button. "The campaign."

"Give that man a prize."

I faced forward. "It's a local council seat. Who gives a fuck?"

"Are you serious?" Her face reddened as her voice rose. "I'm a moderate with a chance to win. If I do, I'm positioned to leapfrog to the governor's seat. Do you know how long it's been since a moderate has been in the governor's mansion?"

"That's what her threat was about? Paige telling the Montgomerys about your voicemail wasn't about their zoning request. It was about affecting your long-term plans for governor. And maybe beyond."

Traffic slowed again, and Elizabeth looked out the driver's side window—a petulant child ignoring a scolding adult.

"She threatened you to stay in the relationship? That doesn't seem like her."

Her head whipped around, and her face pinched. "Then you didn't know her."

"Maybe I didn't." The admission hurt.

Elizabeth smirked. "She loved me." She clucked her tongue. "Can you believe it? We were fooling around like a couple teenagers. It wasn't supposed to be serious. And she had to go and profess her feelings. I love you."

She mockingly said the last three words, but it still felt like I'd been punched in the stomach.

Had Paige really said those words? My hands balled, and I wanted to call her a liar.

The councilwoman's face pinched. "What was she?

Fourteen? For Christ's sake, we were adults."

She angrily honked her horn, but I didn't see an offending car. My face warmed. The words Paige supposedly uttered still rang in my ears.

I love you.

"She should have known better," Elizabeth muttered and jerked the wheel to change lanes. "After she said that, I knew it was too much. I tried to help her see the bigger picture, but she refused. Things had to be her way. Well, not this time. No sir, they didn't."

I remained quiet, thinking about Paige telling Elizabeth that she loved her—something she never said to me—only not to have it reciprocated.

My hands relaxed, and I looked away from the councilwoman.

How many others told Paige they loved her? Levi Montgomery did. I knew that. And we couldn't have been the only two. She must have relished that position of power. Men fell over themselves to please her. Amy said as much.

And then Paige met Elizabeth and finally felt safe enough to say those three words, yet Elizabeth wouldn't say them back. Paige was used to getting her way—she expected it. She probably felt entitled to it.

Hell, she even got me to come back to Seattle when I didn't want to. Paige was a woman who didn't hear 'no' very often.

Then Elizabeth Vanderlinden refused to say the three words back to her.

The councilwoman continued. "I had to get away from her. I couldn't be around someone who couldn't— *wouldn't*—play by the goddamned rules. That's when she went off the rails. Threatening me. *Me!*" She smacked the steering wheel. "It was my own damn fault for that misdial. I'll own that. She didn't make me do that, but she kept the damn things even after she promised she deleted them." She smacked the steering wheel again. "She promised!"

After keeping so many people at an emotional distance, falling in love must have been a monumental development for Paige—scary but exhilarating. Even though she might have known the rules, she got twisted around, upside-down, and inside-out because of love.

It's no wonder she threatened to expose Elizabeth Vanderlinden to keep them together. She had to be afraid of losing the thing she rarely, if ever, opened herself up to.

Elizabeth shook her head before saying, "Then she started seeing that Neanderthal as if that would make me jealous. Hardly." She chuckled. "Like I'm some lovesick puppy."

"Who did you tell?" I asked. "You had to have told someone about the relationship and the voicemails."

Traffic eased once more, and we moved forward several car lengths.

"Nobody."

"I don't believe you."

"I don't care if you believe me. And why would I lie?"

"To get me to go away, but I'm not going anywhere. I've got the disc now."

She glanced at me.

"And so, you know I'm not bluffing, the message about you two taking a trip to San Francisco was sweet. I also liked the voicemail of you telling Paul Montgomery to shove the zoning request up his ass. Nice."

Elizabeth absently wiped a hand over her mouth as she thought. Eventually, she said, "Gary Baker, my campaign manager. He knows things no one else does. I told him about Paige and the voicemails. We were doing a campaign threat assessment. Cleaning out the skeletons in my closet, so to speak." She looked over her shoulder as she changed lanes, moving toward an off-ramp. "I said there were a few harmless pictures, but that Paige deleted them. I did my best not to be in any with her. How those happened— Well, there's no one to blame but me. Like I said. It's the recordings I couldn't be sure of. I never heard them after I left them, but it seems you know how damaging they are. Don't you, Mr. Cutler?"

"Where is Gary now?"

"He wouldn't be involved in any of this. He's not the type to hurt anyone."

She sounded sincere, but while on patrol, I ran across many people who never believed that the good boy next door could commit a violent crime.

"I still want to talk with him," I said.

Chapter 42

We returned to the *Vanderlinden for Council President* headquarters. I rode with Elizabeth as I didn't want her to alert her campaign manager about our impending arrival. That meant leaving my truck in the Starbucks parking lot, but I could figure out a later return to it if need be.

The ride was spent mostly in silence. I doubted she'd grown petulant or introspective. Most likely, she was apprehensive, but she hid her fears behind a mask of apathy. Her eyes, however, told a different story. They narrowed and widened several times as she worked and reworked whatever problem she held hidden inside her head.

The corner location of the campaign headquarters was surrounded by floor-to-ceiling windows, allowing passers-by to witness the excitement of a campaign in full swing.

It no doubt cost an arm and a leg to rent the prime real estate. A moderate like Elizabeth Vanderlinden must have many backers lining up to help pave her way, not only to the council presidency but to a hopeful run for the governorship.

The office was full of professionally dressed young men and women. The one glaring exception was a short, chubby man whose suspenders and loosened tie clashed with the rest of the fashionably conscious volunteers. A pair of reading glasses were pushed upon the crown of his head.

The man was engaged in a conversation with a young

woman seated behind a desk. They appeared to be reviewing some documents.

"That's Gary," Elizabeth whispered.

When the campaign manager noticed Vanderlinden, his face brightened. "Elizabeth!"

Several volunteers smiled at her now, and she acknowledged them with nods and small waves of gratitude.

The chubby man hurried over and familiarly patted her arm. "We weren't expecting you."

"We need to talk," Elizabeth said.

Gary's eyes flicked to me. "Okay," he said, drawing out the second syllable.

"In private," she added.

The campaign manager glanced around the office before whispering, "The conference room." He deftly spun on his heel and headed toward the rear of the office.

The conference room was a basic set-up. A large glass table sat in the middle. On the walls were various charts and maps. A diagram of Seattle was highlighted in different colors with multiple pins stuck inside those colors.

Gary dropped into a chair along the far side, allowing Elizabeth to sit at the head. He smiled politely. "I'm Gary Baker, and you are?"

"He," Elizabeth said, cutting me off before I could introduce myself, "needs to ask you some questions." She settled into her chair.

The campaign manager's gaze remained on me. "About what?"

"Paige McIntyre," she told him.

Gary's head snapped to the councilwoman, but he didn't say anything. A thumb hooked under a suspender.

"Mr. Cutler knows about the voicemails, Gary. He knows that Paige threatened me with them and that I alerted you about them during our threat assessment. I assured him that you hadn't told anyone."

Gary slowly faced me as he ran his thumb along a length of suspender. "I didn't tell anyone. I assure you."

I smiled.

"What's so funny?" he asked.

Elizbeth shifted in her chair. "Yes, Mr. Cutler, what's so amusing?"

"You two. The quick coaching. Nicely done. Now, your story has an alibi."

The councilwoman feigned ignorance. "I don't know what you're talking about. He said he told no one. You should be satisfied now."

Gary's attention returned to Elizabeth like a dog waiting for its next command.

"Is he always your bitch?" I asked.

"Excuse me?" The campaign manager jumped from his chair. "You can't talk that way."

"Who else knows?"

"No one." His face hardened, but it was a feeble attempt at toughness.

I stepped around the table.

"Mr. Cutler," Elizabeth said.

Gary backpedaled.

"Who else?"

The chubby man lifted his hands in defense.

"Mr. Cutler," Elizabeth scolded.

I grabbed Gary's tie as he stepped back. He was now on a leash that tightened around his neck.

"Who—"

"*Mr. Cutler!*"

"Mitchell," Gary squeaked. His eyes immediately snapped to Elizabeth.

"You told her husband?"

"He's the money."

"Why did you tell him?"

"He wants to be kept in the loop."

I turned to Elizabeth, but she was gone. The door to the conference room was still swinging open.

Gary pulled his tie from my hands and tried to smooth the wrinkles from it.

"Where do you think she went, Gary?"

He shrugged.

"Home, maybe?"

He refused to make eye contact.

I yanked his tie from him. "I need to know where she lives."

Chapter 43

The double doors of the Vanderlinden home opened, and a huge man blocked the entry. In my online search of Elizabeth Vanderlinden, I'd seen pictures of her husband. This wasn't him. This man must have been close to six and a half feet tall. A small scar jutted down the left side of his lip to his chin. His black suit contrasted with the shiny blue tie and white shirt. His head was shaved, and his dark eyes bore into me. He never blinked.

A big man, I thought.

Just like the kids at Paige's apartment complex described.

Just like Steve Alfieri said.

Levi Montgomery might have been big, but this guy was massive.

"Leave," he said flatly.

"I haven't even introduced myself."

"The cops are on the way."

That surprised me. Not that the cops were on the way. Plenty of time had passed since Elizabeth ran out of the campaign headquarters. I'd caught a taxi to collect my truck then drove out to her residence using the address Gary Baker provided.

What surprised me was that they were involved at all. This opened the door for me to explain to others why I was there and what Paige had collected. Why was Elizabeth willing to take that risk now? Maybe she wasn't even the one who had called.

Mitchell could have. Gary said the husband knew about Paige and Elizabeth. Would he be willing to expose them by having the cops involved? Was it out of spite or something else?

The man-mountain swung the heavy door, but I jammed my foot in to stop it from closing. It didn't hurt because of my boot. He glanced down, then back up. Again, he never seemed to blink. His tongue flicked out across his lips.

"Mitchell Vanderlinden. Is he home?"

The big man pulled the door back and angrily slammed it on my foot. This time it hurt. He jerked the door back once more and put all his weight behind this swing. I pulled my foot out of the way. It banged shut, the lock turned, and the deadbolt set.

Standing on the porch, I shook a cigarette free from my pack. I lit it and thought about my options.

Maybe Mitchell would come outside now. *That was unlikely.*

Or perhaps he wasn't even home. *If that was the case, the man-mountain could have easily said so.*

Gary Baker had to have warned the house that he gave me their address and that I was probably on the way.

Would Mitchell wait behind the man-mountain for my arrival?

Or would he flee after the call?

Maybe he had been away and decided not to return home.

There was no way of knowing any of this, which meant simply hanging around and hoping I could talk with the man. A Field Training Officer once told me that hope wasn't a plan.

I could call Detective Ahern and update him on everything that had occurred. There were things that he could investigate from behind the power of the badge. But I didn't have to make that call from the Vanderlinden porch. I could do that anywhere.

All of this left me with one reality. Waiting for the cops to arrive meant I would have to answer for the confrontation with Gary Baker. I'd assaulted the man. Getting arrested for yanking a man's tie wasn't how I wanted to spend my afternoon.

And who knew what kind of bullshit they'd create about me standing on the porch of a councilwoman.

I exhaled a plume of smoke, muttered an expletive, and left the porch. If I had been a guest, I might have politely followed the concrete walkway back to the street where my truck was parked. Instead, I cut across the large, well-maintained lawn.

You can catch more flies with honey, I thought. Maybe I should stop acting like a bull in a china shop. They were both clichés but no less accurate. Thoughts of how I should behave differently plagued me as I crossed through a strip of rock landscaping. Another crunch of rock behind me caused me to turn.

The man-mountain punched me in the face.

I stumbled backward, and he grabbed my jacket. He swung me in a half-circle then tossed me back into the lawn. After sprawling awkwardly onto my stomach, I rolled over to face my attacker. He dropped his entire weight across my chest.

The force knocked the wind out of me, and my gun dug into my lower back. For a moment, it was as if my lungs stopped working and the world stopped spinning. Fear gripped me.

I twisted and reached for my gun, but the massive man pinned that arm. He quickly trapped my other arm with his body weight. I felt helpless, and my fear turned into panic.

His free hand slid underneath me.

Frantically wriggling and bucking under the big man's weight did nothing but scare me further.

He slid my gun free from the back of my pants.

My gun!

I couldn't breathe under his weight and couldn't get free. If he wanted to kill me, it was going to happen.

Squirming and kicking didn't work. I swung my head to the side and clipped his temple. When I went to head-butt him again, he pushed off.

As the man stood, air returned to my lungs.

"Your weapon retention is for shit," he said.

He dropped the magazine from my gun with expert deftness, ejected the chambered round, and locked the safety back. He tossed the weapon away to the side.

Greedily sucking air, I sat upright.

He watched me with a calculating coldness. I'd run across a lot of tough men on the street who tried to convince the world of their hardness. This man didn't bother convincing anyone. He just was.

"I give," I said and slowly stood. "Cops are on the way." It felt necessary to remind him.

That brought a sardonic smile. "Pussy."

My face warmed.

"Unless you don't want a second chance."

I swung at his head. It was stupid, amateurish, and precisely what he wanted.

He brought his arm up to his ear, and my hand bounced against his flexed bicep. It felt like hitting stone. Before I could land a second blow, he lowered his height and counterpunched to my stomach. The wind that I had just recovered escaped, and I wanted to vomit. For a big man, he moved with surprising quickness. He stepped to the side and slugged me in the ribs.

Tucking my arms into my sides, I fell to my knees. I wanted to scream, but there was no air in my lungs.

In the distance, sirens wailed. They were the sweet sound of safety—the sound of help.

The big man's arm slipped around my neck. He lifted me off the ground as his arm constricted.

The sirens grew louder.

His breath was in my ear as my hands futilely pulled at his arm. "You're going to die," he whispered.

The big man dragged me to the ground with my back against his chest. His legs wrapped around my waist. I couldn't move. His limbs felt like boa constrictors squeezing the life out of me. I grabbed, scratched, and clawed at the arm around my neck, but he didn't relent.

Darkness pressed in at the edges of my consciousness.

A patrol car skidded to a stop along the roadway, and a door opened. A male officer jumped from his vehicle with his weapon at the ready.

I raised a pleading hand.

The man-mountain released me and shoved me away. "This is the guy," he shouted. "He had a gun!"

Laying with my face on the lawn, I could hear the officer running toward me.

"Stay on the ground," the cop yelled. "Put your hands out to the side."

More flies with honey, I thought ruefully. Why was that so hard?

***

"What the hell are you doing here?" Captain Daryl Crites asked.

With my hands still handcuffed behind my back, I leaned against the fender of a patrol car. "I'm offering support to the campaign."

We were still outside the Vanderlinden home, under a batch of trees lining the drive. Several patrol cars were in front of the councilwoman's house. Elizabeth's BMW was now in the driveway. She'd arrived shortly after the first responding officer and was escorted inside by the man-mountain.

Where had she been?

Two well-behaved Labradors ran around the manicured lawn. Were they inside the entire time?

I eyed the captain. "What are you here for?"

"Damage control."

"For the city or you?"

His lip curled. "They're alleging you came here to hurt the councilwoman's husband."

"For what reason? I don't even know him."

"Why did you assault her campaign manager?"

"I helped him straightened his tie. He should be thanking me."

The captain rolled his eyes. "Uniforms are taking his report now."

"To-*may*-to, to-*mah*-to."

"They've got witnesses, moron."

Using my butt, I pushed away from the fender. "They're involved in Paige's murder."

His face flattened. "Who's involved?"

"Elizabeth Vanderlinden and her handlers."

Crites laughed. "You're kidding. You're trying to connect a councilwoman to the death of a stripper?"

"She had motive."

"What's that?"

"They were lovers."

The captain rolled his eyes.

"Maybe you're a part of this."

His eyes narrowed. "Still the same old Cutler. Trying to cast aspersions to deflect your guilt."

"You weren't surprised by the accusation of a lover."

"People can do whatever they want. Who am I to judge?"

"Are you fucking kidding me?"

Crites innocently turned his palms up. "What?"

"Hello? I'm the guy you dragged through the mud."

"Because you were dirty."

"You judged me."

"You say to-*mah*-to." The salesman smile he flashed was the old Crites I remembered.

Behind my back, my fists balled. "You're feeding Elizabeth inside information."

Crites tsked. "She's a councilperson. I can tell her anything I want."

Both the captain and I turned toward the house when the man-mountain exited and waved at a uniform. The officer hurried toward him. It was the same one who had arrested me.

"Why do they need a bodyguard?" I asked.

Crites shrugged. "How would I know?"

"He knew how to fight. I'll give him that."

"Maybe the councilwoman feels threatened. People approach politicians with all sorts of crazy accusations."

He didn't face me when he made that statement, so I wasn't sure if it was a swipe at Paige. "The big guy wasn't with the councilwoman," I said, "so he wasn't protecting her. I think he's guarding the husband."

That statement intrigued Crites, and an eyebrow went up. He grunted, "Huh."

When the officer and the man-mountain finished their conversation, the two shook hands. The big man went back inside, and the uniform approached us. When he was near, the cop studied me with curiosity.

"What is it?" Crites asked.

"Neither the Vanderlinden campaign nor their campaign manager wants to press charges."

The captain's face slackened. "Did they tell you why?"

The patrol officer had a nervous tic in the corner of his

right eye. "Their security man didn't feel it necessary to share, but I got the feeling it doesn't fit into their narrative."

Crites said, "I don't care what you feel."

The officer's eye twitched wildly. "You can't talk to me that way, Captain." He stalked angrily toward a cluster of patrol officers. Among them was Brock Gatlin. He hadn't approached yet but continued to watch me warily.

"That's no way to motivate your officers," I said.

Crites pointed at me. "Stay away from Elizabeth Vanderlinden."

"Or else?"

"Or else you'll find my boot up your ass."

The captain left me standing alone and headed for his patrol car.

Officer Gatlin approached with a paper sack in his hand. "When you came back into town, I didn't know how interesting things were about to get."

"I'm innocent."

"Aren't we all?"

Crites climbed into his car, slammed the door, and revved his engine before driving away.

"The captain hates you," Gatlin said.

"You think?"

He set the paper bag onto the trunk of the patrol car. It clunked when he did so. "Turn around."

I did as ordered, and Gatlin removed the handcuffs.

"Crites hates a lot of people," the officer said.

"You're saying I'm not special?"

"Sorry to disappoint you." He motioned toward the house. "They're not pressing charges."

"I heard."

"Since you've got a license for the gun, we're not going to put it on property for safekeeping."

I reached for the bag but paused. My gaze drifted to the other officers who were engaged in what seemed to be an intense conversation. "What about them?"

"As bad as you screwed up, John, you were once a cop. That still has some juice over here. And paperwork is paperwork. Nobody wants to do it for a bullshit reason." He patted my shoulder. "Just don't screw up and make us look bad."

Chapter 44

The door to the stockroom opened slightly, and she poked her head through, almost as if she were afraid of disturbing me. "Are you all right?" It seemed an odd question from a woman with a bruised face and busted lip.

"I'm fine."

Amy Mackey stepped into the room and let the door swing closed behind her. "I called asking for you." She crossed the room. "But the bartender said you weren't in a condition to talk."

Sitting on the cot with my back against the wall, I said, "Really. I'm okay."

"You don't look it." She knelt before me. "What happened?"

I reached for my pack of cigarettes, but Amy looked at them disdainfully. "Smoking's bad for your health."

She'd come all this way to check on me, so I tossed the pack back onto the cot.

"Tell me what happened," she said.

"I got beat up by a bodyguard of some sort."

"Whose bodyguard?"

"Mitchell Vanderlinden's."

Her face scrunched. "Who's that?"

"Elizabeth Vanderlinden's husband."

Amy's face remained pinched, but now she shrugged.

"Paige never mentioned that name? Elizabeth Vanderlinden?"

"Nuh-uh."

"She's a Seattle councilwoman. She's running for

council president."

Amy turned her palms up. "What am I supposed to say here? Good for her?"

"I thought maybe you would have seen her name in the paper."

"The news makes me sad. I try to avoid it."

"Paige and Elizabeth had a relationship."

The revelation of that news didn't faze Amy.

"Were you aware that Paige was bi?"

"It doesn't surprise me."

"It did me."

"Because she didn't tell you?" Amy cocked her head. "Did she tell you about past boyfriends?"

"Not a chance."

She stared at me like I was supposed to make the connection.

I didn't.

"Then why are you surprised she didn't talk about past girlfriends?"

I leaned my head back until it touched the wall. My eyes traveled up to the ceiling. "I guess that makes sense."

"Guess nothing. I'm telling you that's the way it is. She didn't tell you because you didn't need to know."

It was a simple truth, but it cut, nonetheless.

"Why did this bodyguard hit you?"

"It was a message to stay far away from the Vanderlindens."

"Why does a councilwoman need a bodyguard?"

"I wondered the same thing, but I think he's protecting the husband."

She reached for my face and winced as if the pain was hers. "Are you going to stay away?"

"There are questions that still need answering."

"Let the cops do it." Her eyes pleaded with me.

"Maybe." That's all I would agree to.

We stared at each other and listened to the nearby hum of a freezer and a refrigerator mix with the music and laughter of the bar.

"What are you going to do now?" she asked.

"Get some sleep."

"With all this noise?"

"It won't last for much longer," I said.

She checked out the cot. "Can I—"

"What?"

"Stay with you?"

I eyed her.

"Not like that." She lowered her eyes. "I haven't been able to sleep since…" Her words trailed off when she touched her cheek. "I want to feel safe for a little while."

Repositioning myself, I pushed to the far side of the cot. There wasn't much room for a second person, but she climbed on and put her back against my chest. I draped my arm over her. Amy clung tightly to my wrist.

The last thing I remembered before falling asleep was the clean scent of her hair.

Chapter 45

In the morning, Amy left to check on her mother. It was an awkward goodbye for two adults who had just slept platonically together. After a shower, I ate a Moons Over My Hammy breakfast at Denny's.

A newspaper was spread open next to my plate. As I enjoyed the hash browns, I distracted myself with the *Sports* section. First, I read about the hopes of the upcoming Supersonics season. One of the things I missed about leaving Seattle was catching the occasional professional basketball game.

Another forkful of hash browns and I moved onto the Seahawks. The football team was already mired in another mediocre season. I made it halfway through an opinion piece that claimed it was too early to give up on them. I liked the Hawks, but they'd broken my heart too many times over the years. After closing the sports page, I tossed it onto the seat next to me.

There was still half a plate of breakfast to go, so I moved on to the local news. It would be less irksome than the national coverage of the presidential election. I wasn't going to vote in it, so what did I care? Let someone else decide the next president for me. Would it make a difference in my life? I doubted it.

I was about to take another bite of my sandwich when a photograph on the inner page gave me pause. Accompanied by a short article, the title sent a chill up my spine. I put my food down and concentrated.

MAN FOUND DEAD IN CAR

Early this morning, a man was found dead inside a car outside the Southcenter Mall.

The only information provided by the Seattle Police Department was the deceased appeared to be a victim of a gunshot wound. Since this was an active investigation, no other information was released.

Homicide detectives declined to be interviewed.

Authorities were alerted to the scene by a security guard who discovered the victim while on his nightly rounds. The police have seized the vehicle, a black Chevrolet Impala, for evidence.

Police are waiting until family notification to release the victim's name. Anyone who has information related to this incident is encouraged to report it to their local precinct.

The accompanying photograph was of several police officers standing around a black Chevy Impala.

I slid out of my booth and hurried to the lobby's payphone.

Amy answered on the third ring. "Hello?"

"Are you okay?"

"Why wouldn't I be?"

I leaned into the phone. "Get your mom and leave. Now."

"What's wrong?"

"Take her someplace safe. Watch for anyone following you."

"You're freaking me out."

"I'm pretty sure someone murdered Steven Alfieri last night."

There was silence on the other end of the line.

"Hello?" I asked.

"How do you know?"

"I saw it in the newspaper. They didn't print his name, but they showed a car like his. You need to go."

"Do you think he told them about me?" Her voice rose an octave. "I don't have the disc anymore." When she realized her implication, she said, "I'm sorry. I don't want anything to happen to you, either."

"Listen. The only thing Alfieri could give anyone is your mother's address."

"Oh, God."

I nodded even though she couldn't see it. "Leave now."

"Yeah. Okay."

"I mean it. Right now. When you get to where you're going, call Finn's and leave me the number."

I hung up.

***

Shortly before noon, Amy stepped into the nearly empty Mickey Finn's. I was leaning on the bar, nursing a cold cup of coffee, and talking with Miles when I saw her. He was bent over, loading several new CDs into the player.

"Great," I muttered.

I slid off my stool and headed for her. Amy hugged herself, and her eyes were wide with fear. I lightly grabbed her elbow and led her to the backroom. When we were alone, I handed her the newspaper that I'd taken from Denny's.

She sat on the cot and read. Her hands shook until she finished, and she tossed the paper to the side. "What are we going to do?"

I sat next to her. "You're going to stay as far away

from this as possible."

"And you?"

"I don't know."

"You should go home. Why stay?"

It was a fair question and one that I was grappling with. After Paige's murder, I wanted to be the one to find her killer, to do something that Levi Montgomery couldn't do. But the more I discovered about Paige, the less I knew her. That didn't change the fact that I once loved her. Even if she never loved me back, maybe finding her killer would close the circle and bring me some peace.

Amy gently touched my forearm. "If you stay, I'll stay. I started this mess by taking the disc."

"You didn't start this." I covered her hand. "Paige started it when she saved those voicemails."

"I can help," she protested.

Standing now, I took her by the hand. "Help me by being safe."

Her car was two blocks away. As I escorted her, I scanned for threats. When she was seated behind the wheel, I knelt next to her.

"Listen carefully," I said. "From now on, don't drive directly anywhere. Take your time, take side streets, and drive through residential neighborhoods. You'll be able to see if someone is following you."

She stared at me.

"Do you understand?"

Amy nodded.

"Call when you're safe."

From the sidewalk, I watched her Cavalier enter traffic and disappear around the corner.

Chapter 46

As the late afternoon sun slipped beyond the horizon, the Vanderlinden house seemed quiet. I parked down the street with a line of sight on the front door and most of the driveway. On the east side of the house stood a tall cedar fence.

Waiting was the hard part. I'd already been there once and gotten in trouble with the police. Coming back again was asking for trouble. They say discretion is the better part of valor, so I tried to convince myself that my caution was an act of prudence and not timidity.

An occasional luxury sedan would pass by on its way to one of the high-priced homes. I didn't smoke while waiting. Doing so would call attention to myself and might alert a curious onlooker. To keep my fingers busy, I rolled an unlit cigarette between my fingers.

I was ready to give up on watching the house when Elizabeth's white BMW pulled into the driveway.

She slid out of the car and closed the door with a thrust of her hip. She wore a black skirt that fell to her knees and a dark wool jacket that went almost to that same length. On modest high heels, she strode to the front of the house and was met at the door by the man-mountain. He wore a tweed sport coat over a black mock turtleneck and black slacks.

The bodyguard nodded as she passed by.

Absently, I ground the unlit cigarette into the truck's ashtray.

A few minutes later, both Elizabeth and the bodyguard exited the house. She tossed her keys to him, and he caught them easily. He repositioned the seat then climbed behind the wheel. The BMW pulled out of the driveway and left the neighborhood.

I followed them.

About ten miles away, they turned into an upscale Marriott. After they parked, the two of them headed toward the hotel. Elizabeth said something that perplexed the big man. He stopped and canted his head. The councilwoman spoke again, and the man-mountain stepped forward and slapped her butt. It didn't seem playful or loving. However, she skipped once then laughed. Then Elizabeth slipped her arm into his as they entered the building.

I tried to figure out what the interchange was. Unfortunately, I couldn't come up with a reasonable explanation. It all seemed wrong. Elizabeth had been so careful with Paige, but now she was openly running around with the man-mountain.

What the hell was going on?

I tapped my steering wheel as I thought. Eventually, I turned around and left the parking lot.

Chapter 47

The woman who answered the door wore a blue cleaning uniform. Her black hair was pulled back, and she seemed uncomfortable with eye contact.

"Is Mitchell home?" I asked.

She shook her head, and then she shut the door.

I stood there for a moment before turning to look at the street. What the hell should I do now? I was running out of options. Maybe I should contact Detective Ahern, tell him what I know, and leave Seattle. Searching for some sort of closure with Paige was a luxury. I needed to get back to my job. I had rent and child support that needed to be paid.

The door opened again, and a neatly dressed man stood there now. He wore khaki slacks and a dark blue polo shirt. Everything appeared perfect—from his salt and pepper hair to his pearly white teeth. He looked familiar as if I'd seen him in a picture before.

"Mitchell Vanderlinden?" I asked.

"And you are?"

"John Cutler. May I speak with you?"

"About?"

"Elizabeth."

He briefly studied me before stepping to the side and waving me inside. When I passed by him, I registered the sweetness of his cologne. He closed the door.

Abstract paintings hung on the walls of the wide hallway.

"Margaret," he called.

The maid reappeared. After he whispered into her ear,

she nodded and went back into the kitchen.

Mitchell led us into the living room, where he pointed to a white leather couch. He sat directly across from me on a black one of the same style. A glass coffee table stood between us.

He crossed his legs and leaned back, resting his arm along the top of the couch. Through the window behind him, I could see the two Labradors playing in a fenced yard. "John Cutler?"

I nodded.

"You were the one who fought with," he hesitated while choosing his words, "our security man."

"Yes, sir." There was no way of getting around that incident.

"Based upon that event, why should I even be talking with you?"

I wondered why he would even have me in his house, but I kept that thought to myself. "There are some things I'd like to know."

"That's not how negotiations work, Mr. Cutler. If you want something, then you need to give something. What are you willing to give?"

I threw it out fast and didn't think of the consequences. "Your wife is cheating on you."

"She is?" His voice remained unconcerned. "With whom?"

"Your security man."

"And how do you know this?"

"I saw them walk into a hotel twenty minutes ago."

"You followed them?"

My brow furrowed. Where was the man's outrage? Where was his hurt? "Your security man intimately touched her."

"He did?"

"It seemed inappropriate for a married woman."

"Let alone a client." Vanderlinden leaned forward when the maid entered the room. "Ah. Here we go."

She carried a small silver tray with a silver pot and a couple of cups.

"Care for some tea?" Mitchell asked.

"No."

I figured it out then. Mitchell's nonchalance was because he already knew that Elizabeth was with the security man.

The maid poured tea into a small white cup. As she did, Mitchell watched her. He seemingly took no interest in me.

"Anything else?" the maid asked.

Mitchell picked up his cup and saucer. "Take the rest of the day off."

When she was out of the room, Mitchell's gaze returned to me. "Please continue with your story, Mr. Cutler."

"How about we talk about Paige McIntyre instead?"

He made a contemplative noise before asking, "What does she do?"

"She's dead."

Mitchell waved his hand. "Don't be that way. Tell me what she did."

"You already know. Gary Baker told you."

"Pretend he didn't. What did she do?"

"She was a dancer."

His face brightened. "A ballerina?"

"Exotic dancer."

"Oh." He sipped his tea then rubbed his lips together. "This is very good. Are you sure you don't want a cup? I'd be happy to pour you some."

I stared at him.

Mitchell's smile returned. "I love how people cover up the dirty things with coded words. Garbagemen are sanitation engineers, and strippers are… Where did she work?"

"Does that matter?"

He sipped his tea again then set both the cup and saucer on the table next to a cordless telephone. "Does that matter? That's a good question. Does it matter? I'm not sure. First, you fought with my security man in front of the house. We dropped the charges in hopes that you'd go away. But you returned to accuse my wife of traipsing off with the same man. Then you ask if I know a dead stripper. I'm wondering why you're here and how it all fits together." His voice never trembled, and he remained unnaturally calm. "So, maybe it doesn't matter where this woman worked. Yet, I still don't know why you brought this woman up."

"Your wife knew her."

"A stripper? I doubt that."

"They had a relationship."

He smirked. "You are full of accusations, aren't you, Mr. Cutler?"

"You never answered my question."

"Which question did I not answer?"

Frustration welled in my chest. "Did you know Paige McIntyre?"

"You never asked that, but I'll answer it for you. No. I did not know her."

Something in the way he answered bothered me. "But you knew *of* her."

He shrugged. "Do we really ever know anyone?"

My face grew hot. "Why are you jerking me around?"

Vanderlinden reached for his tea but stopped short of picking it up. He looked over my shoulder and said, "Hello, Liz."

"Mitchell," Elizabeth Vanderlinden said from behind me.

I tried to stand, but two hands clasped my shoulders and shoved me back onto the couch.

Elizabeth Vanderlinden walked over and sat next to her husband. She crossed her bare legs, making sure her skirt didn't ride up. Her hand rested on Mitchell's thigh.

"Hello, Mr. Cutler. Nice to see you again."

Mitchell set his cup on the table.

I glanced backward to find the man-mountain clamped onto my shoulders.

"Do you see," Mitchell said as he smoothed invisible wrinkles from his wife's skirt, "how you messed up?"

I watched him and the councilwoman.

"Need me to explain it?" he asked.

Fingers dug into my shoulders

"You knew I followed her."

"Of course, we knew. You were outside our house the whole time. Our man saw you there. We wanted to know what you would do."

Mitchell scooted forward to the edge of the couch. "Where is the CD?"

"You knew about her and Paige?"

He didn't answer, but Elizabeth said, "We have an arrangement."

"You're swingers?"

Mitchell laughed. "You told me he was dense, but I didn't imagine he was this bad."

"It's called an open marriage," Elizabeth said.

"Why the sham?"

"Sham?" Mitchell said. "She does what she wants, and I do what I want. We're adults, and everybody stays happy."

"And he doesn't mind my political aspirations, and I don't fault his financial objectives."

"We make a good team," Mitchell added.

Elizabeth held his hand. Their affection seemed

genuine in a weird sort of way. Like they both cared for the other as long as it didn't affect their own pursuits.

"Then what's with the side of beef?" I asked.

The security man cuffed me in the ear so fast I didn't realize he lifted a hand off me. An explosion went off inside my head, and it felt like I might vomit.

Mitchell reflexively pulled back. "Did that hurt?"

"That must have hurt," Elizabeth muttered.

"It hurt," the big man assured them.

To stop the ringing, I repeatedly opened and closed my mouth. It didn't help.

"Where's the CD?" Mitchell asked. "Or does he need to hit you again?"

"Alfieri has it," I said.

The man behind me laughed.

Mitchell shifted his position and put his arm around his wife. "Come now, Mr. Cutler. We know better. Steve told our man that you have the disc. He was quite emphatic about it."

Another piece snapped into place.

"Tell me how Paige died," I said.

"That's irrelevant," the husband said.

"It's what I want in exchange for the disc. Negotiations, you said. You give something, and I give something."

Elizabeth and Mitchell glanced at each other.

The councilwoman shrugged. "Up to you."

Mitchell rubbed his eye with a thumb. "She was blackmailing my wife, and we needed help."

I tried to look up at the big man behind me, but he shoved me down onto the couch.

"Our friend came recommended. He was the one who hired Alfieri to recover the CD and her technology, but he proved to be less effective than originally hoped."

"The break-in," I said. "Alfieri didn't find the CD.

That's why he had to hire Amy."

"The roommate?" Mitchell smirked. "An ill-fated plan. It's a terrible thing when a person's conscience gets in the way of doing the right thing."

"How did Alfieri find Amy's mother?"

"Maybe he was a resourceful man."

I watched Elizabeth until she glanced away. That's when I knew.

"Crites," I said. "A cop would be able to provide you with what you needed. What did he get out of it?"

Mitchell cleared his throat. "A separate negotiation, Mr. Cutler. The terms of which are confidential."

They were telling me a lot to get the location of the CD, which meant if I gave it to them, I was dead. Even if I didn't give them the CD, I was dead.

"Why did you kill her?" I asked.

The security man leaned his weight onto me, pushing me deeper into the couch. "She wouldn't listen," he said. "All she had to do—"

With his attention distracted on Paige's story, I sagged and twisted then. The big man lost his grip and fell forward onto the couch. His hands balled into my coat. I rolled forward, pulling him with me. We collapsed to the floor.

The big man landed on my back. He punched me in the kidney then the side of my face. His fingers slid into my hair, and he smashed my head into the floor. The world swung wildly about as his arm snaked around my neck.

I couldn't buck him off, and I couldn't reach back to him.

Panic rose in my throat. I hollered and clawed at the floor.

As he increased the pressure around my throat, he whispered into my ear, "This time, you will die."

Darkness overwhelmed me.

***

When I came to, I was slung over the big man's shoulder. We were in the garage. In front of us was the open trunk of a red BMW. Had I been more lucid, I might have commented on his and her cars.

The security man shrugged and dropped me into the car.

I clumsily tried to get out, but the man-mountain punched me. I fell backward. He leaned into the trunk then and hit me several more times. Bright flashes continued even after the trunk slammed closed.

When the explosions of light finally stopped, I rolled onto my side and vomited.

Chapter 48

A hard bump jarred me back into consciousness.

Everything was black.

The smell of vomit invaded my senses, and I fought not to do it again.

I heard the roadway underneath. It sounded as if we were driving fast. Maybe a freeway? There were other cars around us. A motorcycle zoomed by.

My gun, I thought. I reached behind my back, but it was gone. The security man must have taken it after the fight. Why hadn't I gone for it when he choked me unconscious? Playing the moment in my head, he was on my back, and I couldn't have gone for it. But the reality was I never even thought about it. I panicked.

Pushing those thoughts aside, I began to work on an escape plan. I searched the underside of the trunk lid in hopes of finding an emergency release pull. All new cars should have one, but this one was missing. Maybe foreign cars didn't come with them? Had the security man prepared Mitchell's car for this moment? Those were thoughts I couldn't worry about then.

My hands continued to fumble about in the dark. In the cramped compartment, I clumsily and painfully shifted my position. My fingers touched a smooth curved item. I pulled it to me.

Like a blind man, my hands danced the length of the item and felt metal, cloth, and thin wires. At the far end was a point, not an extremely sharp one, but a point, nonetheless. The smooth, curved item I initially held was a handle.

Among the occasional bumps in the road, I repositioned myself to be ready when the car stopped.

I touched my face and grimaced when I found tender spots. My tongue passed over my teeth. I was happy to find none were broken.

The illumination button on my watch revealed the time was 8:23 p.m.

After another twenty-two minutes, the car came to a complete stop. A door opened, and the car rocked—footsteps around to the back of the trunk. I clutched my makeshift weapon with both hands.

A small click sounded near my head, and the trunk popped up slightly. A hand slid under the trunk and lifted the lid.

With all the force I could muster, I jammed the umbrella upward.

It caught the security man in the throat, slightly to the left and just below his jawline. A gun fired into the underside of the trunk lid. I flinched but continued to push the umbrella upward.

Scrambling out of the trunk, I ignored the pain lancing through my body and shoved the improvised sword deeper into the big man's neck.

His eyes widened in panic as he stumbled backward. Bright-red blood pulsed and spurted from his neck and splashed down his sport coat.

I let go of the umbrella, and it clattered to the asphalt.

The big man dropped the gun as he backpedaled further away. He clutched his throat with both hands. Two more steps, and he tripped, falling helplessly to his back. His legs kicked wildly.

After retrieving the umbrella, I stood over him with it raised, ready for a killing thrust.

He held one frightened hand up as the life pulsed out from the large hole in his neck. I stayed that way until the security man finally faded. Then I lowered my hands and tossed the umbrella to the side.

For several minutes, I studied the man who had killed Paige. He was dead, but I didn't feel better. It hadn't brought me any closure, and I knew why. The security man hadn't acted on his own. He had gone to Paige's apartment at the direction of the Vanderlindens.

I patted the big man down yet found no wallet or phone. The lack of identification could have meant anything, but I chalked it up to some experience in the killing industry—either covert operations or specialized military training. The lack of the phone meant he didn't want to be tracked by GPS. Law enforcement could search records to determine a person's whereabouts. There would have been nothing to tie him to this location had he killed me.

Sitting in the driver's seat with my feet still on the pavement, I listened to the nearby traffic. I didn't know where I was. This looked like a deserted portion of an industrial park. Night had fallen, and several overhead lights sporadically lit up the area.

Even if I had a cell phone, I wouldn't have known where to tell the cops to come. And to be honest, I wasn't sure I wanted their help.

For a while, I stared at the body. I returned to the umbrella and wiped my fingerprints from the handle. After dropping the umbrella once more, I picked up the gun—a .38 snub-nosed revolver.

Flipping open the cylinder, I confirmed there were still five rounds inside. The sixth had been fired into the lid of the trunk.

***

It didn't take long to get my bearings.

I was in West Seattle near the Duwamish Waterway. I drove for a bit and tried to figure out what to do next. In the rearview mirror, my bruised and bloodied image frowned back.

Outside a convenience store, I stopped at a payphone and dug change from my pocket. An elderly Asian man poked his head out from the store and looked me over. He wore a short-sleeved white shirt.

"Don't want trouble," he said in a heavy accent.

"Yeah. Fine."

"No trouble." He shooed me away. "Go on." He closed the door and spun the lock.

In the reflection of the store's window, I saw myself. Covered in blood and vomit, I looked like I'd just stepped out of a zombie movie. I waved apologetically at the clerk, but he angrily motioned for me to leave.

Turning away from him, I slipped a few coins into the phone. I called the police department's dispatch center. It was a number I still knew by heart. It was answered on the second ring.

"Radio," a woman said.

"Is Detective Donovan Ahern on the air?"

"Who is this?"

"If he's not available, please call him and tell him that John Cutler needs to talk."

I glanced over my shoulder. From inside the safety of the locked door, the store clerk still watched me intently. Again, he furiously waved me away.

"Sir, this number is for official use only."

"Detective Ahern. Please call him."

"Did he give you this number?"

"Tell him that John Cutler knows who murdered Paige McIntyre."

"Where can he reach you at?"

I didn't have my cell phone. It was still in my truck,

but out of minutes. Police radio was recording the call so they could replay the message. If I told them about the Vanderlindens, they could go there now and arrest them.

Is that what I wanted? My bloodied reflection wearily watched me from the store's window. After everything that occurred, did I really not care who brought them to justice?

"Sir?" the dispatcher said.

I hung up.

Chapter 49

I pulled into the long, winding driveway and proceeded to the garage. My body hurt, and my head pounded. My truck was where I had left it. It seemed arrogant in retrospect. What had I been thinking? What was I thinking *now*? Maybe I should turn around, go somewhere safe, and call the cops. There was still time for that course of action.

No, I decided.

Tossing the ball to someone like Detective Ahern wouldn't bring me the satisfaction I wanted. Maybe the metaphorical touchdown could still be scored if he brought the Vanderlindens to justice, but Paige was dead, Amy and Mary Mackey had been assaulted, and I killed a man in self-defense. Too many things happened for me to step out of the way now.

I wanted to be the one to punch this across the goal line.

I wanted to feel the closure.

Would I kill the Vanderlindens? No, but I wanted them to express some remorse over what they had done. I wanted to be there when the cops arrived. I wanted to feel some finality to the whole damn thing.

Walking away and letting someone else handle it wasn't an option.

On the car's visor was a garage door remote. I pressed the button and pulled in after the door lifted. I slipped out of the vehicle but didn't shut the door nor close the garage. Maybe I'd already made too much noise and alerted them. But if I hadn't, why risk it and make more sound?

The security man's gun in my hand felt reassuring as I moved toward the house. The door to the inside was unlocked. Low, unhurried voices came from the living room. I breathed a sigh of relief. They hadn't heard me pull in.

"He didn't have to kill her," Elizabeth said.

"No, he didn't," Mitchell agreed, "but she didn't have to blackmail you either. She made her bed. Let her lay in it. Let them all lay it in."

"What do we do now?"

"Nothing," Mitchell said. "This will be the end of it."

"Unless someone else knows about the CD."

The husband snickered. "If that happens, you'll have to deal with it. At least, the original players have been accounted for."

I peeked around the corner. They faced each other in the middle of the room. Elizabeth had a half-empty glass in her hand while Mitchell stood with his arms folded. He seemed irritated.

"Listen," she said, "you're in this as much as I am."

"Almost."

"Almost? Don't forget you're the one who said we needed a security man."

"Because you screwed up, Liz. I figured you would have had better sense in where you spread it around."

"Nice, Mitch. Real nice."

"An open marriage means you show some discretion. It doesn't mean act like a whore."

She threw her glass at him. He ducked, and it shattered across the floor.

"Maybe if you showed some restraint in choosing your partners."

Elizabeth's laugh was humorless. "Not all of us can screw out-of-town barflies who won't call for a second date."

Mitch pointed at the broken glass. "I'm not cleaning that up."

She turned in my direction, so I stepped from behind the corner. Both instinctively raised their hands.

"How?" Mitchell blurted.

"Where is—?"

"Sit," I ordered.

The husband dropped onto the black couch, but Elizabeth moved toward the minibar. Sitting on top of it was my gun. Someone, presumably the security man, had dismantled it and stacked the pieces on top of each other. The cordless phone was next to the pile. Was she going for the phone or the disassembled gun? I didn't take her to be the type of woman to reassemble a firearm rapidly.

I pointed the revolver at her. "*Sit.*"

She stopped and glared at her husband.

"What'd you want me to do?" he asked. "He got away from the guy we thought was the professional. Like I'm going to take him on."

Elizabeth gloomily walked to the black couch and plopped next to her husband. They looked like a pair of chastised children.

I stood behind the white couch and saw my reflection in the window. I wondered where the two dogs were. "How many deaths was your man responsible for?"

"We never intended for any of this to happen," Elizabeth said.

"That doesn't matter. How many deaths?"

"We don't know," she said.

I lifted my chin to Mitchell. "You hired the bodyguard."

"So? He killed your woman. Not us. We didn't know he'd do that."

"Don't give me that."

I lifted the gun, and he raised his hands slightly.

"Was it worth it?" I asked.

Mitchell looked briefly at Elizabeth before facing me again. "Was what worth it?"

"The power or money—whatever reason you did this for—was it worth it?"

"Only a person who's never had either would ask a question like that."

"That CD," Elizabeth said, "would have ruined my life."

"That's why you had her killed?"

"No," Mitchell said. "We didn't want that. Nobody was to be hurt. Our man went too far."

"Whether you believe it or not," Elizabeth added, "I cared for Paige. We only wanted her to stop with the threats."

"I don't believe you."

"It doesn't matter what you believe, Cutler," a voice said.

I glanced over my shoulder at Captain Daryl Crites. He stood at the edge of the room with a gun in his hand. Looking forward, I could only see my reflection in the window again. Crites wasn't there. I shifted my position slightly so the captain's image appeared.

"Who are you?" Mitchell Vanderlinden asked.

"He's a friend," Elizabeth said.

The husband's brow furrowed.

Crites stepped forward. "Drop your gun, Cutler."

"No."

"Do it, or I'll shoot you in the back and call it self-defense. I'll have two witnesses who will corroborate my story."

My gun remained steady on Elizabeth, the trigger resting against the tip of my finger.

"Shoot him," the councilwoman said, "and we'll play

it however you want.”

Crites stepped forward again. “Do it, Cutler.”

“You’ll drop me if I lower it.”

“If I wanted to kill you, dummy, I would have done it already.”

It was a good argument. He was behind me and could shoot me at any moment. If I whirled around to surprise him, he’d shoot me. I couldn’t move around the couch for cover. Could I dive over it? And then what? Get shot in the back while trying to scramble to my feet. Or worse, get shot on the floor trying to find a place of cover.

I lowered the gun.

“Now,” the captain said, “grab the barrel and give the gun to Elizabeth.”

I held the gun out as ordered. The councilwoman moved around the coffee table and took it.

“Now, Liz,” the captain said, “it’s time you jump in with both feet.”

The councilwoman’s eyes flashed to Crites. “What are you talking about?”

“Who is this guy?” Mitchell whispered.

The captain continued. “Steven Alfieri is dead.”

“That’s the least of our problems,” Elizabeth said, moving back to her husband.

“So, you do know him,” Crites said. “I should have put the pieces together after I ran that woman’s name for you.”

Mitchell’s head whipped toward his wife. “He’s a cop?” he whispered.

Elizabeth lifted a hand to quiet her husband.

“This is the guy you’ve been getting information from?”

“Not now,” the councilwoman harshly whispered.

“An Impala was at the scene of that woman’s assault. Cutler was run over there by the same car.” Crites motioned toward me. "Alfieri owned an Impala. Do you see the trail?"

Elizabeth nervously fiddled with the gun she held. "No one would put it together."

The captain's laugh was a short, mirthless bark. "Want to bet? An enterprising detective will link those things. Now, I can cover my ass, but Cutler here tends to be a talker."

I moved slightly to get a better look at the captain in the window's reflection.

"Easy, Cutler." Crites leveled his gun at me. "Stay right where you are."

"What are you going to do about it?" The councilwoman asked.

"Me? This is your mess."

Elizabeth lowered her gaze to the gun. "What do you expect me to do about it?"

"What do you think? This has to be on you, Liz."

I stiffened.

"You do it," the councilwoman ordered, "you're the cop."

Mitchell mussed his hair as he thought. "A cop," he murmured. "What were you thinking?"

"Shut up, Mitchell," Elizabeth snapped. To Crites, she asked, "Why are you doing this?"

"Sometimes," he said, "we have to work hard for things to happen. Then there are moments we must seize. That's what I'm doing now."

Continuing to watch his reflection, I shifted my weight and prepared to move.

"I've never shot anyone before," Elizabeth said.

"Have your husband do it. I don't care."

"Me!" Mitchell exclaimed.

"Yeah, you."

"But why do I have to do it?" the husband whined.

"None of this was my fault."

"For better or worse, one of you is doing this." The captain waggled the gun between the Vanderlindens. "You dragged me into this, Liz. I'm not getting any more blood on my hands."

What the hell happened to Crites? This wasn't the man I remembered—the true-blue, cheese-eating rat. Although hadn't he punched me when my hands were cuffed? Hadn't he pushed me over the edge by going to Paige's work? Maybe Crites hadn't ever been as clean as he wanted to project.

Elizabeth stared at the captain. "I can't."

"When I saw you with the McIntyre woman, I should have gotten away from you then. I knew who she was."

"Jesus," Mitchell said. "How many people know?"

"When her name popped up as a murder victim," the captain said, "I should have told the investigating detectives what I knew. Instead, I kept my mouth shut."

Elizabeth's eyes narrowed, and she moved to the edge of the couch. "Power corrupts," she said.

He nodded, then shook his head. It was a weird, unconfident effect.

"But you knew what you were doing." Something changed in Elizabeth's demeanor. She sat up straighter, and her shoulders pulled back. Her words sounded more forceful, and she no longer seemed scared. The councilwoman must have sensed something shift in Crites. What was it I missed? Was it the sudden arrival of hesitation concerning his actions? Like a shark, Elizabeth smelled blood in the water. "Don't go all innocent on me now, Daryl. You want to be part of the game. Sometimes it's messy."

"Yeah," Crites muttered. He sounded remorseful. "Messy."

Something in the way he said it caught my attention,

too.

Elizabeth scooted toward the edge of the couch. "What did you do, Daryl?"

"I flagged Cutler's name in the system."

She cocked her head. "And that's bad?"

"It was stupid." He shrugged. "I didn't think it through. I let it get personal."

"Everyone can make a mistake. Help me, and I'll help you."

Crites eyed me. "John called police radio and left a message. They notified me right away because of the flag. There's a record of that."

Now, Mitchell scooted forward on the couch and sat next to his wife. "Then everything worked out fine. We deal with this problem right now, and we're home free."

"Cutler left a message for a detective. Isn't that right, John?"

Both Vanderlindens studied me.

"He said he knew who murdered the woman."

Mitchell pointed at me. "He killed our security man."

The captain lifted an eyebrow. "Is that true, John?"

"He kidnapped me," I said, "and I escaped. He was fine when I left him."

"Not true." Mitchell stood. "Not true!"

"Sit down!" Crites bellowed. He didn't move his gun from me, though. Had he, I may have made a move toward him.

The husband dropped to the couch. "If our man was still alive, he would have called by now. We haven't heard a peep from him."

"If he killed your man," Crites said, "consider yourself lucky. One less witness to what you've done."

This wasn't anything like the Crites I remembered. Was it because he believed his life and freedom hung in the balance? If that were so, he might be able to do anything, including killing me. I needed to move soon.

Crites said, "Radio has informed the detective about John's call, too. That's for sure."

"Then why did you come here?" Elizabeth asked.

"To clean up your mess. The one you pulled me into."

"I'm grateful."

"I'm not here for your gratitude."

Anger washed over Elizabeth's face. "What do you want?"

Crites shrugged. "Nothing you can't deliver. How about chief of state patrol?"

She laughed. "You're delusional. I can't do that."

"When you're governor, you can. Until then, you'll owe me. Mitchell, too."

"Enough of this," the husband said. "Either shoot Cutler or let me do it." He reached for the gun in his wife's hand.

"Listen to him," the captain said, "pull the trigger or—"

It was now or never. I whirled around, and Crites fired. Something sliced my arm, like a knife slashing through butter, but I didn't stop.

Mitchell squealed.

I wrapped my hands around the captain's gun and quickly elbowed back into Crites' face. He refused to let go, though. His other hand covered mine. We were linked at the weapon, and together we spun around.

Another shot rang out, and Crites yelped. He stiffened and fell into my arms. Looking over his shoulder, I saw the councilwoman looking down the barrel of the security man's gun.

Mitchell lay motionless on the couch. The round Crites fired must have hit him.

The captain moaned softly, but he wouldn't release his grip on the gun.

Elizabeth held her gun on us.

"You look pretty comfortable with that," I said.

"Necessity is the mother of invention."

Crites grew heavy against me, and his moaning stopped. His grip on the pistol lessened.

"Mitch," the councilwoman said. She looked toward her husband. "Mitchell?"

I pulled the gun from the captain's hand. I held him up by one arm now.

"Mitchell!" Elizabeth hollered. She reached for her husband and stopped. She pulled back as if horrified. The councilwoman spun and raised the gun. "You did this!"

"Wait."

She fired. The round hit Crites in the back. I don't know if the captain was already dead, but he didn't make a sound. I struggled to hold the man in front of me.

Another round hit Crites and the force resonated through his body. Elizabeth moved forward, firing and screaming.

The captain and I fell to the floor behind the white couch. I pushed away and rolled, coming up with the gun.

Elizabeth didn't hesitate. Jerking toward my position, she fired again. Something exploded behind me.

I fired once, and she collapsed with a shriek. Slowly and carefully, I moved forward to get a better view of her. She awkwardly crawled across the floor, moaning as she went. She positioned herself so that her back leaned against the black couch. The gun hung limply in her hand. Blood seeped from her upper chest. She gasped and sucked for air.

I kept my gun trained on her and picked up the cordless phone. When the 911 operator answered, I set the phone down. They would send someone on the call alone, so I didn't need to say anything.

Checking my right arm where I felt the earlier

slashing, a gash ran along my bicep. The round the captain fired had only cut my arm. I'd gotten lucky. Mitchell and Crites hadn't.

Elizabeth wheezed loudly. "We can… spin this." Her chest heaved as air rushed from her lungs. "We can… turn this…" Her words were labored. "To our… advantage."

I lowered my gun.

"Money," she said. Elizabeth touched her dead husband's knee. "You can—" She coughed blood, and her face pinched. "Be a hero," she rasped.

I'm no hero, I thought.

"We can…" Her head lulled, and she took a long, grating breath. "Spin it," she whispered.

It had already been spun. What else was there to do? Everyone was dead. Paige. Alfieri. The security man. Crites. Mitchell.

Elizabeth lifted her head and struggled to focus on me.

In the distance, a siren wailed.

She sucked for air one more time. The gun tumbled from her hand and clattered on the floor.

I went outside and sat on the front porch, waiting for the approaching patrol unit to arrive.

Chapter 50

The ambulance's interior lights shone shockingly bright as the vehicle's generator hummed loudly. In the cramped confines of its back, an EMT bandaged my arm.

"Is it deep?" I asked.

The female medic muttered, "You'll make it."

Detective Donovan Ahern stood at the open doors and knocked on the side of the ambulance. "Is it all right to talk to him?"

"Up to him," she said. "He's good to go."

I stepped out of the ambulance.

Under his brown suit, the detective wore a white shirt and a printed tie that stopped midway down his belly. He studied me for a few seconds before saying, "Radio said you tried to reach me."

I nodded.

"What happened in there?"

"It's a long story."

"I'm on overtime. Take all the time you need." Ahern pulled out his notebook and pen.

"It played out like this," I said. As I spoke, the detective took notes, scratching out every relevant detail.

Midway through my retelling, Ahern loosened his tie. "Hold on. Wait a minute. Crites did that?"

"I'm not lying."

"I'm not saying you did, but it's Crites. Nobody's going to believe it."

"Check the system," I said. "You'll find his fingerprints. I promise."

Ahern scrunched his nose. "Like where?"

"For starters, he flagged my name. That's how he knew about my call to radio. That's how he ended up here. He also searched Mary Mackey's name. Maybe Amy's, too. That's how Steven Alfieri found both women. That's how I ended up almost getting run over down in Kent."

Ahern wrote quickly in his notebook. He looked up. "You think Crites was involved with your girl's murder, too?"

I shook my head. "No. I think he was genuinely surprised by that, but sometime, somewhere, he saw Paige and the councilwoman together. He inserted himself into the whole mess after that."

Ahern rubbed his chin with the back of his hand. "We're getting too far off course. Go back to the beginning. How did this whole thing start?"

Even though I had already told him this in the interview room, I went back to Paige's phone call asking me to come over. When I finished my story, Ahern stared down at his full notebook.

"That's a lot of stuff to verify."

"You're on overtime," I said. "Take all the time you need."

Chapter 51

Al Green's "Here I Am (Come and Take Me)" floated through the air of Mickey Finn's. It was a few minutes after two in the afternoon, and only a couple of regulars were in the bar. I sat in the far corner booth.

It had been a few days since the shooting at the Vanderlindens. I'd already had several follow-up interviews with Detective Ahern. The crime scene was a mess for investigators to decipher, but luckily it laid out exactly as how I described.

The department found the security man's body where I told them he was. It would still take time for forensics to confirm my blood and DNA were inside the trunk of the Vanderlindens' BMW.

Ahern couldn't confirm it, but it sounded like the department had conferred with the prosecuting attorney and everyone leaned toward closing the file without pursuing any charges against me.

Miles came to the table with a carafe of coffee and two cups. He poured both of us some. Danny tended the bar while we talked.

"Is today the day?" he asked.

I nodded.

"Not going?"

"I paid my respects already."

Miles sipped his coffee. "I guess you did. So, is that it?"

Another nod.

"Got to say I'm going to miss having you around."

I clicked my mug against his. "Gonna miss being

here."

"You can move back. Nothing's stopping you."

"I'm not ready yet."

"You must like flogging yourself for past sins."

The door opened. Sunlight washed the bar, and the two patrons seated there. Amy stood in the doorway and squinted into the darkness. When she saw me, she waved and headed over.

Miles stood. "I'll let you two talk."

He caught Amy in the middle of the bar and said something to her. She nodded and smiled.

Bobby Womack began singing about living "Across 110th Street."

As she slid into the booth, she said, "You're looking better."

"How's your mom?"

"She's fine." Amy pulled the carafe to her. "All done with the detective?"

I nodded.

She wiggled the handle back and forth. "So, are you really leaving?

"Yeah."

"You don't have to, you know? That's not your home." She met my eyes, and a sad smile creased her lips.

"I have to."

"Why?"

I shrugged. "I don't know."

"Then stay here."

"In the bar?"

"In Seattle, goofball. Or in the area, at least."

"Spokane suits me."

Amy fell silent and continued to play with the carafe's handle.

I asked, "Want a cup?"

"No." She pushed the container into the middle of the table. "I just came in to say goodbye. My mom's outside. We're going shopping. Maybe grab some lunch."

"That sounds nice."

"There's nothing I can say that will make you stay?"

I shook my head.

Amy slid out of the booth then leaned in. Her lips lightly brushed my cheek. "Thank you for your help, John." She hurried out of the bar.

Miles hobbled over and dropped into the booth. "That was fast. Where is she off to in a hurry?"

"Things to do."

"So it seems. What's your plan now?"

I lifted my cup of coffee. "Finish this, then go see a young woman."

***

The goodbye with Miles was a simple handshake and a promise not to take two years before returning to Seattle. After leaving Finn's, I stood on the junior high school sidewalk with my hands shoved into my pockets.

When the school bell rang, Erin strolled out of the building with three other girls. She wore blue jeans and a Raiders shirt. Her baseball hat was turned backward. The backpack slung over her shoulder bulged with contents. The four of them laughed as they walked.

The older she got, the more she looked like Maria. I could see it in her movements and mannerisms. Even at twelve, she was becoming a beautiful young woman.

The Hispanic kid from McDonald's broke from a group of boys and called to her. Erin left her friends to talk with him. She seemed sincerely interested in what he had to say. They spoke for a few moments, and then he went back to his friends.

When Erin turned, she saw me. Her eyes widened, and she ran over. "Are you picking me up?"

"Not today. I'm heading home."

Her smile faded.

"I wanted to say goodbye and make sure you know that I love you."

Erin's eyes glistened, and she looked away.

"Hey. I don't have to leave at this exact moment. I can call your mom. Maybe we can go get some fries or something."

She shook her head. I reached for her, but she took a step back.

"Listen—"

"I need to go." She pointed at her friends. "They're waiting."

"Erin."

The backpack swung as she hurried toward the bus. Her friends clustered around her before they all boarded. As the school bus moved slowly by, my daughter's head was down, and she wiped at her eyes.

Her friends angrily watched me. One of the girls even bared her teeth.

After the bus turned down a side street and disappeared, I slowly walked toward my truck.

Why *couldn't* I stay? Why not leave everything in the past and simply start over?

I rested my hand on the truck's handle.

Maybe there was a police department in the area that I could get on with. Without Crites in the mix, I'd probably get at least a tepid recommendation from Seattle PD. Maybe wearing a badge would make me feel like I once did—like the guy I was before her.

I yanked open the door and climbed into the truck.

Paige wasn't to blame for how things turned out. I

was. A badge only amplified my faults.

There was no way I wanted to be that guy again. The problem was the only way I knew how to stop being him was to go away.

The engine fired up, and the truck pulled from the curb.

Did You Enjoy the Book?

Thank you for reading *Cutler's Return*. I'm always grateful when a reader takes time out of their day to comment on one of my novels. If you do write a review, please email me, and let me know. I'd love to say thanks!

About the Author

Colin Conway is the creator of the 509 Crime Stories, a series of novels set in Eastern Washington with revolving lead characters. They are standalone tales and can be read in any order.

He also created the Cozy Up series which pushes the envelope of the cozy genre. Libby Klein, author of the Poppy McAllister series, says *Cozy Up to Death* is "Not your grandma's cozy."

Colin co-authored the Charlie-316 series. The first novel in the series, *Charlie-316*, is a political/crime thriller that has been described as "riveting and compulsively readable," "the real deal," and "the ultimate ride-along."

He served in the U.S. Army and later was an officer of the Spokane Police Department. He's owned a laundromat, invested in a bar, and run a karate school. Besides writing crime fiction, he is a commercial real estate broker.

Colin lives with his beautiful girlfriend, three wonderful children, and a codependent Vizsla that rules their world.

9 781737 112082